JUDGED

A CASEY CORT LEGAL THRILLER

AIME AUSTIN

LOS ANGELES, CALIFORNIA

ALSO BY AIME AUSTIN

Ransomed

Caged

Disgraced

Unarmed

Kidnapped

Reunited

Contained

Poisoned

Abused

JUDGED

A CASEY CORT LEGAL THRILLER

AIME AUSTIN

Judged

This edition published by
Moore Digital Media Inc.
1125 N Fairfax Avenue
Unit 46071
West Hollywood, CA 90046
www.aimeaustin.com

ISBN 13: 978-1-64414-038-3
eISBN 13: 978-1-64414-037-6

Cover Designer: Wicked Good Book Covers
Cover Images © Depositphotos, Shutterstock

Judged/Aime Austin. — 3d ed.

"A wave of notorious child deaths in the 1990s pushed frightened social workers to remove youngsters from their homes first and ask questions later. And most of those youngsters were black."

The Plain Dealer – October 7, 2005

"The color of America's child welfare system is the reason Americans have tolerated its destructiveness."

Prof. Dorothy Roberts, **Shattered Bonds** – 2002

1

Party Night

Olivia Grant

October 6, 2001

I never knew what I was going to encounter when I went home. It was always best if I tackled it alone. I squirmed in the center of the third-row seat of the ginormous SUV. Hugging myself, I prayed silently that my friends wouldn't see anything more than the front door.

"So, who do *you* like, Olivia?" Cate Byers leaned around the bucket seat as she asked me the question.

Beth Fogle shifted so that she too was looking at me. "Yeah, who? Maybe he even likes you back."

I ducked my head, both embarrassed and thrilled to be talking to girls who I'd watched from afar for weeks—enjoying the popularity-by-association conferred by my budding friendship with Cate.

Beth's singsong voice rose above a whisper.

"I know who she likes."

"Who? Who? How do you know?" Cate asked, straining against her seatbelt.

"I bet she likes Marquis Chapman," Beth pronounced.

"No, I don't like Marquis," I said. Overcome by a sudden need to share confidences with these girls, I blurted out, "I like Jon Heath."

Beth and Cate shared a look. "Jon Heath?" Beth flicked her long blonde hair, laughing as she turned back in her seat. "He'll never go out with you."

Mortification stole my voice. I smoothed my hands through hair the beautician had spent an hour straightening. Was it because I wasn't super skinny? I wasn't as pretty as Beth, but I wasn't ugly, either.

Cate leaned toward Beth and whispered something I couldn't hear over the sound of fat tires swishing across wet pavement. When the SUV stopped at the light where the Chagrin, Van Aken, and Warrensville Center streets met, the car was quiet. Beth's whispered response came through loud and clear.

"Besides, if they had kids, they'd be striped like zebras."

My heart squeezed like it was locked in the vice grip of a small fist. I would never fit in.

"Girls, that's enough," Mrs. Byers said, pressing on the gas. Shaker Heights was devoid of traffic tonight. Low-slung, two-and three-story brick buildings stood stoic on the side of the street. The earlier rain had cleared, but I couldn't see a single star to wish on through the overcast sky.

Mrs. Byers cleared her throat loudly. "Olivia, Sheila and I must have gotten our signals crossed," she said, silencing the other girls once and for all. "Your mom, she's a judge now, isn't she?" she continued, as if trying to redeem Beth's earlier slight. "You must be so proud of her. She's gone so far. I'd love to be a career woman like your mother, but I've dedicated my life to my kids," she finished, watching me in the rearview mirror. I met Mrs. Byers' sincere blue eyes and looked away, embarrassed. Nothing Mrs. Byers could say would make me anything but the odd black girl out.

For a few short hours, I'd been one of the gang. Then my mom hadn't come to pick me up after dinner. Embarrassed didn't even begin to describe how stupid I'd felt waiting in that damp, chilly Benihana parking lot for more than a half hour, praying every car that passed was my mother. After the waiters came out, a sure sign the restaurant was closing, Mrs. Byers had said she was happy to drive me home. It was on the way, she had assured me with a firm pat on my cold shoulder.

I turned to look out the window. I'd never be like these girls. Beth was the leader of the second most popular clique at the school. After being invited to Cate's birthday party tonight, I'd hoped to be elevated to a higher status.

I shook my head, mumbling prayers to myself. My mom was at home. It wasn't like she ever went out or anything. She just watched endless hours of television on the white couch, in the white living room of our two-bedroom apartment—then went to bed. The pattern never changed. Usually I was right there with her. The one night I'd decided to go out....

Mrs. Byers interrupted my thoughts. "You're on Latimore, right?"

I nodded then spoke up, giving my house number. We were getting close to my neighborhood, Lomond. While Cate, Beth, and most of the cool kids lived in the northeast neighborhoods of Shaker, my mom and I lived south of the Blue Line—one of the two light rail lines that bisected Cleveland and Shaker Heights. The other kids all lived in 'century' houses—historic homes built at the turn of the century north of the light rail.

I hated living on the other side of the tracks in a neighborhood filled with newer two and three family homes, cleverly disguised by their architects to look like single family structures. School was full of lessons about Pride! and Self-esteem! I tried to feel good about where I lived and not compare myself to the other kids. But on nights like this, I was left wanting.

The SUV got closer to my house. Practiced, I started giving directions.

"Here." I pointed and leaned forward in the car's darkened interior. "You have to make a left on to Lynnfield Road, then swing a right on to Newell, then a left on Latimore."

During our short residence in Shaker, I had given directions to other moms when my mother 'forgot' to pick me up. At twelve going on thirteen, I was already quite familiar with the city's winding streets. "We're the third house on the right."

I stepped between Cate and Beth and opened the large back door of the SUV. Mrs. Byers turned to face me.

"It was so nice finally meeting you, Olivia. I always like to meet Cate's new friends. Tell your mom I look forward to finally meeting her at Mommies and Muffins on Friday."

Mommies and Muffins. Not likely, I thought. My mom's job always came first.

"Thanks for the ride," I said.

Cate and Beth waved through the open door.

When Mrs. Byers started fingering the keys as if she were going to turn off the engine, I tried not to panic. Instead she set the truck's parking brake, apparently intending to wait for me to get inside safely. I balked.

"Oh, you don't have to wait for me. I'm just going inside right here," I said pointing toward the brightly lit front door.

"You kids think you're all grown up." Mrs. Byers gave a knowing smile, her teeth flashing white in the soft glow of the dozen tiny interior lights. "Hope to see you soon."

I jumped from the running board, slammed the door, and ran up the slippery front walk toward the faux Tudor style building. The SUV pulled away from the curb. I breathed a sigh of relief.

I searched for my keys in all the pockets of my purple nylon Kipling backpack. I felt around and found the furry gorilla charm that sucked its own thumb, but no keys.

"Shit," I whispered fiercely, then covered my foul mouth with my hands. The memory hit me squarely between the eyes. I'd left the keys in my room because my mom had promised to pick me up tonight. Looking up at the second floor living room window, I saw that the bulb of a single lamp glowed. Hope burgeoned in my chest. Maybe Mom was awake. I rang the doorbell, pressing and holding the button for long seconds, praying I didn't wake up the landlords downstairs.

I stood for what felt like hours, alternatively ringing the doorbell and listening for the sound of my mother's uneven footfalls on the stairs. But my mom didn't come.

I walked down the cracked asphalt driveway to the back door. Ineffectually, I pulled and twisted the knob. It was locked as well. I came 'round front again.

Panicked, sweat broke out everywhere as I considered my options. I could walk back the way we'd come, down Chagrin to the gas station at the huge five-street intersection at the end of the Blue Line and call my mom, *if* I could find a working pay phone.

Looking around the darkened street, hearing the wet leaves of the towering maples and oaks shake in the wind, I shivered.

Not a good idea.

I studied the front door. It was wood with large decorative glass inserts. I could see the dead bolt, which held the door locked, through the panes.

Without a second thought, I took off my jacket, balled it around my fist and broke one of the eight squares in the door. The shards of glass were surprisingly quiet as they hit the hallway runner. Reaching in, I turned the lock, walked inside, and ran up the stairs.

Grateful to find the door to our apartment unlocked, I pushed it open quietly. My mom was snoring loudly, splayed out on the couch. The television blared the nightly news theme.

It took a few seconds of searching to find the remote, but a satisfying silence fell when I stabbed the red off button. With a sigh, I pulled a blanket over my mom and then went to bed.

2

Qualified Immunity

Sheila Harrison Grant

October 9, 2001

No good parents' children just fell into the foster care system. My chair's ancient springs squeaked as I leaned away from the voluminous file. If Precious Evans' parents hadn't abused the little girl, she wouldn't be where she was today. And today Precious was in hell.

I looked up as a faint knock sounded on the wall next to my open door. Nancy McFadden, my courtroom deputy, peeked around the door.

"Judge, they're ready for you now. Do you need anything on the bench?"

"A glass of water, Nancy. Thanks." I lifted my hand in dismissal, but my deputy remained at the door, expectant.

Whomever said judges had complete autonomy...lied. "Tell them I'll be out in five."

"Will do, Judge," McFadden said, finally leaving the room.

Judge.

I would have to get used to that. Though I'd been on the bench for more than nine months, I was still unaccustomed to being called 'Judge' or 'Your Honor,' or even more formally, 'The Court.' Between Christmas and New Year's last year, the outgoing president, a liberal Democrat, had appointed me to the federal district court in the Northern District of Ohio.

Unlike the judges down the hall, I wasn't a lifer—yet. I was almost as vulnerable to losing my job as the welders at the local steel mill because I was a recess appointee. A seldom-used clause of the constitution permitted the president to appoint me to fill a vacancy of the court, skipping the normal confirmation process.

Recess appointees didn't get a lifetime appointment. Instead, the full U.S. Senate would have to confirm me before the end of the next Congressional session, a deadline less than a year away. If I wasn't confirmed, I'd be out of a job.

Historically, a recess appointment was a vehicle to appoint progressive or minority judges, like me. Even Thurgood Marshall began his judicial career as a recess appointee. Earl Warren was such an appointee to the Supreme Court when it heard the history-making *Brown versus the Board of Education* case.

Though I was the first African-American judge to serve in the Northern District of Ohio, I wasn't sure *that* particular designation would help me survive the confirmation process. After the most controversial election in my lifetime, a far more conservative administration had replaced the previous one, and diversity was no longer a priority.

I shook my head clear of the political sludge I'd waded into. The old-timer judges I sometimes shared lunch with tried to school me in 'playing politics' if I wanted to make my job permanent. Nineteen years at my former law firm had given me some political savvy; after all, I'd become partner. But without Peyton. Damn it, I didn't need Peyton Bennett's help; I could play three-dimensional chess all by myself.

Looking down, I only saw a few drops of liquid and specks of coffee grounds in my mug. Dog tired after reading up on the case I had to preside over, I had been kept tossing and turning all night by Precious Evans. Slamming the file shut, I worked to get thoughts of confirmation out of my head. It was time to get to work. I twisted my pen closed, then pushed myself back from my desk—too quickly. I grabbed my middle when a wave of nausea attacked.

Every damn morning, my skull pounded, and this was no exception. After fumbling with the ornate brass pull for my top right-hand drawer, I pulled out my half-empty bottle of Tylenol, shook out two tablets, and swallowed them dry. I shouldn't be letting this stress get to me.

I pulled my five-foot-six frame to its full height and shrugged on my robe in front of the full-length mirror. The black made me look authoritative, but did little to compliment my looks. According to my daughter Olivia, I might have been 'officially' middle-aged, but I still looked pretty good. Spanning my waist, I was proud to say I wore the same size eight as when I'd graduated from law school. Zipping up the robe hid the pale-yellow wool that better suited my brown-skinned coloring.

"All rise!" the bailiff cried. The people in the mostly empty courtroom reluctantly shuffled to their feet. Glad that my water-filled carafe, glass, and the court's file were in order on the bench, I sat in the high-backed chair. Taking a swig of water, I washed the bitter taste of the pain medication from my mouth.

"Gentlemen. Are you prepared to argue on the motion to dismiss filed by the county?"

"Yes, Your Honor," the attorneys said in unison.

"Prosecutor Richland, it's your motion. You may proceed," I said.

Richland, buttoning his suit jacket, came to the podium.

"May it please the court," Richland began then adjusted the microphone. The thick carpet and velvet drapes adorning the courtroom muffled his voice. "I'm assistant County Prosecutor John Richland representing the Department of Children and Family Services.

"Precious Evans has sued the county for a huge amount of money for pain and suffering, and specialized counseling. The court should dismiss her complaint. The law is well settled that the county is immune from liability because none of the social workers were indifferent to her care. Any time they found a problem, Precious was moved to a new placement. What happened to the girl was just a few unfortunate coincidences."

I had to interrupt him.

Using both my own and the bench's height to full advantage, I spoke. "Prosecutor Richland, I think 'unfortunate coincidences' is rather crude terminology for what happened. Looking at the complaint, it appears that this girl has already been in nine different homes. Is that true?"

"Yes."

"Nine homes and she's been abused at more than one county placement." My head swam as I drifted into silence. Having lost my train of thought, I stopped to read the summary of the case my law clerks had prepared. Regaining my composure, I spoke again in as authoritative voice as I could muster around the bile in my throat. "If my recollection of the record is correct, the girl contracted gonorrhea as a baby at one foster home, was sexually abused by a neighbor of a different foster parent, and was physically beaten at yet another placement. Is this true?"

"Yes, Your Honor," Richland said. "But the county is not directly responsible for any of these incidents."

"You don't think the county is *responsible* for returning this child to an abusive situation with her parents or failing to investigate the abusive foster homes before you put her there?" I asked.

"Every time the county became aware of a bad placement, she was moved—almost immediately."

"So, this child, Precious, who's going to need thousands if not hundreds of thousands of dollars of therapy gets what from the county? Aren't they the least bit responsible for this? They were, after all, the indirect cause of her trauma and abuse."

Richland hesitated under my relentless questioning. Good, I liked them running scared. His voice quavered a little when he spoke. "Your Honor, I go back to our qualified immunity argument."

He wasn't that good of a lawyer. If the law weren't on his side, I'd never rule in his favor. Though I knew my ruling well before I ascended the bench, I wanted to hear from Murphy. Maybe he would say something to assuage my guilt, because the legally right decision wasn't going to be the morally right one. As a mother, the thought of leaving a child in the custody of those who had abused her made my already queasy stomach roil.

"Mr. Murphy, your rebuttal?"

"This girl could only hope for normalcy. Our experts have figured that it's going to take years and a lot of money for this girl to lead a normal life. If Precious doesn't get a chance before a jury to put this travesty of a foster care system on trial, she'll never be justly compensated."

"Mr. Murphy, you've pretty persuasively laid out all this girl has gone through. But since she's already in the county's permanent custody, aren't they already responsible for this girl's care? And if she did go to trial and did win a big money judgment, who would be working with the Probate Court to manage that money?"

I had to give him credit. Patrick Murphy didn't miss a beat.

"Our office is prepared to handle Precious' monetary...arrangement...with court supervision, of course. Sure, the county will care for her, but DCFS is on a tight budget; there are thousands of kids. She's had a bad shake. The county needs to make it up to her now and *after* she ages out."

As Precious' guardian *ad Litem* wound down, I turned my attention to the clock on the far wall of the courtroom. The remainder of the morning docket stretched before me. Precious tugged at my heart, but my job was only to decide the legal issues. And in this case, it was relatively simple. Was the county responsible for the abuse at the hands of foster parents?

No.

The Department of Children and Family Services was immune from lawsuits when they tried their best. They were cavalier, but not deliberately indifferent. The county would win, and Precious would have to fend for herself.

I closed the case file, opening another.

"Gentlemen. You'll have my written decision within a few weeks."

3

Guardian *ad Litem*

Casey Cort

October 9, 2001

My hand-me-down Honda Accord sputtered along Superior Avenue. I tried not to let the red needle hovering around the 'E' on the gas gauge freak me out. I needed to complete the visit to my client DeAndre Nelson today. My wallet was empty, save for a few pennies and some lint. I needed to get my task done and get home before I ran out of gas.

Slowing down and looking at each street sign carefully, I knew this wasn't the case to bolster my bank account. I'd already spent too many hours on it. At forty dollars an hour with a cap of two hundred fifty on fees, I was running against the clock.

Steering with one hand and looking at the map of the east side of Cleveland with the other, I swung a quick left on East Seventy-first Street, then a right on Lockyear, my destination. Checking the address my assistant Leticia had written on the folder, I pulled to a stop in front of the foster mother's house. I peeked at the file again. Kendra James was her name.

Few cars occupied this inner-city Cleveland street. The neighborhood's solitude disturbed me. I reached into the back seat and hauled out the heavy red metal lock, bracing The Club against the steering wheel when I saw several black men loitering on the corner in front of a decrepit mom and pop shop.

I got my briefcase from the seat beside me and walked around to the passenger side to lock the car's doors. The driver's door lock hadn't worked since my car had been broken into during another visit to some foster kids. One more thing I couldn't afford to fix.

I looked for the doorbell. There was none. I knocked carefully at the rotting wood of the screen door, careful not to knock it off its hinge. Waiting by the door, I marveled how these foster parents were nearly as poor as the kids they were 'helping.' Finally, a smartly dressed woman let me in.

"Kendra James." The woman extended her hand, inviting me in.

While she disappeared to get DeAndre, I took a seat on a sunken couch that smelled faintly of things I didn't want to consider. I watched as two little kids, red Kool-Aid rings staining their mouths, sat catatonically in front of a television blaring cartoons.

The uneven acoustic drop ceiling was stained, while bowed wood paneling stood out from the wall like a sail full of sea air. Carpet curled away from the walls. I'd hate to be here during a hard rain. A cherubic baby perched on Kendra's hip as the woman strode from the back of the house.

"So, how's he doing?" I asked after dispensing with the usual preliminary questions. "Any problems? Is the mom getting visitation?"

Babies were the hardest cases. They didn't talk, so I was forced to make custody determinations weighing the opinions of social workers and foster parents.

'Best interests of the child,' the statute said. What's best for someone who can't tell you if cold water drips on him at night or if rats nibble at his tiny toes? Kendra slid the sleepy child into a crank-up swing. I leaned in to have a look. Shrugging inwardly, I supposed the baby was normal—though I hadn't seen many babies in my life.

Kendra sat heavily on a recliner and answered my question.

"The mom's not an issue in this case. The social worker, Ms. Pachencko, said that my husband and I could adopt him in a couple of months."

Had I wandered into some dystopian world? Fostering was temporary by its very definition. I sank deeper into the smelly cushions. The mom wasn't an issue?

The mother was *always* an issue. Parents had fundamental constitutional rights. Even if the new laws cut off parents' rights quicker, it didn't make them any less important.

"Ms. James," I started cautiously. "I think we must have our wires crossed. Right now, DeAndre is not eligible for adoption. The county has only removed him from his mom temporarily. The social worker is a Ms. Pachencko, did you say?" Kendra nodded, so I continued. "She should have a case plan in place so the baby and the mom can work toward reunification."

Kendra James blinked a couple of times as she took in the information. "Oh…but…I'm sorry—I, I thought when we agreed to be a foster-to-adopt home that we'd only get kids we could eventually adopt. I really want to be a mom."

"I'm sorry, Mrs. James, but in DeAndré's case, it doesn't work that way."

"But if the mom's in jail, or dead, why can't we have him?" Her voice was bordering on a whine.

Because babies aren't dogs that you pick up at the pound after a three-night stay. I bit my lip, keeping my opinion to myself.

"Why don't you talk to Ms. Pachencko about that? In the meantime, I need to find out where the mom and dad are—make a determination of whether reunification with the family is a good idea here." Kendra looked so distressed that I softened my tone, mollifying the foster mom as best I could. "We need more people in the foster care system like you and your husband."

With that, I gathered my papers, took another quick peek at the sleeping child, then left the James' residence.

I started the car. I'd just eased my foot onto the gas pedal, hoping to conserve what fuel I could, when a fist banged against my passenger window. Remembering the men down the street, I started then slammed my foot on the brake, bucking the car. It was only Kendra James, though. Turning an engine on and off used more gas than idling, I suspected, and shifted the car to neutral. Leaning across the passenger seat, I rolled down the last manual window in Northern Ohio.

"We paid her, you know."

"Paid who? What?"

"Trish said if we paid her, the next eligible baby would be ours. We've been giving her half the check that comes for the kids. I really want this baby. I...I can't have my own. Please. What do you need from us to make this little boy ours?"

Flabbergasted, I couldn't think of an appropriate response.

"I'm sorry, Ms. James. I can't help you." I pulled from the curb, the tires squealing in protest.

What in the hell was this Pachencko woman up to? This was far from an easy case. Any profit I could have made on this one had just gone up in smoke. Before Carnegie turned into Stokes, the car sputtered to a stop.

Shit.

I pulled the automobile club card from my glove compartment and hoped my membership fee would cover the cost of getting a gallon of gas out here. Maybe I should have taken Mrs. James up on her offer.

My rent was due in a few days. My bank account was looking nearly as grim as my wallet. As I punched in the toll-free number for the motor club, I thought not for the first time, I had to give up these time-sucking, money-losing cases. Doing the right thing was what had landed me in this predicament in the first damn place.

I was tired of being right.

I'd rather be rich.

4

The 'Burbs

Olivia

October 12, 2001

Doodling my way through fourth period Geography class, I drew a heart and penciled in my name and above it, Jon Heath's. Reaching under the scarred wooden chair, I got another pen from my backpack and filled in the lopsided heart with red ink.

The whole Shaker Heights Middle School thing—in the suburbs—was new for me. Since my mom had gotten the job as a judge, she'd said in her lecture voice that it was important to change the way we live our lives. That meant moving from the city to the wrong side of tony Shaker Heights, and my mom acting like a poser in her new Lexus. Gone were the days where I could blend into the background of my Glenville neighborhood.

Every adult I ran into when I was with her mom talked on forever about how Shaker was one of the *finest* school districts in Ohio and how *grateful* I should feel to live there. How it was so much *better* than my Glenville school.

To the outside world, I guessed, the Heights, Shaker, Cleveland, and University looked ideal. But I hated that I was only one of a handful of black students in regular or honors classes. The teachers talked down to me as if I was retarded or something, like I was going to flunk out of school or get pregnant tomorrow. It drove me crazy. But I had enough good sense to know that I shouldn't confront these particular bigots head on.

The white students were friendly enough, on the surface. Like me, they listened to hip-hop music, and dressed in so-called urban gear—even if theirs came from the Beachwood Mall. But other than Cate's one party, I didn't get invited to the others I heard whispered about after class. Worse, the boys didn't even act like I was a girl worth talking to. Some days I just wanted a boyfriend—

"Olivia? Olivia Grant! Are you with us today?" Mr. Donaldson asked, snapping me from my reverie.

"Um, sorry. I didn't hear the question," I said straightening in my chair, trying to look alert.

Mr. Donaldson's sigh was full of exasperation. "Okay, I'll repeat the question for those of you *not paying attention.* What are Russia's five major rivers?"

A sweat broke out on my top lip, as a trickle of moisture ran between the cups of my training bra. Watching teen dramas last night had not prepared me for today's lesson. Desperate for an answer, I flipped through the current chapter, but my gathering tears blurred the information in front of me.

"Uh, the V-Volga," I stammered then stopped, unable to remember any others.

"Olivia, I know you're new here. But I want you to stay after class so that we can discuss student expectations in Shaker Heights," Mr. Donaldson said.

A few students tittered at the rebuke. I sighed and looked down at my new watch with its hot pink wristband. The second hand wasn't moving fast enough. I wanted this class and the humiliation that went with it to be over–now. Watching the thin red clock hand make its sweep, I hid a little smile.

In an unusual fit of generosity, my mom had purchased the watch for me while we were picking up cleaning supplies at Target. Though it wasn't like the other kids' expensive jewelry—I was sure *they* never shopped at discount stores—I was still glad to have something new that was all my own.

Being chewed out by my Geography teacher wasn't enough to get me to pay attention to more boring European river talk. Who cared about the Rhine or Danube?

I was *really* looking forward to my first 'For Girls Only!' club meeting after school. My new guidance counselor, Alison Feingold, had personally invited me.

Alison had been so nice when I had come to her office that first nerve-wracking day. I was anxious about starting in the middle of the school year, but Alison had put me right at ease. It was the first time I'd ever met with a guidance counselor.

At my last middle school, there was only *one* guidance counselor, and she'd only had time for the troubled kids. Alison wasn't like a counselor at all, she was so cool. She'd said I could call her by her first name, and talked to me like an adult.

"Welcome. Welcome to Shaker Heights Middle School." Alison had stood when I first came into her office.

I had looked at Alison shyly. "Thank you."

"Please sit down," Alison said after formally shaking my hand. "It's so nice to meet you. So, this is your first day here at Shaker?" Alison asked rhetorically.

I nodded.

"Well then. Let me tell you a little bit about our school. Shaker is committed to providing you with a great education in small classes and teams, like a school within a school. Obviously, you'll be joining us a bit late in your academic career, but we'll try our hardest to make sure that you fit in socially, and more importantly, academically.

"Each grade is divided into teams. This means that you and about a hundred other students will have the same teachers for your four core subjects: English, Math, Science, and Social Studies. The whole school shares the rest of the teachers for electives.

"I want you to understand that our school is a lot different than your old school. The teachers *here* have your best interests at heart. We all meet regularly to discuss every student's progress. If we believe you have any problems with the work, we'll be there to help you before your academic career goes awry. Our main focus these days is making sure you're prepared for the Ohio proficiency exams that you'll take in the spring."

I took it all in, wondering if Alison ever stopped for a breath. "Your file says that you've come from Bethune Middle School." She paused only after my small nod of assent. "Now, I know that some of the Cleveland schools have good programs. But in the last few years, Cleveland has fallen behind in exam performance. Despite the budget crunch, our schools have been voted one of the best districts in the state. We don't take that honor lightly. Our mission is to make sure every single student can perform at more than a minimal level. And now you're going to be part of that legacy."

I heard the subtext. Don't come here and mess up our numbers.

Fanning her face, Alison blew up at her poufy blonde bangs.

"Whew! I've done all the talking. Tell me more about what your plans are. Have you thought about colleges? What do you want to do when you grow up?"

I watched Alison size me up while I tried to come up with an answer.

"I haven't really thought about it," I answered slowly.

"Well, I see from your file that your mom's a judge! Are you interested in the law?"

I screwed up my face. "Not really." If I knew one thing, it was that I didn't want to be like my mom when I grew up.

Alison closed the folder on her desk.

"No need to talk about all this on your first day."

Had I disappointed the woman? I wanted the counselor to like me.

"We just need to get you settled." Handing me a small slip of paper, she said, "Here's your schedule." Alison pulled the door open and called in another student from the hall. "This is Kristine. She's on your team!" Turning to the pale girl languishing outside, she said, "Will you show Olivia around a little today?" To me, "Hopefully Kris can answer any questions you have."

I gathered my backpack, ready to follow the quiet girl.

"Oh, wait a minute!" Alison ran back to her desk and picked up a fluorescent flyer. "Here," she said, handing the page to me. "I've started a Friday after school club for girls in the school. I'd love you to join us."

When the bell clanged signaling the end of class, I snapped from my memory. Mr. Donaldson finished up quickly, assigning us reading on Russian crops and the latest civil unrest in Chechnya.

I lingered near Mr. Donaldson's desk. I wanted to get lunch. They were serving Boston cream pie today, my absolute favorite cafeteria dessert. Rolling my head, I tried to relieve the permanent tension in my shoulders. I hated being separated out like this.

"We've had a team meeting," he started. Then his eyes pierced mine. "You're coming from a Cleveland school, and we know we're going to have to make some allowances for the learning gap. But we need your participation to make this work. Shaker has certain standards we need to uphold. You understand?" he asked, his face earnest.

I nodded. "Yes, Mr. Donaldson."

He came around from behind the desk and squatted his tall frame before me, coming eye to eye again. "I can imagine it's hard coming from a background that's not like that of your classmates. Hell—excuse my language—I know what it's like to be the first person in your family to go to college. Now that you're here in Shaker, I want you to take advantage of the opportunities presented to you." Rising, he patted my shoulder. Even his pat was condescending. Why did everyone talk to me like I was stupid? "You can make your people proud. Okay?"

I nodded.

"Okay, good. I'll be expecting you to participate fully in class from now on. It's a quarter of your grade." Mr. Donaldson walked back behind the desk and started leafing through some papers. I'd been dismissed.

Briiiing. Briiiing. Briiiing.

Two hours later, the end-of-the-day bell trilled. Glad the school week was over, I ran to my locker, twisted the combination lock, pulling open the metal door. Thinking about the pile of homework I had over the weekend, I stacked most of my books, math, geography, *The Pearl* for English, and my notebook into my Kipling backpack.

Almost felled by its weight, I had to bounce my knees to redistribute the load on my back. The locker door made a soft clank as I closed it. I jiggled the handle to make certain it was secure then walked the long corridor to the library where Alison was holding the 'For Girls Only!' meeting.

The reading room's chairs were arranged in a tight circle with a purple felt hat on the floor in the center.

"Olivia!" Alison bustled into the room. "I'm so glad you're here today!"

I smiled at the greeting. Even though Alison looked like she could be one of the actresses on Ally McBeal, blonde with blue eyes, always in her slim-fitting suits and white collared shirts, she was nice. Most pretty white girls only talked to their own kind, ignoring me.

I heaved my backpack to the floor and took a seat. On each chair, someone had placed a few Post-its. Though I had only observed so far, I was ready with a question today.

Like every other student in the school, I'd received my quarterly report. It wasn't good. The only A I had was in art; the rest were B's and C's. My mom was going to blow her stack when she saw the grades.

Since the move to Shaker, I'd felt overwhelmed by the new school, the new apartment, trying to make friends, dealing with my mother's moods. Instead of doing my homework like I should, I'd zoned out—watching MTV, and sneaking romance novels I'd picked up for a few cents from the Salvation Army.

I unzipped my purple backpack, got out my favorite pink glitter pen, and wrote my question on the paper. Before anyone could see, I folded the sticky-note in half, then quarters, then eighths, then sixteenths before I dropped the square in the wool hat. The other girls, late, frantically scribbled their questions. Alison started the group, her trademark smile and enthusiasm in place.

"Girls! Welcome! I'm so glad you all could be here today. This is the first group of its kind in Shaker, and I think we're on to something. I know for most of you, this is our fifth session, so I hope you gals are getting something out of it.

"Remember, we have ground rules because I want *everyone* to feel at ease and get all they can out of this group." Alison waved her hand impatiently when some of the girls groaned and fidgeted. "One, everything said here is confidential. I don't, and I'm sure *you* don't want to hear your secrets whispered up and down the school's corridors.

"Two, I'm here to help you. If there's *anything* you would like to discuss, but don't feel you can say it in the group, then you can come see me or call me anytime. My home number's on the board. Please write it down and keep it with you.

"Three, please know that while I can keep most stuff confidential, Ohio law requires that I report child abuse and stuff like that to the authorities."

The chairs scraped across the floor as we were all impatient.

"Okay, let's get to the questions." Alison picked up the hat, mixed up the slips of paper, and pulled one out.

"First question: 'I got my period a few days ago, but I'm afraid to tell my parents. What should I do?' Anyone have thoughts?"

Hands rose hesitantly. Alison nodded toward Meredith, a heavy strawberry-blonde girl with more freckles than friends.

"Well, I think she should tell her parents. And she shouldn't be embarrassed because it, like, happens to all girls and parents know that."

Lauren's hand flew up, and Alison nodded toward her. Lauren Eggleton was perfect. She was the most popular girl in school, and she had everything: the latest jeans, sneakers, haircut. There was a girl who never had to figure out what non-dorky thing to wear in the morning.

"I know why a girl might, like, be embarrassed," Lauren said. "It was totally horrible when I got my first period. I told my mom, who told my dad. Then they told my little brother-monsters, and we had a big party at some restaurant like it was my birthday or something. It totally sucked. All I wanted was some alone time with my mom, and some advice on what to do. I want to use tampons, but I'm afraid I won't be a virgin if I do. So, I could see why someone wouldn't want to tell their parents."

Alison nodded sagely while Lauren spoke, manicured hand stroking her chin. "Girls, I think the bottom line is that you have to tell your parents. But maybe the best strategy would be for you to sit down with the parent you feel most comfortable with, tell them. But most importantly, communicate with them on how *you* want to handle it. Maybe with a party—which is acceptable in some cultures that see this as an important passage to womanhood.

"On the other hand, maybe you only want a quiet trip to the drugstore and some tips on handling cramps. It's important to tell your parents what you want, so they don't guess wrong. Guessing leads to mistakes. Think about the terrible gifts you get when they surprise you for birthdays, Christmas, or Hanukkah."

The other girls laughed. Alison stirred up the contents of the hat again with her hand. She pulled another question from the hat. I tried to hold my face expressionless when I recognized my tiny, folded square. The last thing I needed was to be known as the dumb black kid with the single mom—a cable news statistic. I was having a hard-enough time fitting in.

"Okay girls. The next question is one I expected. The first quarter's progress reports came out today."

All of the girls groaned, more or less in unison.

"The question is: 'I got bad grades today. How do I tell my parents?' Any of you have an answer?"

I was ready to commit their answers to memory. I could use all the help I could get. Up until now, I'd always gotten good grades. In Cleveland, the teachers loved me because I was always quiet in class and did my homework. Shaker was very different.

Everyone was striving for good grades. I'd seen students argue, plead, and cajole teachers into better grades. In Bethune, all I had to do was sit down, shut up, and get an 'A.' Here, my grades were low compared to the quality of work I did, but I didn't know how to advocate for myself. So, I'd stopped trying.

"Who has advice for this girl?" Alison asked.

Only Beth raised her hand. I sighed inwardly. Beth probably got the best grades in the school. Every teacher called on her all the time, praising everything she said as brilliant.

"Telling parents about bad grades is hard," Beth started. She hid a quick grin behind her hand when Meredith rolled her eyes heavenward. "Everyone's parents pressure them about getting into good high schools and colleges," Beth continued. "I think you should tell your mom and dad, and then strike a deal with them to do better. Maybe give them a study schedule that you promise to follow, or sign a contract with them or something."

Alison surveyed the room. There were no other volunteers. "I think that's super advice. I'd add that if any of you are having problems with the work here at Shaker Middle, there's peer tutoring. Beth leads that group and I'm sure she or the other tutors could help you in weaker subjects."

The counselor pulled another question from the hat, and the girls continued to give each other advice. Every time one girl would look at another, her hair would swing, and her clothes would move with her, fitting perfectly. Jealousy ripped through my heart.

My hair wasn't right, and my clothes were worse. I had my hair pressed every two weeks at a beauty parlor in Cleveland, but straight wasn't *straight.* And my clothes, ugh.

My jeans tapered unfashionably at the ankles, gapping at my waist. Sure, the discount clothes looked good on the models in pictures, and okay on the racks, but cheap clothes didn't wash well. I looked like a poor relation compared to the other students in their designer clothes.

Nothing I'd said changed my mother's mind about getting me better things to wear.

"*Olivia,*" my mom always said when she was in one of her moods. "You're just a child. I'm not spending my hard-earned money on stuff you're only going to get dirty and wear raggedy."

Lately, I'd caught my mom in good moods less and less. On those days, I'd be lucky to get my mom to drive me to Beachwood Place—where the cool kids shopped. Although I coveted super tiny hipsters from Abercrombie or a hoodie from American Eagle Outfitters, I was grateful to get one bulky sweater from Dillard's. With my mother constantly nagging me about my weight, shopping in a cool store was a no-no.

When I really needed clothes—anything from socks to underwear to jeans and sweaters—we went to Super Kmart way out in Solon. I was sure with the move to Shaker, my mom would never shop there again, but I'd been dead wrong.

"Honey," my mother had said. "You're starting a new school, so let's get some stuff to fill out your closet. What do you need?"

I had ground my teeth all the way to Kmart as I breathed in the new car smell of the Lexus. My mom bought this brand-new car for herself with its leather seats and power windows, but I was still wearing shit clothes.

My mom had said everything would change.

But nothing had really changed.

My mom had glared at me as she pulled into a tight space at the front of the store. Though I tried, I couldn't hide my embarrassment, my anger, or my tears. After a red smocked woman greeted us, my mom grabbed my sweatshirt and pulled me to a corner of the dusty store. The hot faintly alcohol scented breath nearly singed my eyelashes.

"Look, Little Miss Princess, when I was a child and my mother was on her hands and knees scrubbing floors, I would have been happy to have anything that didn't come from the church's donation bin. Take your ungrateful butt in here, and don't embarrass me." To emphasize her point, my mom plucked the skin on my upper arm, twisted, and had pinched–hard.

The jeans I was wearing now, I'd picked out that day. After gym class, I'd changed in a corner so the other girls wouldn't notice how I had to cinch the pants to get them to fit. Happy that I had a big terry hoodie to hide my discomfort, I wondered if I should cut my mother a little slack. After that disastrous Kmart trip, a few weeks later, my mother had come home in a better mood.

"O-liv-ia," my mother had sung out. Uncharacteristically enthusiastic, my mother bounded up the stairs to our living room. "Poppet, come here! I've got a surprise for you!"

I closed the magazine I was reading—Cameron Diaz could wait—and ran down to the living room. When my mom had a surprise, it could be really good. I'd never forgotten the time my mother had gotten me a Barbie computer. It was still one of the best days of my life.

My heart almost stopped when I saw it: the biggest shopping bag Nordstrom offered. Denim poked from the bag. My breath hitched as I gauged the chances of one hundred-dollar Lucky jeans being in there.

"Poppet, first help me with my stuff. Then you can see what's in the bag."

I hefted the yellow leather tote and briefcase, running to put them in my mother's bedroom closet. Then I hastened back downstairs.

Shifting from foot to foot, I tried to calm the butterflies somersaulting in my belly.

"Can I look in the bag or not?" I tried not to whine. That could trigger a slap in a heartbeat.

I flinched as my mother held up a hand. But it was to give pause, not to cause pain.

"Wait. Let me just tell you, these aren't new clothes."

I could feel confusion squinch up my face.

"I had lunch with some people from the firm today. You remember Nelson, right?" I nodded even though I had no idea who Nelson was. "His wife's daughter planned to donate some stuff to Goodwill. I know you like designer stuff, so I offered to take it off his hands. Look through here and whatever you don't want, we'll drop at the Salvation Army."

Excitement replaced dread when I sorted through the bag. I pulled out flared jeans that fit my curves, straight leg cords, and even a really cool striped cashmere scarf I could wear looped around my neck. My mom clapped as I modeled different looks.

We even dug out an old People magazine and made me look like one of the teen stars featured in there, braiding the scarf just right. My mom's beaming face joined mine in the mirror over the mantle. Then my mom hugged and kissed me like I was a little kid. We couldn't stop laughing.

It was a tug on that scarf by Alison that brought me back to the present.

"Can I speak with you for a second?" the counselor asked, her face looking serious. "If you ever need to talk one-on-one about your personal life, or any problems, I'm here for you. I always promise to keep stuff confidential."

Making the lonely walk down the hall to the back door and the late bus, I felt another tug at my black and white striped scarf.

"Nice scarf," Beth said. And the two girls with her laughed.

Lifting my lips hesitantly, I accepted the compliment at face value. "Thanks."

"Where'd you get it?" another girl asked.

Before I could think of a suitable lie, Beth answered.

"At the zoo!" There was a pause as the other girls looked at me and each other quizzically. "Get it? It's the love child of Olivia and Jon Heath."

The pause before the laughter was short. Heat streaked through my cheeks as I laughed with them, ignoring their casual cruelty.

5

Juvenile Court

Casey

October 9, 2001

“Has my client, Rosa Coleman, checked in?” I asked.

The bailiff gestured toward the files sloppily stacked on her desk, “What’s the child’s name?”

I held the pig leather briefcase in my arms like a baby while unzipping the top.

“Aliyah Coleman.”

Making little effort to move the folders and papers around the desk, the bailiff concluded, “Nope. She hasn’t checked in. You new to the case?”

I shook my head.

“Not exactly. I was appointed to represent Rosa when the county took permanent custody of the oldest. I got a notice, and assumed I was on the new permanent custody matter filed."

Pushing up her wire-rimmed glasses, the bailiff looked at me more closely.

"I don't think I've seen you around here before. What's your name again?"

"Casey. Casey Cort."

"Cute name."

Like I'd never heard that one before.

"You've got a doozy of a case here," the bailiff said. "This family has been in and out of here for the last five years. Good luck. I wouldn't let the mom care for my cat, much less my kids."

Initially offended, I had to wonder if I'd let Rosa care for my own cat Simba.

"If my client doesn't show up, what will the judge do?"

"Set it for another pre-trial." Gesturing to the stack again, the bailiff continued. "None of these files is complete. The prosecutor needs to finish the psych exams, the GALs need to see the kids," she said, falling into court jargon and turning back to the behemoth of a computer on her desk.

Retreating to the hard wood benches lined up like church pews along the corridor, I looked at my watch. The court was already a half hour behind. Shifting uncomfortably between an overweight mother with a wiggling four-year old on her lap and a sullen blue-haired teenager, I couldn't help feeling like I didn't belong here.

It had been nearly six years since I'd made the stupidest mistake of my life.

"I need you to represent me!" I had said, barging into Professor Sinclair's office.

Richard Sinclair had jettisoned his reading glasses and smoothed his hands through his curly graying hair. Overlooking the vanity that had always annoyed me during class, I had tried to even out my breathing.

"Ms. Cort, right?" Professor Sinclair had asked, maintaining the silly formality that separated law school from all of my education before. "You want to talk about Transactional Litigation before the final? No need to be nervous. You've always been one of my best prepared students. You lived up to your reputation."

I reached into my backpack and pulled out the letter/summons and placed it on Sinclair's desk. "This is why I'm here. I'm super confused about this letter I got."

I took another deep breath. How could this be happening to me? If I could just convince someone as smart as Professor Sinclair to come to my aid, surely it would all be fixed.

"I'm being brought before the law school's judicial board. You have to defend me."

"What exactly did you do? Cheat? Sleep with one of my colleagues?" As if seeing me for the first time, his gaze traveled from my dishwater blonde hair, down to my small breasts and larger hips. His eyes shifted to an ornate brass and wood clock on a credenza as if his quick survey had found me wanting.

"No," I said sharply. "I didn't do anything."

The professor sighed. "I have a half hour. Close the door and sit down," he said, gesturing to the leather couch.

Relieved that he was going to hear me out, I closed the door, dropped my backpack, and made a space for myself on the paper-cluttered couch.

"I'm not sure—"

"Wait," he said, eyes alight with recognition. "Did you rat out Ted Strohmeyer?"

I hated everyone calling me a rat, when it was Ted who'd done the sneaky, rat-fink thing.

"I didn't do anything."

My voice was a plea.

I sighed, sank deeper into the couch cushions and laid out my case. "Last year I was named executive note editor for the law review." He nodded. "I was looking for something to publish from a student in the fall issue. And Ted's topic was interesting, and the writing was really good. Not boring or dry."

Sinclair nodded.

"I was doing a search to make sure some other school hadn't just published something similar, but there was an article just like it from Valparaiso. I started reading it to see if maybe I could figure a way to get Ted's note in..."

"And?"

"Ted's was the same, not just the idea but whole paragraphs and even footnotes."

"Why didn't you move on to someone else's? No one would have faulted you for not publishing a plagiarized note."

"You sound like my boyfriend. It didn't seem right that he got to put law review on his resume, when he didn't do the work. I looked at the honor code and reported it to Dean Condit."

"Ms. Cort, can I call you by your first name?" Relief flooded my veins. If they were going to work together on my defense, he wouldn't want to call me by my last name all the time.

I nodded.

"Casey is fine."

"You knew the note was written by Ted Strohmeyer, right?"

"Why should that make a difference?" I was bewildered by the focus on *who'd* done the plagiarizing.

"Off the record. Ted Strohmeyer's great-grandfather started the Strohmeyer Beer Company. You know, *'You'll be a high-flyer, when you drink Strohmeyer,'*" he sang a jingle, as familiar as my own name. "His dad's a modern-day hero in Cleveland. He has naming rights to the stadium, and negotiated with the NFL to keep an expansion team in town."

"What does that have to do with me? *I* did the right thing—outing plagiarism, saving the school embarrassment. Why am I being scapegoated?"

"That's the way the world works, Casey," Professor Sinclair said matter-of-factly. "Why do they want to remove you from the law review post? Losing that post could end your legal career before it even begins."

I pushed the wrinkled envelope I'd laid down earlier closer to him. I'd torn open the letter, but couldn't make heads or tails of it through the blur of tears. Professor Sinclair's upturned hand urged me to continue. I slipped the letter I'd picked up at my parents' house across the desk. Reading glasses perched on the end of his nose, he read silently.

"Dereliction of duty? Sounds like you were in the army and didn't scrub enough toilets to get promoted from private."

"I'm not sure what it means either."

He scanned it again, then spoke.

"Bottom line: they're saying you can't do the job."

I held my breath in check, trying not to whine, 'why me' like a seven-year-old.

"I've worked really hard. I go to every meeting. I wanted us to be well-respected like Harvard."

Professor Sinclair's cough almost sounded like a laugh. He'd gone to Columbia, been editor-in-chief, he had to understand. "Have you had conflicts with other students on the board?"

"No," I said quickly.

He pounced. "Don't rush to answer," Sinclair said. "People are never brought down for the big stuff. It's always the little things."

It was such a small thing.

"The editors were mad at me the first couple of weeks."

"Why?"

I told him about how I wanted to solicit the best writing from students all over the country, and how the other editors had only wanted to publish their work. I knew I'd gone on too long when Professor Sinclair reclined.

"Maybe you should resign."

I shook my head vigorously. "I worked really hard these last two years. I was elected. I *deserve* this."

"Do you have a job after graduation?" When I nodded, he continued. "You're lucky. Coming from a lower tier school, most kids in your position would sit back and take it easy until the bar exam."

Professor Sinclair's chair still reclined. His level of outrage didn't match mine.

"Are you going to defend me before the board?" He didn't answer right away. "I don't think I can do this on my own." I hated the pleading tone in her voice.

His chair bolted upright with a large squeak. "I'll take this on." he said. "Leave it with me."

Stupidly, I'd left it with Sinclair. He'd caved into pressure from the editors and their faculty rep in the first few minutes. After that, my life had collapsed like fallen dominoes. Two weeks later, I had lost it all: my position on the law review, my job, and my well-connected boyfriend, Tom Brody. Just like that, my dreams of living better than my parents, having sophisticated clients and the perfect husband had vanished. Instead I was here in juvenile court.

"Miss Casey, I'm here. I'm here!" Rosa yelled. She ran to me, crumpled papers in hand.

I heaved a sigh of relief.

"They haven't called the hearing yet. Let me check you in with the bailiff. Then I need to talk to you."

I snagged the court's file from the bailiff and took Rosa to a couple of chairs in a corner. I shushed my client as I reviewed the facts the court had. At thirty years old, Rosa was the mother of five children, three to seventeen, and she'd been involved with Children and Family Services nearly all the years she'd had those kids. The county was going for permanent custody of the remainder of the kids in custody.

Though Rosa looked fine to me, albeit rough around the edges, she was supposedly an alcohol and drug addict prone to violence. Last year she'd threatened to stab the father of two of her children.

The hallways of juvenile court were as clogged as an artery after Thanksgiving because of the Adoption and Safe Families Act. To prevent what had been coined foster care drift, the new law shortened the period the parents had to work toward reunification. Of course, Rosa was running out of time.

"Where have you been? It's nearly two o'clock. You were supposed to be here by one. Do you understand that they're trying to take away your kids *permanently?*" Rosa nodded, but I didn't think her client had a proper sense of urgency. "I can't do this by myself, Rosa. This is your case."

"I've been doin' my stuff, Miss Casey," Rosa said, contrite. She proffered the crumpled papers from her hand. "These are my certificates, a letter showing I have an apartment, and a pay stub," she said.

I smoothed out the wrinkled papers as best I could. If I'd had corporate clients, they would be handing over crisp sheets of paper or sending me documents via e-mail, not this.

Sighing, I looked over them. There was a parenting class completion certificate, some kind of letter scrawled on notebook paper, and a handwritten pay stub. The only outward sign of my frustration were lips I couldn't help compress.

"Did you get my letters, Rosa? I need these kinds of things on official letterhead. We have to *prove* to a *court* that you've done all these things," I said.

"I got some of your letters. My mom read 'em to me. But why can't the social worker just call to check? I can get her the phone numbers," Rosa said.

I put the papers in the outside pocket of my leather case. "The time for that has passed, Rosa. The social workers are not on your side anymore. If they win, you will never see your kids again. Ever. No phone calls. No visits. Nothing." I paused for dramatic effect. "The judge is not going to take your word for it.

"Like this letter you brought," I said, trying not to tear the notebook paper I eased from the briefcase's pocket. "This may well be from your landlord—but without letterhead—without it being notarized, we don't have enough proof."

Rosa pouted. "I wish I had me some money. If I could get Johnnie Cochran, I'd get my kids back for sure."

I silently damned O.J. Simpson. If I had a penny for every time I'd heard that, I could easily pay off my student loans. Letting the insult roll off my back, I tried again. "Let's look at this. Did you do the ninety-day inpatient drug treatment?" I flipped through the file again. "CFS referred you to the Clean Cleveland program."

Rosa shook her head. "I couldn't do no long thing like that. I couldn't even get into that place. I went to A Better Start. It was a thirty-day program. I did real good there. Now I'm working with Margo on the outpatient thing."

I clicked my pen, taking notes on my legal pad. "That's good. Do you have Margo's number, a certificate of satisfactory completion?"

"Call over there and ask for her. She knows me," Rosa said with confidence. I rolled my eyes involuntarily, but made a note.

The rest of our short interview went the same way. This was why two hundred fifty dollars didn't stretch far. When clients didn't have to pay for their lawyers, they weren't inspired to do any of the heavy lifting. I knew I'd spend at least an hour tracking down these folks, getting them to fax me letters on actual letterhead, and this was only *if* Rosa's information was accurate.

"Coleman!" the clerk yelled. "The judge is ready. Are all parties here?" I rushed to the courtroom as fast has my weight would allow.

Prosecutor Dick Foster was permanently planted on the left side of Judge MacKinnon's courtroom. A young woman, county ID badge dangling between her breasts, joined him at the table. Another, older woman—probably the guardian *ad Litem*—stayed behind the bar.

Dorthea MacKinnon was a popular judge. She was reasonable, listened to all the facts, and tried to make the best rulings given the circumstances. Despite that, how she'd gotten to the bench was an open joke among the bar. One couldn't walk more than a few steps in the courthouse without hearing tales of Judge MacKinnon's many failed attempts at running for office. Most of the judges in the county had been on the bench forever or had come from judicial family legacies, where surname recognition had launched their careers.

Weather-beaten billboards with the text, "Dorthea MacKinnon, Judge" had littered Cleveland for years. She'd won, most thought, because the billboards had been up so long that the voters had finally given into the constant visual assault. No matter a judge's pedigree, everyone rose when they came to the courtroom.

MacKinnon plunked down her afternoon coffee before taking a seat. Attendance taken, the bailiff pressed record on the tape recorder that stood in for a court reporter and left the room.

"Good afternoon. Sorry we're late today. Judges' monthly luncheon ran over. I see we're here on the Coleman/Andress children. Ms. Coleman, I remember you. On the record we have Prosecutor Foster, Sonia Casiano. Are you the social worker?"

The young dark-haired woman at the prosecutor's table nodded her head.

"I see Glenda Ober in the back. You're the GAL?" Then she turned to me. "Now you, I don't know."

I brought myself to my full five-foot height.

"Good afternoon, Your Honor. I'm Casey Cort. I was appointed a few months ago to represent Rosa during the disposition of her oldest daughter's case. Now I'm here on the PC matter." I used my best authoritative voice.

"Miss Cort. Nice to meet you. Now let's get down to the nuts and bolts of this case. We're here on a pre-trial hearing in the matter of Aliyah and Aaron Coleman, and Angel and Alexa Andress. In a previous hearing, Aliyah was committed to the permanent custody of her maternal grandmother. That case duly severed, we're only going forward on the three youngest kids, right?

"Mr. Foster, what's the story on the fathers in this case?" MacKinnon asked, looking at him over her reading glasses. Foster spoke softly to the social worker for a few seconds, then flipped through a thick manila folder. "Jimmy Coleman and Roy Andress," MacKinnon prompted.

"We haven't been able to find either Jimmy or Roy to administer paternity tests. Although Jimmy doesn't need a test because he was married to Mom. I'll stipulate on that one."

Judge MacKinnon turned to me. "Do you have any further information? Are the dads going to be here? They face losing their kids."

I turned to Rosa. Blank stare.

"My client doesn't have any further information."

Judge MacKinnon made a note. "We'll have them served at their last known address," she said. "Absentee fathers," MacKinnon muttered under her breath, her head shaking vigorously. "Well, Mom, at least you're here. Let's hear from the county and the guardian. How are the kids doing?"

Sonia Casiano stood.

"Aliyah is going to school and doing real well with her grandmother." She read from her notes. "Aaron and Angel are living in the same foster home, but they're facing some challenges. Now that we've had the time to have them tested—they've been diagnosed with ADHD. But they're on meds and responding. Their foster parents have been real good with training on meds and stuff.

"Alexa isn't doing so well. She's acting out with boys. We're thinking a more restrictive setting like an all-girls group home would be good." She turned toward Casey and Rosa. "Mom said that she's completed parenting, drug treatment, that she has a suitable house, but I don't have any certificates yet—"

"I got my papers right here!" Rosa interrupted, shooting her hand in the air like an eager grade-schooler. "I gave them to my lawyer—"

"Counselor!" I squirmed in my seat under the judge's rebuke. "Please instruct your client that she's not to speak at this hearing. Please continue, Miss Casiano."

"Anyways, I visited Mom's new apartment. There's enough rooms for all the kids, but there aren't any appliances. The department wouldn't send the kids home without a stove or refrigerator."

"I'm getting my stuff next week. The guy promised to put it in," Rosa said.

"Ms. Cort," the judge warned. Heat stole up my cheeks. I laid a firm hand on Rosa's bouncing knee. The judge turned back to the social worker. "These kids have some challenges. I'm sure the county will address that. Moving forward. Let's set a date for the permanent custody hearing. One afternoon enough?"

I opened my Filofax at the same time the guardian snapped the stylus from her Palm Pilot. The bailiff came into the room, judge's calendar in hand. "How about December sixth? One o'clock? Good for everyone?"

"Works for me, Your Honor," I said.

"I'm free Thursday afternoon as well," the GAL said.

The judge rose from the bench and walked into her chambers, signaling the hearing was over.

"Miss Cort," Rosa pleaded. "I've got to get my kids back. They belong with me. I'll do right this time, get a job, make sure the bills are paid. I promise."

"I hope you get that chance." I wrapped a hand around Rosa's emaciated arm, escorting her from the courtroom. In an alcove away from everyone, I willed Rosa to meet me eye to eye. "You need to work with me. We have to prove that you are ready to have your kids back."

Rosa put on her coat, pulling a pager from her pocket. She casually scrolled through her messages. I jerked Rosa's arm. The pager fell to the floor with a clatter, earning us a reproachful glance from the sheriff monitoring the hall.

"You need to listen to me. That prosecutor in there will have evidence and witnesses ready to tell the judge your kids are better off in the system. We need to be ready, too. To win this, you'll have to fight this."

Rosa rescued the cherry red pager.

"I'll call you tomorrow, Ms. Cort. I promise." Rosa was out the door before I could get in another word. I looked around for the guardian, but Glenda's head was shaking, repelling my approach. With one big sigh, I readied myself for the cold long walk back to her office. I suspected I wouldn't hear from Rosa until December.

6

Home Fires

Sheila

October 12, 2001

The brass keys rattled in my shaking hand. Finding the lock, I pushed through the door. Olivia was lying on the couch as if there wasn't a room needing cleaning or homework that needed doing.

Cookie crumbs fell off my daughter's belly spreading light and dark brown flecks all over the white couch when my daughter shot up, lowering the volume from blaring to annoying.

"Get your feet off that couch. How many times…? Never mind. Come here and help me with this."

My sister Deidre and I would never have gotten away with this. As soon as our mom and dad came home, we'd have rushed to the kitchen to add vegetables to a stew, or make sure the potatoes were ready. Not this one. She'd gotten her responsibility genes from her father.

Olivia grabbed for a thin brown paper bag in my hand. I stepped back. My daughter, never graceful, almost toppled over.

"Livvy, don't be a klutz. Grab my briefcase. It's the heaviest."

My daughter relieved my sore back of the briefcase and a leather tote that held spillover work. Shrugging off my jacket, I walked to the kitchen and shoved my purchase to the back of a cabinet out of Olivia's reach. Leaning against the gold speckled Formica counter, I violated my house rule of always putting things in their proper place, and kicked off my heels. Curling and stretching my stockinged feet, I let the cool tile relieve the ache in the arch of my foot.

"What have you eaten today, Olivia?" I watched my daughter straddle a kitchen chair, eyes glued to MTV.

"Cafeteria lunch. Some cookies after school."

Even at twelve, Olivia was moving past what I would have called 'healthy.' It was showing in her face and butt. I tried not to imagine what my colleagues thought when they saw Olivia. My former partner's children were all gangly kids, engaged in year-round sports. The only exercise my daughter got was working her fingers on the remote control.

"I don't know why you eat that junk. You have to learn it's all about calories in, calories out. What do you want for dinner?" I gestured to the cold, empty stove. "I'm going to order in."

"Whatever."

I pulled a menu from the drawer and dialed the phone.

"I'd like to order two small antipasto salads for delivery." I paused, trying to concentrate on the usual litany of questions. “Yes, no. No dressing. If you must, put it on the side.” She gave our Latimore address. “Olivia. Handle this delivery when it comes. I’m going upstairs to change. I’ll be back when the food gets here.”

Barely able to pull her eyes away from the swirl of television color, Olivia took the proffered cash, jamming it into her pocket.

Decibel by decibel, the volume increased. Olivia would go deaf if I didn’t keep an eye on that girl.

Teenagers.

After opening the cabinet, I removed my favorite glass. Its diamond design mimicked the crystal Peyton had in his apartment. The heft of the glass belied its true origin. Pulling a bagged bottle from the back of the cabinet, I poured enough of the golden liquid to fill half the glass. I put the bag back, and topped off my glass with plain cola. Picking up my shoes, I moseyed up the narrow stairs to my third-floor bedroom. Lying back against the pillows, I sipped the bittersweet liquid. Peace.

“Close the door behind you,” Peyton Bennett, Junior had said.

I had been with the firm for more than a few years, and I’d never been behind a closed door with anyone. Not sure if I should have been nervous or happy, I’d sat, bouncing a yellow pad on my knees. Peyton, who’d been an associate when I’d joined, had recently made partner. Not that the son of the firm’s founder firm getting a promotion had come as a shock.

Peyton looked at his watch, its gold gleaming in the faint light from the slim window.

"You want something?" I didn't answer as Peyton turned and helped himself to something from his decanter. He turned back, crystal in hand and looked at me. "Drink?"

Lead crystal had never been something real people did. The characters on the drama-filled stories my mother was always trying to catch were filled with old white men in leather chairs, cigars and decanters at the ready. What the hell? Maybe a little something would calm my nerves.

"Sure," I'd finally replied.

Peyton filled a second glass then pushed it across the desk. I took one sip of the liquid. The burn was unexpected, and I tried to cover my mouth as my throat closed up, sputtering and coughing in protest.

"Oh God, I'm sorry," Peyton said, moving papers and bottles. "Topping it off with some ginger ale might help."

Keeping up with the guys was important. I took another sip of the doctored drink. It slid down much better this time. My insides were warm, despite the cold January sun. My knee stopped bouncing.

"I'm planning to start an informal mentoring program at the firm."

"What did your dad think of that?" I blurted. My face grew warmer as regret stilled my heart. Damned alcohol had loosened my tongue. Peyton Bennett, Sr. was no fan of coddling associates. They could all sink or swim for all he cared. I was barely treading water.

He leaned forward and smiled at me. From his clear blue eyes to the quirk of his lips, the smile seemed genuine. "Fortunately, BFB is not a dictatorship. We put it to a partner vote, and the majority ruled."

I took another sip. It felt good to lose the knife edge of nerves that I perilously stood on every day, afraid to make one fatal slip.

"Where do I come in?"

"I'm your mentor."

"Does this mean I'll make partner?" I'd had to ask. Never ask, never receive, my father had always said.

Peyton let out a hearty laugh. I had to laugh as well, glad now that the door was closed and the hallway was not filled with our giggles.

"You've always had a one-track mind. I picked you because I don't think the firm is strongly behind your long-term career. I want you to get as fair a shake as the other associates. I don't know a lot about you though." He paused.

Thought.

Considered.

"Can I ask you a question?"

I hesitated. Honesty was not the best policy in the legal world. Making a truth that fit a narrative was better. I laid the pad and my pen on his desk. "Peyton, I..."

He grasped my hand, a friendly gesture. Awareness of Peyton as a man came unbidden. Our eyes locked, and his smile disappeared. I snatched my hand back like it was on fire.

He refilled both our glasses. I drained mine this time, no coughing or gagging. He sipped thoughtfully. Neither of us talked about the tension in the room, as thick as the evening fog rolling in from Lake Erie.

"I wanted to ask you what you'd do if you didn't make it here."

My stomach bottomed out for an entirely different reason, this time. My left thumb stroked the smooth metal of my wedding band. My husband Keith would want me to quit and have a house full of kids. But I had to make it. I needed the security of a permanent job.

"Of course, making partner is paramount. I want to contribute to the firm, build on the legacy of Bennett—"

"I know all that. But what else?"

"What are you asking me?"

"I'm asking you what else you've dreamed of? I'm not asking you as a partner, or your mentor. I'm interested in you, Sheila. You keep very quiet here. Hold yourself apart from the others. Hole up in your office, like we'll give it away if you're not in there all day and night. I want to know what makes you tick. I've never known anyone like you."

Black, from the east side is what he probably meant. Though black and white people had been living together in Cleveland for at least a hundred and fifty years, we might as well live an ocean apart, not just a few miles. I chose my words carefully.

"I've always thought about being a judge, maybe."

There, I'd said it. My biggest dream. Something I knew would probably never happen. Cleveland judges were elected, and the political machine didn't elect a lot of black ones.

"Cool. Who knows? Maybe one day you'll leave us to do that. Turn the tables. Judge us instead of us judging you." And that had been it. He hadn't laughed or made fun of me. Instead he'd talked about the kind of cases that I'd have to handle to succeed at the firm.

"Mom, the food is here," my daughter called from below.

Taking my time, I sat on the edge of the bed and stared at the empty glass in my hand, remembering the weekly mentoring sessions with Peyton.

He'd tutored me in the finer points of the law—and expensive alcohol. I'd once heard another mom call the evening drink 'mother's little helper.' There was a lot of truth in those three words.

Without a man's strong hands to help ease the kink of a knotted muscle, I rolled my shoulders and dropped my head to loosen the tension that settled between my shoulder blades. There was no rest for black folks; working twice as hard only to get half as far as white folks.

I had a judicial appointment that wasn't all the way there, after leaving a partnership that I'd clawed my way to, only to have it slip through my hands like sand. Putting on what my mother would have called a housedress, I girded myself for dinner.

"Mommy!" my daughter shouted again.

"Honey," I called down. "I know you're not putting that salad dressing on there. It's nothing but fat and calories you don't need."

When I came down, I could see the leaves and meat glistening all the way from the dining room door.

"Mom, an antipasto salad is *meant* to have dressing," Olivia retorted. This girl.... Lifetime habits had to start now.

"How was school today?"

My daughter swallowed hard. For a moment, I felt a twinge of guilt for taking her out of Bethune, but that was quickly swept away by the thought of the opportunities she'd have from a real school like Shaker High.

"School's okay so far. But the kids are really standoffish. No one talks to me." She sighed as if she had the weight of the world on those narrow shoulders. "I wish I had more friends than just Cate. She doesn't even want to talk to me or sit with me at lunch all the time–"

"Olivia, I'm not friends with a single person I knew in junior high. You don't need these kids. Just keep your head in your books."

My daughter's light brown cheeks flushed red. "How would you know, Mom? You don't have any friends. I don't want to grow up to be old and lonely like you."

I gripped my glass so hard I thought it might break. I had never talked back to my mother.

Never.

Behavior like Olivia's would have earned me a full-on beating with a switch, or a slap if I was lucky. But you hit kids these days, and they were calling nine-one-one in a heartbeat.

"Olivia. You do not want to be anything like those white kids. Keep your head down, do your work, and make sure your grades are good." I took a long drink, letting the liquid give me patience. "Don't worry if these damned kids like you or not. You need to worry about getting A's, getting into a good college, and a better graduate school. You're gonna need a good job to support yourself so you don't have to rely on any man. These privileged kids can goof off partying and they'll be just fine. They're not worrying about you, so don't you worry about them."

Glad to see the message received, I pushed aside my half-eaten salad. Olivia devoured hers like she was starving.

Come to think of it, I hadn't seen much in the way of tests or grades since the school year had started. "When are your progress reports due?" I asked. "Seems about time for you to have gotten some kind of grades."

Olivia shifted, suddenly uncomfortable in her seat. Her cheeks grew red again.

"We haven't gotten them yet," she said. "It's sometime next week, I think." I could see my daughter's belly poking out over her jeans, and yet she pulled a piece of Italian bread from the foil packet and spread a thick layer of butter.

"Are you going to eat that, too?" I asked, incredulous. "You've already had salad and dressing. You can't still be hungry."

It was as if my daughter didn't hear me. Instead, Olivia spread the butter thicker, swallowing the bread in two bites. After chasing the bread with cola, Olivia shuffled from the dining room back to the living room couch.

I swallowed the remaining contents in the glass but thirsted for more. The faces of four twenty-something actresses flashed on the screen, an old Beatles tune, a theme song for the show. Why did my daughter take such solace in this fake world where everyone had perfect hair and teeth, nice clothes, and big houses—though you never saw them do a lick of work. I didn't have the energy to parent this child tonight, to steer her on the right path.

Maybe tomorrow.

I got one more drink to relax before joining my daughter for another night of escapism on the couch.

7

Progress Report

Olivia

October 19, 2001

I didn't know what jolted me awake, until I opened her eyes and saw a very angry mother standing over me. My body turned leaden with dread.

"Well, Princess, I'm glad you finally deigned to wake." Mom's voice was scarily calm. She brandished a folded paper under her nose. "Perhaps you can tell me the meaning of this?" Calm turned accusatory.

Despite great effort, fear prevented me from getting my mouth and brain to work in concert. Not waiting for an answer, my mother went on with morning red eyes that were the stuff of horror movies. I shrank back as far toward the wall as I could.

The shouting started then.

"Why in the hell am I busting my ass to keep you in Shaker Heights? We left Glenville so that you could go to a school that challenged you—and you come home with these grades?

"To have the nerve, the absolute *nerve*, to hide these from me—for a week, no less. Have you lost your ever-lovin' mind? Where do you think you're going in life with grades like this?"

The finger came out then, jabbing me hard in the sternum. That would hurt for days. I hoped it didn't leave a bruise I'd have to explain away during gym class.

"How many God damn times do I have to tell you that black people don't get a fair shake in this country? Unless our credentials are stellar, we get passed over.

"Before you were born, I worked my ass off for years, finally making partner at Bennett Friehof. Then despite this family and no support from anyone, I got appointed to this judgeship—a job where some white man can't fire me. Do you know that it was hell for me finding a job? I had straight effing 'A's in college and law school, but hiring partners didn't care.

"I got in when they couldn't turn me down and worked day and night, turning in flawless memos and briefs, only to be passed over for partner, year after year. I watched boys who'd graduated years after I did—who I *trained*, order me around on cases, telling me what to do, closing the door on me when decisions were being made."

The lingering smell of alcohol on my mother's breath surrounded me like a cloud. I didn't dare wipe away the spit that had flown from my mom's mouth and landed on my face.

"With this kind of mediocre performance, you'll end up just like your father, lucky to have any piece of shit job at all."

My ears perked at the mention of my father. Mom hardly ever talked about him. Maybe I could live with him one day, if I could find him.

He might not have a lot of money, but at least he didn't drink. My mom was still yelling. "You watch all that God damn TV—talking about how you want to leave 'boring old Cleveland'—wantin' to work for some glossy New York magazine or at a television network. Well, *none of them* are going to want some roly-poly black girl with a second-rate education.

"Aren't you going to answer me?" My mother's hands curled around the covers and snatched them to the floor. The cool air only had a moment to hit my body before my mother yanked me out of the bed by my left arm.

At once, I was standing up and rubbing the shoulder of the arm my mother had pulled so hard. When I thought my mother wasn't looking, I stole a glance at the clock radio. Crap. Not only was my mother on the warpath, but at this rate, I was going to miss the school bus and have to ride with her, too.

Mom continued, "Go wash up and get dressed in those overpriced clothes you're always asking for. I'll take you to school today."

I ran to the bathroom, and even though I tried hard to hold it all together, my eyes smarted, and my nose dripped. Thank God my mother didn't see. There was little room for emotion in my mother's house. I did my best to pull it all together for school in less than ten minutes.

My mother just didn't understand.

School was boring.

What was the point?

I had never seen any adult doing equations or filling in blank maps. As long as I understood what the teachers were going on about, I wasn't worried about my future. I knew I'd be fine as soon as I could get to college and away from my mother.

I didn't say any of that to my mother, of course. The angry diatribe continued all the way down Shaker Boulevard. There was no time to look at the mansions and imagine the fairy tale lives of their occupants. My hope for tense quiet was misplaced.

"Don't just sit there with your mouth stuck out," my mother hissed. "What are you going to do to fix this? I didn't raise no idiot." My mother shook her head vigorously. Then she pressed down on the gas, hard. The car shot forward, barely missing the bumper of the SUV in front of it. My mother hardly noticed. "You're going to hunker down and do what's necessary to get straight A's. There will be more working and a lot less TV watching."

We pulled onto Belvoir Oval, my mother finally taking a breath.

"Now get in there and learn something—you sorry excuse for a child."

Tasting freedom, I pushed open the door, when I felt the vicious pinch of the flesh on my upper left arm.

I knew from experience that no reaction was always better, but I couldn't contain the exclamation of pain and the tears that sprung to my eyes. I jumped out with my backpack and felt nothing but a whoosh of air as the car door slammed behind me.

Six hours later, I walked to the Friday afternoon 'For Girls Only!' meeting alone, head held high. Beth galloped toward me in the hall. Despite the early morning fight with my mom, I was pleased with myself for getting my clothes right today. My Britney Spears newsboy cap, flared jeans and long-sleeved tee looked like everyone else's clothes.

"Hey, Olivia," Beth called out, her glossy lips in a wide smile.

"Hey," I answered, playing it cool. Something fluttered near my heart. I couldn't believe Beth was talking to me *in school*, in front of *everyone*.

"Cate's party was awesome, huh? I'd never had Japanese before. That guy with the knives, cool right?"

"Yeah, it was pretty neat," I said, then mentally kicked myself for sounding like such a dork.

Beth graciously held the library's glass door for me.

"Oh, and by the way, that's a great hat that you're wearing today."

"Thanks," I said, the warm feeling spreading outward from my center, making me smile. Maybe this new school wasn't going to be so bad. Maybe Beth *was* really nice, underneath. Maybe Cate, Beth and I would all be good friends one day.

"Is it some kind of special holiday?" Beth asked. "Are all of you wearing hats today?"

I looked around the library, but no one else sported a cap.

"Who?"

"You know. All you guys."

I shook my head, not comprehending.

"The black kids? Marquis and some of the other homeboys were wearing hats today. Did you guys plan it? Was it some kind of new holiday like Kwanzaa?"

Happiness bubble deflated, my head sagged.

"No, I don't think so. It musta been a coincidence," I answered mechanically then walked over to get paper for my weekly question. Sitting alone on the far side of the room, I got out my favorite pen and asked about the one thing that was really bothering me.

When the wool hat went around, I dropped in her question. My stomach did flip flops, worried that anonymity wasn't guaranteed. Alison fished out a slip of paper and read it silently.

"Okay," Alison said, her brightness hard and brittle as winter ice. Even her neatly pressed gray pantsuit and purple silk blouse seemed to droop a little. "Today's first question is: How do I know if my mom drinks too much?" Her ever-ready smile dimmed a few watts. "Okay, girls," she said to the suddenly dead quiet room. "What do you think?"

Beth's hand shot up.

"Alison, I think that anyone in a situation like that should seek out counseling from a trusted adult like you," she said with a kiss-ass smile. "Or a priest, minister, or rabbi. Something like that is too difficult for anyone our age to handle on their own. This girl needs an adult to help her."

I swung my legs with the urge to kick blonde Beth where it hurt. I needed real advice, not something I could have picked up in a stupid magazine. A few of the other girls had similar suggestions. None of it helped at all. After a while, I couldn't hear anything past the whooshing in her ears.

Skip this.

I needed to get home. If I got perfect grades like I used to, maybe my mom wouldn't be so mad or drink so much. I leaned down and packed up my bag, but couldn't work up the guts to leave the meeting early.

After the meeting, I walked toward the back doors to the late busses waiting behind the school. The other girls left together, planning a pizza night at someone's house. Of course, I wasn't invited. Accompanied by the shouts of the school's athletes, I started to push the huge bar that opened the back door. A hand grabbed at my left arm, hitting the spot still sore from my mom's pinch that morning.

"Ow!" I whirled around, ready to confront one of the loud boys, but it was only Alison, purple hat still in her other hand.

"Olivia, is it possible for you to come to my office for a quick second? Right now." Alison's voice was a few octaves lower, serious.

I gestured toward the students filing through the back exit. "The late bus leaves now. I don't have a ride home." With no stay-at-home-mom who could pick me up at a moment's notice, the walk from Shaker Middle to my house on Latimore had to easily be four or five miles.

"This is important," Alison said in a low but fierce whisper, leading my unwilling self into the guidance wing, parting me from the student throng. "*I'll* drive you home."

I sat down in the flowery smelling office, shrugging my coat off my shoulders. It wasn't quite winter, but the steam heat was going full force, fogging Alison's window.

The normally chipper counselor wasn't smiling as she cocked a hip on the edge of the desk, facing me. Her stare held accusation.

"I know you were the girl who asked about the mom drinking."

I gasped, immediately clamping my hand over her mouth, all chance of denial down the drain.

"I recognized your turquoise sparkly pen," she said, a nervous smile returning. "It's like I promised, the questions *are* confidential. I don't tell any other teachers or counselors what's said in the group. And I certainly don't tell any of the girls who wrote a question." She paused, deliberately softening her tone. "I've been worried about you. Your midterm grades weren't that good, though your IQ scores show that you're smart."

Something dislodged in my chest, but I didn't speak. I'd been warned for as long as I could remember about black folks 'putting their business out in the street for white people to know.' But I'd been bottling up secrets for so long. Before I could stop them, the words bubbled forth.

"Alison," I began, voice trembling. "I hate going home at night. My mom always comes in with a paper bag—like I'm not supposed to notice—with a bottle of rum with its red, white, and gold label."

"Does she drink every night?" Alison asked, kneeling to meet my eyes.

"Almost. When she thinks I'm not looking, she leans all the way to the back of the cabinet, pouring rum in a glass. Then she tops it off with Coke." For the third time that day, I worked to hold back tears.

"Are you ever scared that she's going to hurt you?" Alison's eyes darted away for a minute. "Or even hurt herself?"

I shook my head. "She doesn't fall or anything. She just falls asleep on the couch, or goes to her room. Sometimes I wake up and her TV's still going."

"What's wrong with your arm?"

My right hand reflexively moved to the back of my left arm. My eyes slid to the floor.

"Nothing."

"Let me see." Before I could protest, Alison had pushed the sleeve of my tee all the way to my arm pit. The bruise, already turning green, seemed to pulse like a neon light. "Where did you get this?"

"I tripped and hit the bed post when I was pulling on my pants this morning." I jerked down my sleeve and shrugged on my jacket.

"Does she pass out? Like, forget what happened when she was drinking?"

A bad feeling started in the pit of my belly and radiated through my body. I'd made a mistake. Alison was too interested. It wasn't so bad, my life. I needed to get home as soon as I could.

"She's fine. Can I go home now?"

"Let's go," she said. But the questions continued in the hall. I kind of wished I'd stayed to make sure Alison knew it wasn't serious. That I wasn't some kid in a Lifetime movie. "Have you talked to your dad...Keith Grant...about this?"

I pulled up my hood, and spoke to it rather than Alison.

"I haven't seen him in a while. He lives on the Westside. My mom and him don't really get along."

Slipping into a black leather blazer and getting out car keys, Alison pushed open the door we'd abandoned earlier. "Let's get out of here."

Despite my worry about what Alison might do, I was awed walking toward the faculty parking lot. I knew teachers were real people, but I couldn't believe I was going to ride in a counselor's car. The car was a super cute blue Volkswagen. Maybe I'd drive something like it one day.

The car's dark interior was quiet as we made the short drive. Pulling up in front, Alison turned to me. "Are you okay to go home tonight?"

"It's fine," I said. "Things are okay at home. I don't want you to think it's like some movie or something. My mom will probably surprise me with dinner out tonight."

Before I could pull the handle, Alison was asking questions again.

"What happened to your front door? Did someone break in?"

I shifted as close to the door as I could, the lip of the leather seat poking me in the butt.

"No, um after Cate's mom dropped me off a couple weeks ago, I forgot my keys and couldn't get into the house."

"And?" The question was loaded with disapproval.

"I, uh, just broke that little window pane, to turn the lock. The landlord put that cardboard there until it gets fixed." I pulled at the handle, but Alison had yet to unlock the doors.

"Why didn't your mom let you in?"

"She was supposed to pick me up. But she fell asleep. I forgot my keys, so it was really my fault. My mom always says I should wear my keys around my neck or attached to my backpack." I nervously fingered the zipper on my bag. "Sometimes I forget…."

Alison's face was neither smiling nor carefully neutral, two expressions I had gotten used to. There was a pinched look to her face, a deep crease between her brows. But she finally popped the locks.

The cool fall air was a relief. Swinging my feet out onto the damp tree lawn, I looked back. "You're not going to tell anyone what I said, right? Cause, you know, things are really okay with my mom. She's got this great new job. We moved to Shaker, and things are a lot better. We just had a rough time because my grades were—"

"Don't worry, Olivia. I'm only here to make things better for you."

8

Clients Don't Pay

Casey

October 6, 2001

I jammed my card back into the ATM. I hated using the bank on weekends; the machines always ran out of money. Maybe if I only asked for twenty instead of sixty. I glanced across Shaker Square at the long line of brunch patrons. Damn, I should have put my name on the list *before* I went toe-to-toe with the bank.

The card spit out again. I shoved it in one last time, checking my balance. A small receipt crept out of the printer. I snatched it up.

$16.03.

My bank balance was sixteen dollars. I looked at the damp line shifting behind me. So much for breakfast.

Balling up the receipt, so no one could laugh at my balance, I shoved it into the overflowing trash bin next to the machine.

It was too late to cancel my plans with Lulu now. Rounding the square, I investigated the contents of my wallet. I had enough for fruit salad or oatmeal, but not both. Today was going to be the first day of my new starvation diet.

After putting my name on the list, I leaned against the iron railing separating the waiting diners from parked cars on the square. Names were called. The rain dwindled from drizzle to fog. Finally, Lulu came running toward me, waving her hands to get my attention. The arm flailing was unnecessary. No one missed Lulu.

My friend Lulu Mueller was a self-styled Jewish Diva. She'd always said that's what the two letters on her law degree really stood for.

Today, in addition to her gold Cartier glasses, she was sporting a skinny belted gold raincoat tied in a big Christmas like bow at the widest part of her pear-shaped figure. Not a great look on any woman of eastern European descent. I did everything I could to downplay my own frame. But I wasn't going to be the one to burst Lulu's fashion bubble.

Lulu pulled me into a bear hug.

"Girl, so good to see you. We gotta talk about what's going on with you." Since Lulu was the child of a gastroenterologist, I'd always considered her ghetto talk a put-on. But Lulu insisted that growing up in increasingly black Cleveland Heights, her speech was a natural byproduct of integration.

Despite my admittedly homely appearance and Lulu's, well, diva look—we came from very similar backgrounds.

We were the children of immigrants. First generation achievers. Lulu's parents were from Eastern Europe, by way of Israel. My family were Polish and German.

We'd barely made it to the back of the packed restaurant, hung our jackets and folded our umbrellas when a harried waitress plunked two water glasses on the table and pulled out her pad.

"You ready to order?"

Fuck it, I thought. Lulu could pay. I needed leftovers since groceries were off the list for today.

"I'll have the Killit Skillet." The popular entrée came in its own cast iron skillet with eggs, hash browns, bacon, sausage—all covered in melted cheese—and chased down by a loaf of ciabatta bread.

"I'll have the sunrise special, drop the hash browns. Give me some grits. Y'all have cheese grits up in here today?"

The waitress tapped her pad. "Only butter grits."

"Okay, I'll have those. But maybe you could sprinkle some cheese on there."

When the waitress walked away, I looked at the mini menu standing between our salt and pepper. "Nowhere does it say anything about grits."

"Girl, you're on the Eastside now. Every diner has grits."

"But it's not on the menu."

Lulu shook her head.

"I hope you don't kill that skillet. That's a lot of food, and you've been getting a bit thick since law school."

"Maybe I'm going to save it for lunch, dinner, and breakfast. Maybe if I could afford a gym membership, I wouldn't be packing it on. Maybe—" The tears came before the hysterics could take over. God, this was embarrassing. I pulled my thin napkin from my lap and hid my eyes.

"Hey, I was only kidding," Lulu said, her usually strident voice softening. "You look fine. What's wrong?"

"I have to quit my practice."

"Why? Things are going great, right? Everyone envies your spunk. Tom's probably sorry he dumped you."

I quieted the flutter in my heart at the mention of Tom Brody's name.

"Jealous. Yeah, right. The traitors I graduated with? I hate seeing any one of them with their new lakeside apartments, their new and *working* cars, their damned European vacations. Jealous of me. No fucking way. At least they earn more than their secretaries. Hell, their secretaries earn more than me."

"Are things that bad?"

I had to close my eyes against her pitying face. When I opened them, I decided to get very honest very quickly.

"Do you know how much I have in my checking account?"

"A couple thousand? That would be hard to get through the month, but—"

My snort was unladylike. "Two thousand? I'd be happy to be at two hundred. At twenty. Ha." I shared the balance with my friend. "That's it. I'll be lucky if they don't cut up my credit card when I try swiping for this breakfast."

"Holy shit."

"Holy shit is right. My rent is due in *both* places on the first of November, and I can't pay *either*. I may have to move back in with my parents—at–thirty-two." I pasted my right index finger and thumb against my forehead. "Loserdom, here I come."

"Why didn't you tell me before?" Lulu asked, her affected speech disappearing.

“Because I’m mortified. This isn’t the way it’s supposed to be. Everyone thinks lawyers are rich. It’s one of the reasons *I* went to law school. I didn’t want to live like my parents—worried about money, making do, fearing the next layoff.

“I grew up looking east over the Cuyahoga River, thinking everyone who lived there had money, education, culture—everything the hourly workers on our side of the river didn’t have. And it’s not working out. I should have sued the law school when I had the chance. The law review thing—they ruined my career. I don’t think I’m ever going to recover.”

“Do you really think it’s the plagiarism thing? Did Dean Condit or Tom’s family really sabotage your job offer?”

“Only one offer got pulled in our class. Mine. The firm didn’t go out of business. Only my slot disappeared. That’s not coincidence.”

“Have you seriously tried to get another firm job?”

It took a lot of will to not let my frustration from my last few years, months, days, spill over on to my friend. I had to assume she was nothing but sincere. Maybe it *was* all unbelievable to the someone on the outside.

“I tried calling everyone I know. Your firm wasn’t interested. Remember? I even tried a headhunter. Without my personal information on my resume, I get screening interviews. After they meet me. Nothing.

“Even I can’t blame the Brodys or Dean Condit anymore. Now that I haven’t practiced ‘real’ law for five years, I’m a legal pariah. The hiring partners treat me like I’ve been doing baby law and can’t play with the grownups and your oh-so-sophisticated practices.”

We sat in silence for a long moment. The rain had started up again. I watched the cars splashing through the puddles on Shaker Boulevard.

"Tell me I'm not crazy." There was a pleading not in my voice that I didn't like.

Lulu sighed.

"You're not crazy. At my firm, we call them 'common pleas lawyers.' He's the guy in the ill-fitting suit who's smart enough to pass the bar, but not smart enough to get a firm job. But you're different. I went to law school with you. You were on law review, at the top of our class. Any firm worth its salt should be gunning for you!"

"Then where are they?"

"Have you thought of leaving Cleveland behind? You can waive in, now."

"My parents aren't getting any younger. But I've tried D.C. and Philly. When I call, firms are like, Cleveland State? You'd think I went to an unaccredited school in Timbuktu."

Our food came, and I tucked into my skillet. I tried not to be disgusted with myself as at least five thousand calories disappeared from my plate. For all Lulu's posturing, she barely touched her food, only eating two forkfuls of her improvised cheese grits.

Lulu's persona came back. Serious talk was over.

"What are you gonna do? You need some mad scrilla up in there."

"If I had the time, I'd use half of it pursuing the big money cases, rainmaking. Reality? I think I'm going to extend out my student loans to the twenty-five-year plan. Right now, I'm going to take as many appointed cases as I can get. The county may pay badly, and pay late, but they always pay."

9

Black Out

Sheila

October 5, 2001

I looked at the white princess phone next to my bed, tapping its plastic surface with my fingernails. I needed help. Parenting was kicking my butt. Maybe my ex-husband was the answer I was looking for.

Keith had always loved Olivia. He'd probably be involved in her life now, if he wasn't hiding out from child support enforcement. Pulling open my nightstand, I got my address book out. It was woefully thin, empty save twenty or so people.

Cora Bigham's number was in ink under the B's. Keith's maternal aunt had lived in the same house for more than fifty years. Cora and Keith had always been close. She'd know where her nephew was. I picked up the phone and dropped it again. What could Keith bring to the table? He hadn't really been in Olivia's life after his mother died.

Without nagging from his mother-in-law, it was like my ex had lost interest in fatherhood. I put the empty glass down and looked at my bare ring finger. It wasn't the divorce that was a mistake, it was the marriage. I lifted the receiver, holding the phone.

The dial tone changed to a series of short buzzing noises. I placed the receiver down, more carefully this time. Keith wasn't the answer. How could he show up for his daughter when he hadn't even shown up for the divorce nine years ago?

"Grant versus Grant!" The bailiff had shouted.

Everything on Judge Miller had glittered. She had looked more like a drag queen than an officer of the court. The rock on her finger lit up the room like a crystal chandelier. The jewels at her throat and wrists sparkled. Oddly, the judge hadn't found all the opulence out of place in a courtroom of mostly indigent litigants.

Peyton and I stepped to the bench.

Judge Miller looked down at us from the bench. Her gold-rimmed, diamond studded glasses slid down her nose.

"Are you Sheila Grant?"

Peyton answered for me. "Yes, Your Honor."

Judge Miller pushed up her glasses and scanned the papers in front of her. "You have a three-year-old daughter, Olivia Grant?"

Peyton answered again. "Yes, Your Honor."

"Let's see, husband Keith Grant hasn't answered these divorce papers, though he's been served. Does your husband work?"

I answered for myself this time, clearing the frog that seemed to have lodged in my throat when I'd entered the neoclassical building. "No, Your Honor."

"Oh, they never do..." The judge looked away. Something in the papers had caught her eye.

"Well, well, Mr. Bennett. You're far from your home turf. It's rare that we see folks like you from Bennett Friehof around these parts. Word is that you don't like to get your white shoes dirty here."

The judge laughed heartily at her own joke, then turned serious.

"From these papers, Ms. Grant, I see that you're earning a sizable salary at Bennett Friehof. I'm going to order that your soon-to-be ex-husband pay the statutory minimum child support of fifty dollars a week. In addition, I'll order Mr. Grant to immediately seek work so that we can attach his wages for this child support order. Be sure to come in for a modification upwards when you know he's working.

"Ms. Grant, I'm going to ask you a few questions. Do you want a divorce here today?"

"Yes, Your Honor," I said, swallowing my pride. Admitting before God and everyone that I'd failed at something was painful.

"You have asked for a divorce on the grounds of irreconcilable differences. Are you and your husband unable to live together as man and wife?"

"Yes, Your Honor."

"I'll grant you a divorce today. Good luck." The judge moved the green folder to a thick pile, and the bailiff called the next case.

I held myself tall as I walked down the full courtroom and out of the heavy leather padded doors. Peyton grasped my arm, stalling my progress down the hall, and pulled me to one of the wood benches lining the hallway of the ornately decorated early twentieth century building.

In a movement familiar to both of us, Peyton's larger hand enveloped my smaller one, and he placed our joined fingers in his lap. As if sensing my unease, he spoke.

"I'll tell you a story about Judge Miller."

I looked down at our hands, then up at my mentor. No matter the ups and downs in our relationship, our connection had always remained strong. I nodded, letting him take my mind off the anticlimactic end of my marriage.

"Ten years ago, my father had a barbecue at his house. I'd mentioned it casually at some bar luncheon, and Judge Miller invited herself along. My dad would not have wanted her company so I told her some tale about having steaks and that we'd already given the caterer a number.

"So, the barbecue comes along and you'll never guess who showed up, but Judge Miller. And here's the best part—she brought her own steak!" Peyton chuckled, then laughed, then guffawed.

Although I couldn't join in his laughter, I saw the humor in the situation and appreciated Peyton's attempt to take my mind off my divorce. The judge's bailiff came out and handed the court's file to Peyton.

"If you walk it through, the clerk's office will issue the final decree today."

Not taking his hand from mine, Peyton took the folder, thanking the bailiff profusely. If I had learned one thing during my years of practice, it was to be nice to the court's staff. Today's divorce court bailiff could be working on multi-million-dollar civil cases tomorrow. One misplaced word could make or break your case.

The bailiff stepped back into the chambers and left us in the empty hallway. Peyton slid down the bench a few inches so he could look me in the eye. His gaze caught me up short like it always did. My throat dried, my heart beat so loudly, I couldn't hear anything else, and I couldn't remember why I always pushed him away.

"The last time I asked you, Keith was your excuse."

I swallowed against the lump in my throat.

"If I ask you in one hour, or three, will your answer be any different?" He tapped the file against his knee. It was the only chink in his armor. The only indication that the next words I said could change everything. I didn't know how long we'd sat that way, but the spill of litigants from Judge Miller's room broke the spell. "I'll see you back at the office in an hour," he said at normal volume. "Say yes," he said in a more intimate tone.

I nodded noncommittally at Peyton, stood and walked down the long corridor, my heels clicking on the cold marble floors. I knew without looking back that I was going to let this last chance at possible happiness slip through my fingers. Peyton would never have forgiven the secret I'd kept from him these last three years, nine months, and twenty-three days. I'd have to live with that.

Sleep was the only thing that saved me from repeated thoughts about what might have been. A stiff drink eased the transition from wakeful reminiscence to dreamless sleep. At 2:42, I jolted awake. The faint sounds of a television filtered through my sleepy haze.

"Olivia!" I yelled. "Get up from in front of that TV and get to bed!" It took a few minutes, but I heard Olivia tiptoe past my door. Slipping on my own house shoes, I took my empty glass downstairs. After I pulled the bottle from the back of the cabinet and eased it from the paper bag, I hesitated, wondering how this would look to someone from the outside. I wondered if I might have a problem with drinking. That voice quickly quieted.

I had one of the most stressful jobs in America. Singlehandedly, I was responsible for the fates of defendants, deciding who won or lost millions of dollars, making judgments in cases that could mean the success or failure of businesses—and the people employed by them, and the shareholders invested in them. If I needed a drink to unwind, that was okay.

Leaning against the counter, I sipped my final drink of the night. It was too quiet in this house. Climbing the stairs, I emptied the glass, and clearing my mind of Peyton and Keith, eased back to bed and into a fitful sleep.

10

Hotline

Alison

October 22, 2001

"696-KIDS, how can we help you?"

"Hi! I mean, good morning," I started, nearly dropping the phone in my nervousness. "I'm calling to report something...I feel may be...unhealthy...for a child I know."

"What's the situation?"

"I think the child's mother has an alcohol problem."

"Child's name?" the operator asked.

"Olivia Grant," I said.

"Address?"

I rustled through the file on my desk, having forgotten where I'd dropped Olivia off in my nervousness. "2603 Latimore Road in Shaker Heights." Although I had heard the operator's pen scratching the entire duration of the phone call, there was sudden silence.

"Excuse me," the operator cleared her own throat. "Did you say Shaker?" The operator paused. "We hardly get any calls from there."

I was speechless for a moment then started speaking rapidly to cover my awkwardness.

"I am a little hesitant reporting this. But I think I'm required to make this report by law."

The operator sighed audibly. "Can you tell me what you've observed that would lead you to suspect abuse in the home?"

"I can't exactly tell you that," I said, feeling a little like Pandora. Had I opened a box I wouldn't be able to close? "Things aren't right. The girl is smart, but she's doing poorly in school. And she confided in me that her mother drinks every night."

"Mm-hm."

My voice rose.

"Olivia had to break into her own house when her mom passed out one night. And her mom is verbally abusive. It may even be physical."

"Did she use those words?"

"Not exactly. I'm just summarizing what she said to me. You see," I started. The operator sighed. I pushed on. "I have this all-girls peer group here, and Olivia's been asking questions which make me think there are a lot of problems in her house."

"Anything else you'd like to add?"

"I think maybe I saw her mom yelling at her and twisting her arm. I can't exactly be sure. It happened so quickly during a drop off."

"Thank you for your report. We'll forward this to the appropriate social worker for review and investigation. Did you want to remain anonymous?"

I paused for a moment. I didn't realize that I didn't have to give my name. The operator breathed heavily into the phone. Anonymity versus outing myself ping-ponged in my mind. On the one hand, as a school official, I knew I was required to report *anything* I suspected. On the other hand, maybe if I remained anonymous then Olivia would never find out I'd betrayed her trust.

"I want to remain anonymous for now," I said. "But can you note that I can come forward if the social worker needs my corroboration?"

"Thank you for calling 696-KIDS."

11

An Inauspicious Visit

Sheila

October 23, 2001

By ten in the morning, I already felt as if I'd worked an entire day. I'd been on the bench for nearly two hours, working to clear my docket of civil matters. During the ten-minute recess I'd called, I added two more aspirin to the Tylenol already floating in my empty stomach, all *before* the bailiff called the last hearing. Standing and zipping up my black robes, I came to the bench.

"Please be seated. Last on the docket we have Busby versus Amalgamated Conglomerated, Limited."

Two older men in suits came forward.

"Good morning, Your Honor," one man said. "I'm Jacob Schmidt representing the plaintiff."

The other attorney, not to be left behind, quickly stepped forward to the other table. “I’m Stephen Hewitt of Hogarth, Clovis, and Banning. We represent Amalgamated, Your Honor.”

“All right, gentlemen. You should have worked any discovery disputes out yourselves. But you’re here. What’s the problem?

Both men started talking.

“One at a time,” I warned. The plaintiff’s attorney blamed the defendant for stonewalling—hiding damaging information. The defendant accused the plaintiff of going on a fishing expedition.

The attorneys spoke in turn, their voices rising with indignation. While they made themselves red in the face with anger, a young black woman came in and sat at the back of the spectator’s gallery. Momentarily turning my attention from the angry voices, I looked at the woman quizzically. A twinge of unease snaked through my belly, but I chalked it up to the painkillers on an empty stomach.

The woman wasn’t dressed like an attorney, and I couldn’t remember seeing her before. Maybe she was visiting the courtroom. Occasionally, the public exercised their right to observe the courtrooms their tax dollars supported.

I turned my attention back to the two men. They’d blown off enough steam. It was time to rein them in.

“Counselors, I have a solution to your problem.” I looked pointedly at the plaintiff’s attorney. “Mr. Schmidt, you need to have your client available for depositions. No excuses. Mr. Hewitt, Amalgamated isn’t going to pull one over on this court. Don’t think that because I’m up here on the bench, I’ve forgotten the practice of law.”

I turned my gaze on Hewitt, narrowing my eyes for emphasis. "You will provide the requested documents in thirty days. Inform your client that if the documents mysteriously disappear, I'll find them in contempt and fine them. Bottom line: get the documents to the plaintiff, and let's get on with the case."

Schmidt was smirking like he'd won a round of boxing.

"Mr. Schmidt, don't get too happy. I'm not Santa Claus, and this ain't Christmas. Your case looks weak. You'll get your documents. But after discovery is done, and I've reviewed the motion for summary judgment that I'm one hundred percent sure the defendant is going to file, and I find out you don't have a case, I'll dismiss this action faster than you can cross Superior Boulevard.

"Gentlemen, do we understand each other?" They both smiled, thinking they'd come out ahead. "Good, then. My clerks will prepare the order," I said, dismissing the lawyers. I rose from the bench, ready for a break in my chambers, then I remembered the young woman in my courtroom. If the girl were a potential law student, I could spare five minutes. I looked back, and the young woman rose as if to speak.

"Can I help you?" I asked from the top stair of the bench.

"Yes, I think so," the young woman said, unsure.

I waited.

"Are you Sheila Grant?"

Taken aback by her lack of formality, I straightened my robe. Adding steel to my voice, I said, "Yes, I'm *Judge* Grant."

The woman paused a beat too long. My patience was wearing thin. I waved my hand, urging the girl to get on with it.

"I'm Celeste Young with the Cuyahoga County Department of Children and Family Services," Young said, attempting to hand over a card.

The bailiff, charged with protecting my personal safety, approached Young, hand firmly planted on the holster of his gun.

"Ma'am. Step back. Do not approach the judge," he warned.

Suddenly sorry for the lost woman, I said, "I think you're in the wrong place, that's all. The family court is over on Lakeside." Softening my strident tone, I continued. "People make this mistake all the time. These buildings are almost identical. If you follow Superior through Public Square, and go down Ontario toward the lake, you can't miss it." I turned back toward my chambers. The woman continued her approach.

"Ma'am. Step back." The bailiff's warning was final.

"Um, I don't think I'm in the wrong place. I really need to speak with the Judge," she said, proffering the card again. That woman needed some damned backbone. She'd never succeed professionally with all the hemming and hawing. "It's about her daughter, Olivia."

Whipping around, I heard my own voice went go steel to shrill.

"Oh, my goodness! Is there something wrong with Olivia? Is she okay? What's going on?"

Young again looked unsure. "Ma'am, um, Your Honor, I think I need to speak with you privately."

My confident countenance gave way to uncertainty.

"Does this concern my daughter Olivia?"

"Yes." Young nodded.

"Is she okay?"

"She's fine," Young said. "She's at school right now. Everything's fine. But I do really need to talk to you."

Relief flooded through my veins.

"George," I said to my bailiff, "I'll see her in my chambers in ten minutes." I resumed the walk to the back. It would take me that long to shake the fizzy vein feeling the rush of adrenaline had caused. Damned woman had almost given me a heart attack, mentioning Olivia. This was probably about some damned volunteer hours I'd missed, or something. While I balled and released my hands, one of my clerks approached me.

"Not now," I hissed, stopping the clerk in her tracks.

I slammed the door of my office and threw my robe on its hook. "Celeste Young, Intake Worker," was penned in light blue ink on the card in my hand. How was this official? Anyone could write her name on one of these. Lifting the phone, I dialed the number on the card and got a recording.

Moving my eyes from the handwriting on the card to the phone, I punched in the extension. A voice that sounded like Young's came through on the voice mail. If she was legit, what was wrong with Olivia? Panic, previously subsided, came back with a flash, dampening my palms, making the area under my bra uncomfortable with sweat.

"Nancy. Have George show the young woman in," I requested via intercom.

Within a few seconds, Young entered my office. "Have a seat." The woman plopped down. "Now tell me what's going on with Olivia."

"Ms., um, Judge Grant? I'm an intake worker with the county. I'm responsible for removing children from unsafe homes."

Those new suburban girls were going to be trouble. I knew it. I tried to hold in my exasperated sigh.

"Which one of her friends is in trouble?"

Young shook her head briskly, hesitating before she spoke.

"We're removing Olivia from your custody."

I went from cordial to livid in a millisecond. "What in the hell are you talking about?" My heart hammered in my chest. Who would dare to take my baby? Who would dare to accuse *me* of not doing my job as a parent?

Young fumbled with her pigskin briefcase, pulling papers out.

"Ms. Grant, today the prosecutor's office filed a petition for emergency custody. Based upon information from a credible source, we've determined that Olivia is at risk in your home."

Abruptly, I stood. I glanced at the chair spun wildly behind me, nearly keeling over then turned my full attention toward the woman.

"I'm going to get my daughter at her school, and get to the bottom of this." I grabbed my coat and bag from the tree by the door.

"But, Ms. Grant. I have to fill out this intake form," Young said, waving a stack of blank forms in the air.

My voice held venom. The young woman shrank back from my mother bear wrath.

"Ms. Young, I'm sure you have your job to do. But I have to resolve this mix-up before anything stupid happens." With that, I stormed from my chambers.

12

Removal of the Child from the Home

Sheila

October 23, 2001

My hand stifled a yawn. Mr. Donaldson should be prescribed by doctors instead of the pills dancing in commercials. The minute his mouth opened, my eyes closed.

"Not only is it important to your understanding of geography, but it will contribute to your knowledge of history as well," Mr. Donaldson said.

I yawned again, not bothering to hide it this time. I'd already memorized the state capitols from a Schoolhouse Rock CD my dad gave me years ago. The beat caught my imagination, and I started drumming my fingers on my desk. My dad and I had fun when he'd played that during one of my last visits. For once, I'd get an easy 'A." Maybe my mom would lay off when I brought this good mark home.

The droning stopped abruptly when someone knocked on the closed classroom door. All twenty pairs of eyes zeroed in on Alison Feingold walking into the room. Alison looked unusually nervous as her normally steady eyes glanced around the room while she whispered and gestured to Mr. Donaldson.

Instantly alert, I was dying to know what had happened that would cause Alison to interrupt my class. Did someone's mom die? Did another airplane fly into another building? Was the school going on lockdown because someone'd brought a gun? After watching Columbine unfold on TV, I was a lot more scared than when I was in elementary school.

The mystery was solved, in part, when Mr. Donaldson nodded in my direction.

"Olivia Grant. Gather up your books. You need to go with Ms. Feingold now."

The low murmur in the room rose audibly. I shook with worry. Maybe it was my mom who was hurt. I snatched my backpack from the floor and frantically shoved my stuff into the bag. Throwing it over my shoulder without zipping, I took the long, mortifying walk from the back of the class to where Alison was waiting, wondering how I'd ever live this down. I'd spent weeks trying to fit in, only to be called out in class twice in two weeks.

"Alison, what's going on?"

The counselor avoided my eyes.

"Let's talk in my office."

"Is my mom okay?" Mom might not be ideal, but she was the only one I had. My mind started ping-ponging around. Where would I live if something happened to my mom?

With my dad? Could someone find him? Or would I live with Auntie Deidre and all her kids? Both my grandmas had died. Great auntie Cora was too old.

"Your mom is fine—no one's hurt," Alison soothed. My relief came out on a whoosh of breath. "Hurry now."

We walked swiftly toward the front of the building, finally stepping into Alison's office in the guidance wing. I was caught up short to find two adults already in the office, a black woman in some kind of shiny ruffled dress, and a white guy with a blue-black uniform and a gun. I dropped into a chair, my backpack slipping from my shoulders.

I jumped when the officer slammed the door behind me. Froot Loops from breakfast rose up, threatening to choke me and spill from my mouth into a multi colored mess on the floor. I swallowed back the bitter bile. My eyes darted from the cop to the black woman to Alison. No one would meet my gaze. Finally, Alison sat down at her own desk.

"Olivia, we're all here to help you." Gesturing toward the black woman, she said. "This is Bernice Johnson, a social worker with the Department of Children and Family Services. And this is Officer Fitzpatrick."

The sting of betrayal spread from the backs of my eyes to my fisting fingers.

"Alison, *you promised*!"

Bernice Johnson spoke up. "We don't think your mom's capable of taking care of you right now."

"That's a lie. My mom's just fine. Look at me. I'm clean, I eat—a lot." I grabbed at the tiny roll of fat my mom always pinched around my waist. "Anything you heard is a lie. Call my mom. She'll tell you we're just fine."

Bernice continued like I hadn't spoken. "This is only temporary. You'll be with a good family until she gets better."

"But I have a good family," I said, choking on my words. The tears that pricked behind my eyes spilled over. Swallowing the lump in my throat, I hung my head.

How did they find out about my mom, if it wasn't Alison? Had she gone to the same liquor store too many times? Did some detective threaten Mr. Ossman at East Town Eagle until he spilled the beans? Could the landlords downstairs have heard Mom yelling at me? I'd never felt good in Shaker. Everyone was staring.

"Oh, Olivia. Don't cry," Alison's hand awkwardly reached across the desk and patted my arm. "We're going to make sure you're happy, and most of all, safe."

Happy without my family? Safe?

"Where am I going? Now? Am I going to finish school today?" I asked.

Hesitation and silence from the adults, then Bernice spoke up. "I'm going to place you in an emergency home." Her voice changed. I didn't believe a word she said. "There's a loving foster family who's ready to provide a home for children like you right now. It'll be like going home."

I didn't care anymore if everyone saw me cry. Maybe they would see that this was all a mistake. Maybe they'd let me go back to class and take the bus home. I half stood.

"Wait. I want to go home—to *my* house," I wailed. "Where's my mom?"

Bernice sighed, her veneer of patience wearing thin.

"Olivia," she snapped. "This is all for your own good." She walked closer, pushing me down in the seat. "Does your mom drink a lot?"

I looked from Alison, to the officer, to Bernice. It didn't matter what I said. I shrugged and sniffled all at the same time.

"I have to tell you that most moms aren't like that. We want your mom to be all better–for you." Bernice's head snapped to the side when a commotion started in the hallway.

The guidance officer's door swung open, bouncing off the doorstop. Thank God.

My mom was here, full of authority and anger in her forest-green power suit. This was the first time I was happy my mom was a judge. She'd tell all these people what to do. She would put them in jail, if they didn't do what she said. I got up, books scattering unnoticed, and threw my arm around my mom's waist.

"Take me home. These people say I can't go home with you. Fix it, Mom."

13

The Best Interests of the Child

Sheila

October 23, 2001

I took Olivia into a hug, smoothing her straightened hair, missing the tight spiral curls that had bounced around my daughter's face most of her childhood. I wiped the tearstained face, looking into the hazel eyes that reminded me of Olivia's father. How had I let grades or fat matter?

This child was my heart, from the scar on her ear caused by a playground accident, to all but two fingernails bitten to the quick. Setting my daughter aside for a moment, I picked up Olivia's books. It was time to take her home. Maybe we needed counseling. Something had gone woefully wrong here. I turned away from the exasperated look Bernice threw at the officer.

Like my own bailiff had earlier, the sheriff got between Olivia and me. I started to push him away then thought better of it. I couldn't mother my child if I was dead. He pulled a thick bundle of paper from his belt.

"Ma'am, here's the court's order allowing the county to take emergency custody of the minor child," the officer said. He shoved the typed pages at me.

I quickly glanced at the pages, my lawyer's brain absorbing what my mother's brain couldn't. Some judge had signed over my daughter to the county. Olivia had wormed her way around the officer, and was clinging to me again. It would only be for a night or two. I couldn't win this battle. Not here. Not now. This was war and needed to be fought in my domain, the courtroom.

As gently as possible, I pried open Olivia's grasping fingers. I shook my daughter's shoulders, gently.

"Poppet, a judge has said that you have to go today—"

"But Mommy, you're a judge. Can't you cancel that out?"

The question was like a blow to the solar plexus. I could send grown men to jail and fine multi-million-dollar corporations, but I couldn't keep my daughter from the county's clutches. If it were only as easy as Olivia thought. It wasn't going to be like fixing a playground squabble where the moms were on even turf.

"Stop crying and listen to me."

Olivia wiped away the tears, and nodded at me.

"You have to go with them. But I'll be able to pick you up in a couple of days when I get this misunderstanding cleared up, okay?"

My daughter's movements were lethargic, but she took the backpack from me anyway.

"Olivia, let's get your jacket from your locker. Then we'll be ready to go." The woman had to be another worker from the Department of Child and Family services. I had to turn my back when the social worker led my daughter from the room with the sheriff picking up the rear.

Alone in the counseling office with some young woman, I raised an impertinent eyebrow. One that had experienced lawyers cowering.

"And you are?"

The school employee rose from her desk unsteadily. Who had populated the world with unsure young people out to do me harm?

"I'm Alison. I run the 'For Girls Only!' peer group that Olivia belongs to."

I rose to my full height, and using all the coolness I could muster, postured like I was on the bench.

"I hope you're not behind this fiasco. There's absolutely no problem in my house, and I resent your involvement and the county's hand in our lives. When I get to the bottom of this, no one and I mean *no one* from the school better be involved. As a judge, I promise you that I have all the tools and resources at my disposal to prosecute any misconduct to the fullest extent of the law."

I stalked from the office, through the hallway now thick with pre-teen hormones, and strode to my car. The new car smell mocked me after I unlocked the door. I threw the court papers on the passenger seat, leaning my head against the steering wheel. The horn blared, but I didn't give a shit what people thought. How had this happened, just when I'd fixed it all? Just when my personal and professional lives were finally coming together?

14

The Blue Wall

Olivia

October 23, 2001

My down vest hissed like it was blowing off steam when I leaned against the plastic bucket chair. Officer Fitzpatrick had left me here in a police station, with my only company a stressed-out looking receptionist. When I asked where I was going, Fitzpatrick had said it wasn't his territory, signed some papers, handed them over the counter and walked out the door.

My new babysitter said it was one-thirty. Normally, I'd be in art class right now. Sadness spread through my body when I realized that I'd be missing ceramics, the unit we were starting this quarter. I had been looking forward to making a mug that would be glazed and fired in the kiln, coming out shiny and crackly like the demonstration models along the windowsill.

At two-thirty, I scooted my chair back on the shiny linoleum floor to get out of the hot sun streaking through the window. The receptionist threw me a look at the scraping sound. I pulled the geography book from my backpack. Maybe I'd read the next chapter. My mom had always told me that I'd do better in school if I got a head start on the other kids.

By three-thirty, my brain but was numb. What had happened to Bernice Johnson? The social worker had taken her own car, while I'd been escorted in the back of the police car. My sadness was turning to anger. Why had it been such an emergency to get me out of school? Here I was, just sitting and waiting with nowhere to go.

When the big hand on the large wall clock struck four, my stomach growled. I'd have been home by now, watching something good on TV and eating cookies. I couldn't remember what we had at home, but it would have been better than the nothing I'd had here so far. I craned my neck and spying a vending machine, I found and peered into my pocket, I pulled out and tore open my Velcro purple wallet. Except for a picture of my mom and aunt from a few summers ago, it was empty.

"Excuse me," I said, knocking on the bulletproof glass separating me from everyone else. When a heavyset woman rolled her stool to the shiny metal microphone, a speaker cracked to life.

"Do you know when I'm leaving?" I asked with an unexpected quaver in my voice. After I spoke, I realized the woman at the front desk had changed. The overworked, frowning woman was long gone, and this one was in her place.

"Who are you, young lady?"

I put my hand on my chest to still my beating heart.

"I'm Olivia Grant. A social worker is supposed to take me somewhere, but I haven't seen her in hours, and I'm kinda hungry."

"Have a seat," the receptionist said without irony, gesturing to the blue plastic seats I had only vacated a moment ago. She opened and closed a few drawers, then squeezed her hand into the tight pocket of her blue polyester uniform pants, pulling out a few quarters. "Here," she said, dropping the coins in the metal tray near the window opening. She rolled out of my sight.

Taking the change, I walked over to the vending machines. I quickly calculated that a drink *and* food were out of the question. Looking around, I saw an ancient water fountain. All three quarters jingled through the machine, and a bag of Funyuns dropped into the dispenser. The sound of the bag, the smell of the artificial flavors, calmed me almost as much as the first crunch. I hadn't eaten an orange stack since I'd been back in Glenville last spring.

My mom had been late. It had been Shawn's birthday. Shawn Upchurch had been my very best friend for as long as I could remember. We'd always lived on that same block, six houses between theirs.

The birthday party had been fun, catching up with the kids I'd known forever. Shawn's mom had finally allowed cupcakes now that the five of us girls were too old for the icky rectangular supermarket cake. The other three girls at the party had been picked up or walked home, but I was still there, because walking all the way to Shaker Heights was out of the question.

"Olivia," Mrs. Upchurch said, "what do you think happened to your mom?"

"She probably got caught in traffic," I said, though there was never any traffic to speak of on Cleveland's east side—especially on a Saturday afternoon.

I made myself useful, balling up cupcake foils, wiping cake crumbs from their pink and gold speckled Formica kitchen table. Despite my helpfulness, I still felt like a third wheel on a bicycle.

Mrs. Upchurch, who liked my dad, but never much liked my mom, handed me the cordless phone.

"Why don't you try your mother's cell phone again? Make sure she's on her way."

I dropped the green sponge into the nicked sink, black iron showing through the white enamel, and took the offered phone. Walking to the darkly wallpapered dining room, I dialed my mom's phone.

Voice mail.

Her cell must have been off. Pressing flash, I dialed home. Four rings, then the answering machine.

I hung up without leaving a message. Sinking into a heavy dining room chair, I avoided the bustling in the kitchen. A good excuse as to why my mom wasn't here was what I needed.

Shawn sidled into the room, her newly changed starched dress rustling against the heavy, velvet dining room curtains.

"Liv? Maybe you could come to dinner with us," Shawn said. "It's just going to be my mom, pop, and crazy cousins from Hough. I know my parents are making a big deal about having *reservations,* but I'm sure Charley's Crab could fit one more in."

"No thanks," I said. Everyone knew Charley's Crab was expensive. Would I have to pay for my own dinner? Would I break their budget? Would they let me in wearing jeans and a sweater? "I'm sure my mom's going to be here any second. Besides, you're all dressed up."

Shawn, summoned by her parents, walked me to the vestibule. Pulling the opaque fabric aside, I looked at the empty street through the front door's glass panel. Shifting from foot to foot, I waited. Shawn's parents whispered to their daughter, then I heard more clattering in the bedrooms upstairs. The cupcakes in my stomach turned to stone.

When Mr. Upchurch came downstairs, adjusting his unfashionably narrow tie, my mom's Lexus finally pulled up, its tires banging against the curb. Grabbing my jacket from the coat closet, I waved to Shawn's father, opened the door and ran to the car.

"Sorry. Sorry. Time got away from me," my mother said, hugging me with one arm and steering from the curb with the other. Two wheels were on, then off, the sidewalk. I closed the door before I fell out of the car. My mom was in one of *those* moods. I remained quiet, but my mom was garrulous.

"How's Shawn?"

"Fine."

"The Upchurches were always a nice family. Have they put your friend in private school like they said?"

"No." Shawn's family never had private school aspirations but had said so under my mom's cross-examination.

"That's too bad. She's a smart kid. But if she stays in the Cleveland public schools, she'll never go anywhere."

I wanted to defend my friend, was aching to point out that she and my dad had gone to Cleveland public schools.

Were they nowhere?

I bit back my retort, instead grabbing the door handle when my mom made an erratic turn from St. Clair to East One Hundred Fifth Street. We pulled into the small parking lot of East Town Eagle. I sank into my seat, intractable when my mom urged me in.

"I'll stay in the car."

"Olivia, c'mon. Mr. Ossman has been asking after you for a while. Plus, you can get whatever you want."

With heavy feet, I shuffled after my mother into the little store. I looked through the front display racks, considering my potato chip options, when my mother moved to the back of the store. I'd picked up a jumbo bag of Funyuns when she was summoned.

"O-LIV-I-A," the yodeling of my name by my mom made my skin crawl. "Come say 'Hi' to Mr. Ossman, girl."

Scuffing my feet along the floor, I inched along the tile floor before coming to the back counter.

"Hello."

"C'mere and give me some sugar," Mr. Ossman said, pulling me around the counter into a bear hug, smacking a juicy kiss on my cheeks. Mr. Ossman, a redboned bear of a man, had worked at East Town Eagle for as long as I could remember. For the last few years, I'd gone with my mom every few weeks or so. My mom stocked up on rum, and I was allowed to get anything I wanted, no matter how unhealthy. The visits had stopped once we'd moved, and I hadn't missed them or the junk food, really.

"How you doin' out there in Shaker? Don't think you're too good for us over here. You should stop-on-over more often." He pulled me so close, I was halfway on his lap.

Mom answered for me.

"Olivia's doing nicely. The schools in Shaker are exceptional. She's already talking about college. Aren't you, Olivia?"

I'd never said a word about college. I shifted, uncomfortably hot on Mr. Ossman's lap. My mother had fixed me with a piercing glare.

"Yes, sir, Mr. Ossman. I'm enjoying Shaker."

Duty fulfilled, I had jumped down from the store owner's lap. "Can I get these, and a pop?"

Seizing the moment, I had run to the front of the store and pulled a strawberry soda from the refrigerator case. Mr. Ossman had dropped the pop into a plastic bag with my chips. My mother's own brown bag had already disappeared into her oversized tote.

When the police station's front door opened, I looked down, surprised to find my snack demolished. Two cops walked in behind a tall, thin, dark-skinned guy in handcuffs. Sizing up the room, the perp nodded at me. I stared back, never having seen anyone in real handcuffs before.

The officers left the guy on the chair next to me, unlocking the door to the back. They talked to each other about some fight between my new seat neighbor and his girlfriend, complaining that it was just a fight when they'd expected a gun.

I looked away from the guy, when I saw his knuckles were puffy and red. They were just going to leave me here, all alone, with a criminal. Ready to pound on the glass again, I looked up to see Bernice Johnson in full stride.

"Sorry it took so long, but there were some snags in finding you a place for tonight."

If I had no place to go.... Hope chased away the fear.

"Does that mean I can go home now?"

"No." Bernice's answer brooked no argument. "I *had* some problems. I've found you a nice place to stay—far away from your mother."

Oh. For five hours I'd wanted to be anywhere else but here. Now I'd happily stay here, next to the handcuffed guy all night. But Bernice was tapping her foot with impatience. Balling up the cellophane bag, I pitched it into the bin and smeared my yellowed fingers on my pants. I slipped my wallet into my backpack and hefted it onto my shoulders, following Bernice out the door.

The floor of the aging Ford Escort was filled with plastic toys, greasy Happy Meal remains and girls' plastic barrettes. I looked down the yellow stains on my pants, immediately regretting my carelessness. The bag in the trunk only held school books. What was I going to wear tomorrow? Sleep in tonight? Rubbing my tongue along the film of the corn snack on my teeth, I realized that I didn't even have a toothbrush.

When I worked up the nerve to speak, I asked, "Where are we going?" The social worker was intently focused on the street outside the car's windshield. It was a long time between her sigh of exasperation and her answer.

"We don't have anywhere permanent for you. For the next few days, you're going to stay with Sadie Watkins. She loves kids."

I clutched at my seat belt when Bernice consulted a wrinkled paper, making a sudden left turn on to East Seventy-ninth Street. She stopped her car in front of a simple wood-framed house, pulling the emergency brake up with a jerk.

"Here we are." Her voice was full of false brightness. "Look, I'll be back here in a few days to get you into someplace more permanent." Bernice opened her own car door.

Paralyzed with fear, I stayed put. Darkness shrouded the all the homes on the street. Was I supposed to call this mine for the night?

"C'mon," Bernice urged. "Let's get going. It's getting late."

Side by side, we walked up the five steps to the porch. There was no sound inside after Bernice rang the doorbell. She rapped loudly on the screen door. I jumped when it rattled on its hinges, prompting a baby's cry. A disheveled person silhouetted against the screen. The door squeaked open, and in the shadow stood a brown-skinned, thickset woman in bathrobe and slippers. I wondered if the woman was home sick. It was nowhere close to bedtime.

"Hello, Miz Johnson," the woman said. "Is this the girl I'm takin' tonight?"

"Yes, Sadie. That's Mrs. Watkins to you," Bernice said, facing me. "This is Olivia Grant. She came from school, so she doesn't have anything. We'll try to get some vouchers out to you right away. If you don't have any questions, I have to go. It's long past the time I'm supposed to clock out." Bernice pointedly looked at her watch.

"I know what to do with these chi'rens, Miz Johnson. You be goin' now," Sadie said.

I looked down from the porch, past the dry brown weed patch that passed for a lawn, watching the social worker drive away, and with it, any hope of home.

"C'mon in, child. Don't be shy. You'll be fine here. Miz Johnson tol' me on the phone that you're having some problems with your ma. Don't you worry, the county will take good care of you while your mom gets better. The county sure does good by us." Mrs. Watkin's laugh turned into a phlegmy cough.

From the darkened hallway, I could see a small room on the right dwarfed by a huge projection TV. A talk show with wisecracking guests blared larger than life. Miss Sadie steered me to the dining room and kitchen on the left. Smoothing my hair back, the woman pointed to the only corner without clutter. "Call me Miss Sadie. No need for all that missus stuff. Now, put your bag there. Are you hungry, chile? I was just puttin' some supper on. Sit down at the table."

Miss Sadie shuffled over to the kitchen, got some floured pork chops from the counter, dropping them into a black skillet sizzling with fat. "You lucky to be heah, girl. Tonight, we're having a right good dinner, candied yams, fried pork chops, and even some okra from the yard." I squirmed in my seat while Miss Sadie eyed me up and down. "You're a skinny little thing. Hope you have a good appetite."

Despite the combination of nerves, hunger, and acid in my belly, I smiled. I'd never thought of myself as skinny. And the food did smell really good. Maybe this wouldn't be a bad place to be while my mother straightened everything out. The house was a little messed up, but Mrs. Sadie Watkins seemed nice enough.

Six was early for dinner, but Miss Sadie set a full plate before me. Swallowing past the fear, I spoke. "Miss Sadie? Can I have something to drink?"

"Sure thang, baby." Miss Sadie opened the olive colored refrigerator and removed a plastic pitcher. Something purple and sweet smelling poured out into a plastic cup. She handed it to me along with a fork and knife. "I need to check on the baby, hon. Make yourself at home."

I got up from the table and turned on another TV, sitting atop a tarnished brass stand. I retrieved the remote I spotted on the windowsill and flipped through the channels. The woman had Showtime and HBO! I turned to the beginning of *Bring it On!*—one of my favorite movies. The pork chops weren't bad, either. The food displaced my unease. By my second serving, I wasn't even worried about where I'd sleep.

15

Emergency Custody

Casey

October 23, 2001

I was gunning for Tricia Pachencko. Several knots of social workers gabbed over morning coffee. With faces full of youthful enthusiasm, or knowing resignation, they were easily spotted. I squinted. Read one tag after another. None was my Pachencko.

What would a bribe-taking, baby-selling, civil servant look like exactly?

I refused to be intimidated by a labyrinthine process I was just beginning to work out. Instead, I took a deep breath and shouted, "Nelson! Anyone here on the Nelson case?"

A squat, ill-dressed social worker broke from the crowd, answering the call. Her piggish eyes assessed me, finding me lacking. "Are you the G-A-L on the case?"

"I'm Casey Cort." I tried not to recoil when Pachencko pawed a quick hand through stringy hair, wiped it on her blouse, and then took my hand.

"Trish Pachencko. Been working cases here ten years. Haven't seen you before." Did my law degree come with an expiration date? "This is your lucky day. Cases don't get any easier than this."

Righteous indignation dried in my mouth. In spite of my choice of profession, confrontation wasn't my thing. The dull roar of the hallway filled my ears. What if the foster mom was lying, and she hadn't paid Pachencko?

The social worker patted my shoulder. "All the mom's other kids have been removed. And since she's in jail, we've got grounds to get this one. C'mon, Casey, visit the foster mom and the baby. You'll see that it's a good home. The kid—"

"I've met Mrs. James," I interrupted.

"Then you know. One month. The kid gets a permanent home, and you get paid." Pachencko walked away without a backward glance, melting into the crowd.

Girding myself, I sat down to wait. I was about to throw a wrench in the slow grinding gears of juvenile justice. Magistrate Chambers opened his door. I recognized the officer who did nearly all the emergency custody hearings. I snapped my briefcase shut, hoping mine was the first to be called. No such luck.

"Grant!" he shouted down the hall. "Is everyone here on Grant?"

It was nearly a half hour before I got into the room. Rarely did these hearings last more than a few minutes. What in the hell had happened in here, I wondered? Everyone looked a little shell shocked.

The magistrate actually smiled at me as the room filled with Pachencko and the prosecutor.

"Easy one?" he asked, looking hopeful.

I tried not to look away.

He closed the door behind us and started talking into the tape recorder.

"We're here in a petition for permanent custody—" Chambers stopped the tape mid-sentence. "Lunch is out the window today. What in the heck do we have here? Valerie?"

The room was silent as the prosecutor familiarized herself with the complaint. No shrinking violet, Pachencko spoke up when the prosecutor didn't.

"Your Honor. This is the deal. The mom here had the baby in prison. She's lost all her other kids to permanent custody, already. Obviously, in jail she can't do a case plan and get ready in the next six months, so we're going straight for PC. Casey here can tell you the kid's in a good foster-to-adopt situation. The mom's not here, so I think we can close this one."

The magistrate nodded, doing his best imitation of pensive. Pachencko slipped her file into her shoulder bag, ready for the court to rule in the county's favor, and get on with her day. The prosecutor was still flipping through files. The hearing officer glanced at me.

"Casey, is it?"

Here went the wrench.

"Magistrate, I think permanent custody is the wrong way to go."

Everyone stilled. Great, I loved talking into a room full of silence.

"I visited the mom. She's not in prison, exactly. She had the baby in Franklin because that's where everyone in custody has to go. She's in pre-release, scheduled to come out in six weeks, and she wants her baby back." I took out my own thick file, ready to answer any questions. The research, the visits, the whole thing had taken up two long days. I'd be lucky to get minimum wage on this case when all was said and done.

"Valerie?"

The prosecutor had finally found what she was looking for. "Okay. This mom has five kids total. The others we got permanent custody on."

"Why?"

The prosecutor read aloud.

"Because she was incarcerated for five years on a drug charge."

I opened my own file and decided to hit them with some facts. "The court did grant PC on the mom's other kids because of the sentence, but not for abuse or neglect. Her boyfriend was dealing drugs, and she got busted when the cops came to their house. She got charged with possession and intent, same as him, based on what was in the house. He admitted during his plea that he was the dealer, that she didn't know about it, and had nothing to do with it. He was dealing at his day job as a delivery guy. Drugs with your pizza, I guess.

"The mom's got parents willing to help her, a high school diploma, and other than this, no blemishes on her record. I think this baby needs to be in emergency or temporary custody until Mom gets out. I can't see any reason why this can't happen."

"Any objections, Valerie?" The prosecutor shook her head, mute. "Ms. Pachencko?"

Pachencko glared at me. I stared right back, giving Pachencko a look that said, 'you cross me and the bribery stuff goes all over the record.' The social worker nodded mutely, though her face shone purple with indignation.

The magistrate pressed the tape recorder again and recited the case number. "The county has modified its petition for permanent custody to a request for temporary custody. All parties agree. It is so ordered."

16

Emergency Custody, Part 2

Sheila

October 23, 2001

Late and discouraged by my trip to the wrong juvenile court building, and rough handling by the sheriff's deputies there, I walked up to the right building and did my best to bolster my flagging spirit. The last time I'd been here had been nearly two decades ago when I'd taken on some poor kid in a pro bono case.

That last visit did nothing to prepare me for the sheer number of people teeming around the building, or the carnival atmosphere. Parents patronized roadside carts, buying restless kids hot dogs, soda, and candy while attorneys hammered out deals on the courthouse steps. The quaint brick building used to house children and have courtrooms. With the war on crime, the kids had been moved somewhere else, and it was nothing but wall-to-wall courtrooms as far as the eye could see.

Look was all I did as I bypassed the circus. I had to give my briefcase to one guard, while walking through the airport style metal detector. When I beeped, I was grabbed by a third guard who waved a wand over every inch of my body.

The guards' eyes met.

"She's clear," one said, while the other handed me the open and disarrayed briefcase.

Going straight to a large reception desk, I was blatantly ignored while a young woman held up an airbrushed nail and finished her obviously personal call.

"What you need?" she asked, finally addressing me.

Tamping down my impatience, I said, "I have an eight-thirty hearing before Magistrate Chambers."

"First room on your left," the receptionist said, pointing to a long hallway thick with bodies.

Locating the small room, I swallowed, my throat painful with frustration and worry, and struggled to keep my cool. My one goal was to get my daughter home. Whatever hell the juvenile system had for the rest of the poor families in Cleveland wasn't my concern. I would soldier on, battle through today, and never have to come back here to be disregarded and disrespected.

A thickset woman lumbered to the door. "Did you sign in?"

I looked down at the numbered list affixed to the clipboard. Pulling my gold pen from my briefcase, I signed my name with a flourish. But there was no magic today.

Usually adding my signature awarded millions or put someone in prison. Today my name was just one on a long list. Looking for a place to sit, I found every bench full.

A young dishwater blonde called the name 'Nelson,' and rose from the bench. Working to keep my suit crisp, I smoothed my clothes before wedging myself between a surly teenager and a woman bouncing a fussy baby on her lap.

I fought panic and hysteria as long minutes passed. When Olivia's name was finally called, I walked into a hearing room the size of a janitor's closet.

My God, I thought when I had a good look at the room. This magistrate can take people's kids away, but he doesn't even have his own courtroom? Where were the bailiff and court reporter going to fit, I wondered as I occupied the last empty chair. When the magistrate closed the door, immediately pressing a red and black button on a tape recorder, I was stunned.

Like everyone, I'd heard stories about the stunning lack of progress in the juvenile court system, but tape recorders were as backwards as anyplace could get.

Get Olivia home.

I repeated it to myself like a mantra. Procedural problems could be ignored.

The magistrate stated the case number. "We're all here in the matter of Olivia Grant. Representing the county, we have Valerie Dodds," he droned, motioning to a twenty-something black woman in a baggy green suit.

Chambers scanned the room, his eyes landing on Celeste Young. "You're the intake worker on this case?"

Young nodded.

He looked quizzically at me. "And you are?"

My voice carried, echoed in the small room. "Sheila Harrison Grant. My daughter is Olivia."

Chambers squinted at me, assessing. "Ma'am, are you represented?"

I sighed. "I'm an attorney. I'm sure I can handle this hearing today."

The magistrate jammed his finger on the stop button. The plastic mechanisms ground to a halt with a squeak. "Going off the record." He took in the three women in the room, each one erect with righteousness. "What's the story here? Allegations? Can this be worked out?"

Dodds tipped her hand to Young.

"Your Honor, well. We have allegations that Ms. Grant here is an alcoholic and abusive mother."

"Who made these allegations?"

"You know we can't reveal that. But we have good info on this case."

Chambers rested his chin on his folded hands, taking that in. He looked me in the eye.

"Okay, counselor. This doesn't look good for you. I'm sure you know the standard of proof at EC hearings is preponderance of the evidence. If I find it's more likely than not the allegations against you are true, your daughter will be committed to the agency's custody.

"I've never seen you around here. This is not downtown. Do yourself a favor and get an attorney who's familiar with how things work around here."

Chambers turned his back on us, pressing buttons to continue the recording.

"The parties are not in agreement regarding custody, so we're going to take some testimony today. The county is represented by prosecutor Dodds, the mother, Sheila Grant is unrepresented. You all know the score. Ms. Young, raise your right hand."

Chambers swore in Young. "Miss Dodds, go ahead."

The prosecutor turned in her chair and began questioning the witness. She dispensed with the preliminaries, name, job title. "In your capacity at DCFS, have you had a chance to become acquainted with Elizabeth—excuse me..." Dodds shuffled her files. "Olivia Grant?"

"Yes," Young answered.

"What allegations led you to investigate the family?"

"We got a call on our six-nine-six kids' line. They said the mother drank and was physically and emotionally abusive."

"Have you talked to the mother?" the prosecutor asked.

"She refused to cooperate."

"Have you had any contact with the father?"

"No."

"Has paternity been established?"

"I don't know."

"Where is the child currently?"

"She's in an agency foster home."

"And how is she doing?"

"Great," Young said.

I took a deep breath, my ribs grating against the ladder back chair. How could these hearings pass a due process challenge? This was stone cold nuts. Not a single person in this room looked disturbed by not having a single shred of evidence of anything, but they all looked ready to snatch my daughter from me and put her God knew where in the ghetto. Dollars to that big ol' box of doughnuts the staff was eating outside this room that they weren't going to put her up with some rich suburban family and send her to private school.

"No further questions," Dodds said.

Magistrate Chambers turned to me. "Now, as I said before, I'm no fan of parents representing themselves. If you weren't an attorney, I'd just refer you to the PD's office. But if you want, you can cross examine the witness."

This was it. Olivia's get out of jail free card. I had to play this hand just right. I rose from her chair. Standing was an intimidation tactic I'd learned very early in my legal career.

"Good morning, Miss Young. I'm Sheila Harrison Grant, and I'm here today to ask you a few questions about the testimony you presented."

Unseasoned, the young case worker looked disquieted by the unexpected formality of my introduction. Good. She stuttered out a greeting. Keeping her off-kilter, I continued.

"What evidence do you have to sustain the allegations in the complaint?"

"As I said before, we received a call from six-nine-six kids indicating there was a problem in the…in…*your* house."

"Who was the call from?"

"Objection," prosecutor Dodds shouted. "I don't think Ms. Grant is familiar with court procedures and the revised code section that protects anonymous reporters."

"Your objection is sustained," Chambers said. "Ms. Grant, it's the policy of this court to keep the complainant confidential. You may continue."

Despite the calm exterior I projected, I fumed inside. This excuse of a hearing would never pass any kind of appellate scrutiny. What would stop anyone with an axe to grind from calling the hotline and having someone's child removed?

"Well, Miss Young," I continued. "Do you have any other evidence, beyond the hotline caller to support the allegations you've made?"

"The information from the call, and your refusal to meet with us was enough for me to believe your daughter was in danger," Young said, better on familiar footing.

Without incriminating myself, I couldn't fathom what else I could ask. The gall of these so-called social workers who thought they could remove my daughter without any evidence.

"No further questions," I said, taking my seat.

The magistrate deliberated for a few moments. The pretense likely for my benefit. He'd decided the damned case before I'd ever walked in the door.

"Okay. It will be my pre-trial order that the child be committed to the emergency custody of the Department of Children and Family Services, pending the next hearing.

"Ms. Grant, I'm aware that you're an attorney, and apparently a competent one, but I'm going to suggest that you retain counsel for the next hearing. Juvenile court has its own set of procedures. We have a number of excellent attorneys who specialize in these types of cases.

"Now, we don't have a hearing date for the TC, but you'll all be receiving notices in the mail. Let's see..." the magistrate paused, flipping through several stacks of papers on his desk. "We don't have a GAL on the case either. Gloria!" he called.

The woman had exchanged doughnuts for diet coke. "Yes, Magistrate?"

"Can you pull in someone from the hallway? We don't have a GAL on this case. I think I saw Patrick, or maybe Ed out there."

Aghast was the only word I could come up with to describe my feelings. In my limited experience with this side of the law, a guardian *ad Litem* was crucial to protecting a child's interests. And they were going to pick any live body from the hallway to protect my daughter?

"Excuse me, Your Honor." I paused and modulated my voice. "Isn't there some procedure for appointing guardians in these matters?"

"Counselor, if we go through the juvenile court clerk's office, chances are we won't have a guardian until well past your next hearing date. That would further postpone matters. Since you seem so *eager* to resolve this case, it's best for you if we clean up what we can now while we're all here."

Gloria pulled a forty-something woman from the corridor. "Magistrate, I've found Sherry Otis," she said.

"Counselor, good morning," Chambers said. "I've just put a…" He looked down at his notes, "thirteen-year-old child into emergency custody. The mom here," he gestured toward me, "is non-cooperative and an attorney. Do you think you can handle this one?" I took note of his patronizing tone. "It may be pretty time-intensive."

I worked to maintain the same unassuming posture I'd displayed during the hearing. I hadn't yet digested that I'd lost this preliminary hearing. That I was being dragged kicking and screaming into this crazy ass place. I hadn't expected to visit the juvenile court building more than this one time.

For a long moment, Otis sized up everyone in the room. "Thanks, Magistrate. I'll accept the appointment."

"Okay folks, that should wrap this up. Why don't you all go discuss this in the hallway? The temporary custody hearing will be in about six weeks. The clerk's office will notify you." With that, Chambers pressed 'stop' on the tape recorder, closed Olivia's file, and opened another folder. "Gloria! Can you call Garcia?"

The prosecutor stayed in her designated seat, reaching down to fiddle with the pile beneath her chair, coming up with another manila folder. Dismissed, I shuffled from the small, now too-warm, room with the guardian and social worker.

I rounded on Celeste Young. "I need to make arrangements to see my daughter. After four-thirty would be perfect. I need to see how she's doing. Make sure—"

"I'm sorry, Ms. Grant." Young's face held little sympathy. "I can't do that. I'm only the intake worker. A regular 'ongoing' worker will be assigned to the case. She'll be able to arrange visitation. I can tell you right now, though, we don't have daily visitation. It's usually every other week or so, depending on the availability of the drivers and most of the visits occur at Metzenbaum. So, you should keep that in mind."

"Ms. Grant," Sherry Otis butted in, her maroon lipstick crawling into the lines around her thin lips. "I understand you may be an attorney. But let me reassure you that I'll treat you exactly the same as every other parent I meet. No special treatment. I haven't read your complaint yet, but I'm sure that if you're here, something's wrong at home." Otis barely paused to take a breath. "I'm here to represent the children. The children *only*."

I closed and opened my eyes. Surely Otis wasn't wagging a finger at me. But there it was, a chubby, ringed finger waving before my very eyes.

"If I find out anything is going on that's not in the best interests of the child, you can be sure that heads will roll. That not only goes for you and the dad." The next was under her breath. "If he's around." She returned to full volume. "But also, for any foster parents. You can be sure that I'm going to visit the girl and make sure that any disposition is in her best interest."

I watched Sherry Otis very carefully. I guessed Otis to be around fifty. From her purple crepe dress to her ruby toned hair and her home shopping gold jewelry, a sense of superiority oozed from the woman. I wasn't entirely sure what kind of pull Otis might have, but I couldn't afford to get on the wrong side of anyone until I got her daughter out of the system. Then and only then could I go at these people, guns blazing. Until that day, I knew what I had to do. I pretended I was walking down a sidewalk in the south and figuratively stepped into the gutter to spare some white person the ordeal of being near me.

I extended my hand toward Otis. And like that colored woman in the south stepping out of her place, it was ignored. Taking a deep breath, I spoke. "I look forward to speaking with you about my daughter. This whole process has been one big mistake. I plan to get this all straightened out before long," I said.

"Well, Ms. Grant, you'll just have to believe me when I tell you, I've heard all that before." Otis dug through her purse, extracting a business card and extending it to me. "Here. Please call my office to arrange a time when I can meet with you and view your home." Distracted by movement in the hall, Otis looked at her watch. She flipped open her overstuffed Filofax. “I can’t talk more now. I have a dozen hearings this morning.” Without so much as a goodbye, Otis stalked off.

The hallway was still packed with black and Latina women nearly as defeated as I felt. I looked at my own watch, realizing I needed to get back to my own courtroom and prepare for my afternoon docket. Other people’s problems paled in comparison to my own, but I propelled my unwilling body forward.

Though I knew I had the expertise to handle my own case, maybe I should hire an attorney. Once past the metal detectors and out the front door, I retrieved my cell phone from her bag. I dialed a number I’d known by heart for years. When the receptionist picked up the phone, I asked for a familiar name.

“Peyton Bennett, please.”

17

Happy Clients Never Sue

Peyton Bennett

April, 2000

I pulled my eyes from the documents I was scouring and grabbed the trilling telephone from the expanse of my mahogany desk. I barked my name into the receiver.

A no nonsense voice came from the other end. "We have a problem."

Dennis Traxson had to have been the inspiration for the "Boy Who Cried Wolf." I sighed. "What now, Dennis?"

"There's a big problem with my client, Arron Medical Systems," he whined.

Instantly alert, I sat erect. "Isn't Sheila Grant handling those cases? She's the billing attorney, right?" I asked, seeking confirmation for what I already knew.

"Yes, your little protégé is the problem, Peyton. She screwed up a discrimination case," Traxson said as if a black woman should be an ace at cases of that sort.

"Come to my office. Now," I commanded, disconnecting the internal call.

I'd worn a path in my burgundy and blue Esfahan Persian rug in the ten minutes it took for Traxson to walk the forty feet to my office. Traxson shook my hand and patted his shoulder as if we hadn't seen each other in six months rather than the six hours since we'd run into each other at the Arabica coffee shop downstairs earlier that morning.

Reaching over Traxson's shoulder, I slammed the door. "What's the story with Sheila and Arron Medical?"

"Got a call from Jerald Stazcyk, EVP over at Arron. He's frantic. They're being sued by some guy. He's Chinese...no, Korean. Asian. Anyway, he came after Arron claiming discrimination after they fired him. But they are pissed. Sheila advised that that it would be no problem terminating this guy."

"But it's a problem, right?" I asked. Traxson nodded his head in confirmation. "Shit." I banged the desk, putting an exclamation point on the explicative. Heavy brass fittings rattled.

Traxson moved from his perch by the door and made himself comfortable, leaning back in one of my brass studded leather chairs. He smiled unctuously. "Your little filly out of control?"

"Uncalled for, Dennis. I was Sheila's *mentor*. Kimberleigh and I have been happily married for years." I shook off the slight. "Let's get down to business."

We strategized for an hour and came up with a plan to turn Sheila's sow's ear of a blunder into a silk purse.

A week later, Traxson, Sheila and I, along with several associates, assembled in a borrowed courtroom. Though the windowless courtroom was paneled from floor to ceiling in warm oak and the recessed lighting cast the room in a golden glow, the room was ice cold.

An associate in judge's robes sat at the bench. Twelve men in sweatshirts and jeans filled the plastic swivel seats of the jury box.

"Call your first witness," the 'judge' said.

I rose to my full six-foot height. "We call David Park to the stand."

An Asian actor walked to the cloth-covered witness chair. There was no swearing in during this mock trial.

"How did you come to live in Cleveland?" I questioned.

"I was born in Koreatown in Los Angeles. I'd lived there all my life. After my wife got her medical degree from UCLA, she got an offer from Cleveland Clinic. It was hard to leave our families, but we came to Ohio."

"And how did you come to work for Arron Medical?"

The actor looked down, speaking to his chest. "I couldn't find a job right away. This is the kind of town where it takes years to be accepted. My wife and I mostly kept to ourselves. Nearly every vacation and holiday we went back to L.A."

"Your Honor," I said.

The judge directed the witness to answer the question asked.

"My wife Kyo-jin finally talked with her bosses at the Clinic and they got me an interview, and finally a job at Arron."

"What was your job at Arron Medical?"

The Park impersonator nodded modestly. "Arron makes imaging machines. The designs, testing, et cetera is done here—the manufacturing in China. I was on a team that designed and did quality control testing on the newest products."

"Did you have any problems with the machines you tested?"

"At first things were going well. We designed some innovative scanners and sales were through the roof. Then we started having problems with the latest batch of bone scanners. Buyers were complaining. Our own testing showed a failure rate near fifty percent."

"In your opinion, what was the source of the product failures?"

"Arron tried to get manufacturing on the cheap. The first set of machines from China were fine, but the newer models were further subbed out from our Chinese manufacturer to Sri Lanka. The designs were sound. The quality control during manufacturing was not."

"Did you have a falling out with your bosses at Arron?"

"I suggested we tell the customers about the high failure rate and offer to replace the machines. Jerald Stazcyk said we shouldn't until a scanner failed—waiting out the warranty if possible. But my wife—she's an oncologist—said lymphoma and leukemia were too serious to mess around with."

"Then what happened?"

"Going to work went from bad to worse. They had always made jokes, like saying 'Hello sexy girlfriend' every time I walked into a room or comparing me to David Carradine's Chang character. That I could handle." The actor put his head into his hands for a moment then resumed speaking. "But when they started complaining about how my lunch smelled bad or asking if my wife was good in bed, had she been trained by her grandmother in the ways of the Japanese, I got really upset. When they started calling me a ..." The fake Park paused for dramatic effect. "...'Gook,' well...I didn't think anyone had used that since the Korean War."

There was a hush among the voluntary jury members.

After 'Park' left the stand, I presented a few more of the plaintiff's witnesses. Traxson played Sheila's role as Arron's lawyer and presented the medical manufacturer's case. Then the twelve volunteers went to the jury room to deliberate the case. Unlike a real deliberation, a secret process sacrosanct in the American justice system, this one was piped into the courtroom via closed circuit TV for the attorneys viewing.

During the deliberation, one juror started crying. The name on the brunette's shirt read: Luz Dalangin. "I can't believe they made a joke about comfort women," she said, sniffling. "Where my parents came from in the Philippines, that's not something we joke about. I just...I just found out my grandmother was one of the *Lolas* those assholes at Arron found so funny."

Another female juror shook her lowered head. "These men were mean because he was Asian. I don't know if he was doing a good job or not, but they shouldn't have said those things."

Later in the deliberation another juror who'd been quiet the entire time spoke up. "I don't normally think there's anything to these race lawsuits. But in this case, Arron is guilty."

The jurors decided on the issue of Arron's liability and started arguing damages amongst themselves. Traxson and I, box lunches in hand, walked to a small conference room down the hall from the deliberation.

"And Sheila didn't think this was a problem?" Traxson asked, excess turkey club mayonnaise filling the corners of his mouth.

Reflexively wiping my own mouth, I answered. "Maybe Stazcyk didn't give her all the facts."

"I've known Jerry for years. We were at University School together. Sheila? Who the hell knows what she was thinking?"

"Sheila's very smart. We recruited her straight from Michigan."

"That's affirmative action for you," Traxson said, stuffing the remainder of his sandwich in his mouth and tossing his napkin toward the wastebasket. He missed.

A young associate hesitantly poked his head through the door. "The jury's reached a verdict."

I returned to the courtroom, sitting at the counsel table. Traxson joined the firm's other lawyers at the defense table farthest from the jury.

The 'judge' came back to the courtroom. He nodded toward the jury. "Have you reached a verdict?"

"We have."

"What say you?" asked the bombastic young associate, enjoying his role.

"In the matter of David Park versus Arron Medical Systems, we find for the plaintiff, Mr. Park, in the amount of ten million dollars."

I slumped back into my wooden chair, resigned. I cast a quick glance toward Sheila who had gone unnoticed in the gallery. While an associate paid the jurors their one hundred fifty-dollar fee for a day's work, we lawyers gathered their papers. Before leaving the building, I pulled Sheila aside in a small corridor.

I looked at Sheila, seeing her clearly for the first time in a long time.

Instead of her usual direct stare, she lowered her eyes. “We’re in trouble, aren’t we?”

“I don’t know what’s going on with you. I’d always been so proud that we hired you. I know the firm hasn’t always treated you fairly. But you’ve always, always been on the ball.”

“Peyton, I’ve given my life to this firm.” Her tone was pleading. “I’ve lost my husband. I barely know my daughter. This—you are all I have.”

“Us doesn’t exist anymore. I was your mentor. But now I’m your partner.” We were standing only a hair’s breadth apart. “I have fiduciary responsibilities to all of the partners. I’ll need to contact our ethics guy about this.” I paused, grasping for words. “This was malpractice.” I cupped my hand along her jaw, touching her one last time. “I’m very sorry. I’ll do what I can. But you have to know that you can’t stay.”

Sheila

Slinking home that day, I waited for the axe to fall. It didn’t the next day when I went back to work, nor the next month. But in December I was called to Troy Holman’s office.

Holman was the firm’s elder statesman. Before joining the firm three years before, Holman had enjoyed a twenty-year career in the House of Representatives as a congressman for Ohio’s Eleventh District, the west side of the Cuyahoga river.

Back in his day, Holman had been a young partner with Bennett Friehof. After he retired from public service, like many others in Washington, he took up his legal career right where he'd left off. Except he didn't practice law, exactly.

Holman worked at the art of making connections between the firm's top lawyers and the many Midwest based corporations that had business before agencies in Washington. Though Holman was outside the Beltway now, he still greased wheels, made introductions, and was proving invaluable to the firm's clients.

When I walked into Holman's office, I knew the other shoe was going to hit the expensive Oriental carpet.

"Good to see you," Holman boomed. "Good to see you." He pumped my hands up and down. "So, tell me, how do you like Cleveland? Not planning to move anytime soon, I hope," he laughed, though there was no joke that I could fathom. "Seriously, though, how are you doing for money? Firm paying you okay? Have a house payment?"

I had no idea where this was going, so I was less than candid. "The divorce set me back a bit. But I think I'll be able to save for a down payment—maybe buy something in Cleveland or Shaker in the next couple of years."

"Let me get to the point, Sheila. That Arron case was a nasty business, but things are definitely looking up for you. I've got an opportunity that I think will interest you. But it'll be a bit of a pay cut. Though I must say that hasn't dissuaded many." Holman's laugh was quieter this time. "I've been talking to some people and it looks like the president is ready to fill some of those judicial vacancies that are always making the news. Before he leaves office, he's going to make a number of recess appointments." Holman paused.

I nodded like I was in full agreement though my head was spinning with thoughts of losing one job, but getting another lifetime one in its place.

"If you're interested, there's a vacancy in the Northern District that has your name on it. What do you say?" Holman held up a hand before I could speak. "The president is holding a press conference in Washington day after tomorrow."

"When would I get confirmed?" I asked.

"Ah, the kicker. The kicker." He paused a long time. I should have known something this good couldn't fall into my lap without a caveat the size of a Mack truck. "You'll get your temporary commission in January, if memory serves me right. There'll be some meeting with Ohio senators and members of the Judiciary committee. The hearings will be in late spring or early fall."

I sat back in the chair, crossed my legs and mulled over the offer. I realized two things. Peyton had really come through. He'd called in one last favor, and for that—and Olivia—I'd be forever grateful. The other thing was I didn't have a choice. No matter how pretty a bow Holman was trying to wrap it in, if I didn't take this judgeship, I'd be unemployed come January.

"I'll pack my bags, Troy." Standing, I shook his hand. "I look forward to meeting the president."

Peyton

A week later, I watched the scene unfold on C-SPAN. Sheila was in the oval office meeting the president. I watched as she stood, smiling stiffly, and the president doled out his signature charm on the small group of women and minority lawyers who looked as shell shocked as Sheila. Turning to the small press gathering, the president spoke eloquently about the nominees, about justice, and then about his life beyond the White House.

When it was Sheila's turn at the microphone, she said she'd do her best to uphold the constitution of the United States. That she'd administer justice fairly and equitably. Silently, I wished her the best, snapping off the television with the remote.

18

Bennett Friehof & Baker

Sheila

October 25, 2001

I walked into the reception area of Bennett Friehof and Baker, and for a moment it was like a homecoming. The firm had been my home away from home for nearly twenty years. And even though the firm had moved from its old digs in the Huntington Building to the newly renovated Skylight Office tower in my later years, the overall atmosphere and culture of the firm had not changed.

I had started at Bennett Friehof during my second summer of law school. In the early eighties, there weren't too many black women law students. Getting a job at a white shoe firm was damned near impossible, but I had done it. The height of the affirmative action era and two successive

Reagan administrations had yet to cast a pall over the issue of minority hiring.

During minority recruitment fairs, Bennett Friehof had stepped up to the plate. Despite being one of the first, I wasn't the only black hire. In the ensuing years, the firm's reputation for hiring and developing minority talent was well deserved. I had been the second black and third woman partner of the firm.

While the elevators *whooshed* me up to the top of the twelve-story building, I strategized on how to approach my impending meeting with Peyton Bennett. He'd been a friend and mentor all through my years with the firm.

Peyton had guided me through two of the most difficult times in my life—navigating the minefield of my climb to partnership and representing me in the divorce from Keith. I had made a vow never to ask favors from anyone at Bennett Friehof—especially after the firm backed my appointment to the bench—but for Olivia I was going to make an exception.

After hugging the receptionist and exchanging pleasantries, I was directed to Peyton's office. He was expecting me. I walked through the firm's lobby—sumptuous by any standard, with plush Turkish carpeting, leather seating, priceless artwork—to the back decorated in cube farm beige where the associates slaved.

It had taken me years to work my way up from the darkened corners of the library to a corner office with a bevy of associates under my supervision. Despite all those hours over all those years, only a couple of raised hands and jutted chins greeted me.

Though I'd done two times the work to make partner, it hadn't been a decision supported by everyone. Even after all those years and all those wins, it was whispered that I was an affirmative action choice. But like I had done when I worked there, I held my head high and strode with confidence.

Bonnie's greeting was the most effusive yet. "So good to see you, Judge Grant.

Pulling back from the warm hug, I asked, "How are your daughters?" Bonnie's two girls had to be college aged by now.

"They're good, Sheila—excuse me—*Your Honor.*" Bonnie's curly hair danced as she beamed. Lowering her voice, she said, "Since you left, I've been stuck with nothing but young attorneys who think they're God's gift."

I laughed. Some things never changed. Secretary and paralegal assignments were often problematic. On any other day, I would have reminisced with Bonnie, taking her out to a long lunch. But my anxiety replaced congeniality. "Is Peyton available right now?

Taken aback by my abruptness, Bonnie's professional mask slid down. "Yes. He's just finished up with Kimberleigh. Go right on in."

Without further prompting, I pushed open Peyton's door. My stomach clenched at the lingering smell of his wife's perfume. Mentally pinching myself, I refocused.

Peyton sat regal behind a huge mahogany desk, brass fittings gleaming. The small squeak in his brass studded leather chair was the only acknowledgement of my arrival. I remained standing, trying not to notice how the bespoke charcoal suit complimented his newly silver hair.

Eventually, Peyton stood in greeting. "Good evening, Sheila. It's good to see you. How's the federal bar treating you?"

I declined his extended hand. “Things are good. The case load is pretty hectic. But I’m getting the hang of wearing the robes.”

“Too bad you have to recuse yourself on any Bennett cases. It’d be good to see you in action.” Peyton sat, gesturing for me to sit as well. “What brings you here?” Small talk was over quickly. There was once a time when we’d never run out of things to say to each other.

In the few short minutes I had been in the office, there had been more foot traffic than necessary past Peyton’s office.

Gossipmongers.

I lowered my voice.

“The county has Olivia in foster care.”

Peyton shot up and slammed his door.

“What in the hell?” he asked when he got back to the other side of his desk. “Did Keith do this? I thought he was in the wind.”

“I don’t know how this happened. Someone must have called child welfare. The county filed a complaint alleging I have a drinking problem. They gave temporary custody after a sham hearing. No one at the juvenile court has ever heard of due process.”

“Did you go to the hearing alone?”

“I thought I could handle it myself. There was no evidence. I assumed I could clear it up, and Olivia would be home with me now.” I paused, indignation rising. “I never expected to be in this fucking position. I have confirmation hearings coming up. A hint of scandal will kill my job. And what I’ve heard about county foster homes.” I worked to clear Precious Evans from my mind. “Olivia could be scarred for life.”

Silence permeated the darkening room. Something nearly imperceptible shifted. Peyton pried his fingers apart, leaned forward and spoke.

"But Sheila, what can *I* do for you?"

Undaunted by his tone, I spoke. "I need representation. After all I've done for this firm over the years, all I'm asking is that you spare a couple of associates to help me fight this. I need to get a handle on this right away.

"The county doesn't have a lick of evidence against me. With the firm's help, I can get Olivia home now. Then I can concentrate on the Senate hearings," I explained patiently. Mentally, I was already picking which lawyers I'd prefer and figuring out how I'd divvy up the work between them—with one handling procedure and the other law. If he only gave me one....

"Why can't you have your clerks do this?" Peyton interrupted my thoughts.

"I hired these people late. Don't get me wrong, they'll probably be good clerks, but they're not on par with Bennett's associates. I need a couple of bulldogs on this."

"We'd really like to help you."

"But?" I couldn't be hearing right. They would not abandon my daughter and me like this. Not now, after nearly two decades of loyalty.

"We put you in this judgeship. You were destined to leave this firm one way or another. You got a second chance at your career and an opportunity to save face. We kept our hands clean."

I jumped through mental gymnastics. "You are not holding the Arron Medical Systems shit against me. Are you?"

"You dropped the ball on that one. You know what it took to get it back on track and settled. That's why the judicial appointment was perfect. It allowed the firm to support you, yet have you leave in an amicable way."

I couldn't believe it. Nearly twenty years of service, and he was denying me based on one small mistake I'd made last April. Anyone could have done what I did. *Would have.*

Peyton continued. "At the time, I suspected some kind of substance abuse may have been behind it. But I gave you the benefit of the doubt."

My mind reeled. *Benefit of the doubt.* After all I'd done for these—

"Frankly," Peyton interrupted my thoughts, "I'm not ready to put the firm's reputation on the line over this."

The brass handle rattled as he opened his right-hand drawer and removed a monogrammed pad. He scribbled something, folded the sheet in half, handing it to me. "Here's the name of a friend of Kimberleigh's. We've known her for years. Madeline Montgomery's handled some matters—discreetly, of course, for some of the partners around here. You'll find her fees quite reasonable. I'll tell her to expect your call."

Peyton stood up. I was dismissed. "I hope I've been of some help."

For the second time in as many days, I was rendered speechless. After all I'd done, serving the Cleveland legal community, doors were closing on me everywhere. I quietly gathered my self-control and my coat. I opened his door, but I couldn't leave him with the last word.

"I can't believe it." I shook my head. "You've become your father's son."

19

Common Pleas Lawyers

Sheila

October 26, 2001

Offering no explanation to my staff, I left my chambers mid-morning. Nancy, my courtroom deputy, looked up as I swept from the anteroom.

"I'll be back in an hour."

I could sense Nancy wanted more information, but my stern look kept the woman mute.

I walked east from the Metzenbaum courthouse—named for Ohio's long-time senator—down Superior Avenue to Madeline Montgomery's office a few blocks away. In no time at all, I reached the twenty-two-story neoclassical building filled with lawyers. The gray columned Walker and Weeks was built in the 1920s and the interior exuded eighty years of smells. I checked the building directory in the marbled lobby and located the attorney's name.

Stepping into the ancient elevator, I eased slowly, creakily to the eighteenth floor. Though the building was spotless, the musty smell pervaded. When I saw the long list of placards affixed to the door, I wasn't thrilled.

Anonymity was paramount.

The three other attorneys who shared office space wouldn't be charged with keeping my secrets. It was my experience that confidentiality went out the window when lawyers worked in close quarters. Out of choices, I pushed open the heavy door with a sigh.

Several women, knee deep in paperwork, filled the reception area.

"I'm here to see Madeline Montgomery," I announced.

A youngish woman, pinned to her chair by a box of papers, acknowledged me.

"Have a seat, ma'am. She's not back from court yet, but asked you to wait. You're Judge Grant, right?"

At the mention of my title, all activity ground to a halt. Judges were rare in attorney's offices. Not willing to wait amid scrutiny, I took a different tact.

"I'm very busy. Have Ms. Montgomery meet me in my chambers when she's done with court today. Whose room is she in?"

The woman finally removed the box of papers from her lap and consulted a computer.

"She's over at domestic relations, Judge Flanagan's room."

I opened the door to take my leave.

"Tell Ms. Montgomery I'll be waiting."

Off the bench and on the computer two hours later, I looked up when Nancy came in unannounced.

"Judge, there's an attorney Montgomery here to see you. Is this an ex-parte meeting? Do you need any files, the court reporter? She's not on calendar."

"I don't need anything but privacy," I said. "This is a confidential matter. Show her in."

Madeline Montgomery was more or less what I expected. A tall, thin woman with Irish coloring and an aggressive haircut entered my office. Briefcase, purse, and cell phone clattered about her. I was familiar with the type: fortyish white woman, dark hair, huge diamond.

Montgomery was the kind of woman I always thought of as playing at the practice of law. With husbands at home to fall back on, they weren't serious about their work.

I stood up, taking Madeline's hand in a firm grip.

"Ms. Montgomery. Sheila Grant. Nice to meet you."

After we sat, Madeline scratched out the answers I gave to some preliminary questions on a yellow legal pad.

"I'm not quite sure what's happened," I began. "Someone called child welfare and reported that I couldn't care for Olivia because I drank. Then everything moved so fast. Olivia was in foster care before I could blink an eye. And the so-called 'emergency hearing' was a sham." I shook my head, annoyed with myself for believing in the justice system even one tiny bit. "That's not the point. The point is that I need a lawyer who knows this crazy juvenile court system and can get my daughter home." I met and held Madeline's eyes. "Are you that person?"

Under direct questioning, Madeline faltered, but only for a second. "Judge, I may not practice in federal court, but I'm good at what *I* do. I know my way around the family courts here. I handle nothing but divorces, juvenile cases, guardianships and adoptions. I've also handled a number of high-profile clients like yourself. I don't like to brag, but I'm one of the most well-respected attorneys in Cleveland. My husband and I graduated at the top of our class from Cleveland State. The judges know us, our families, our children. Those personal relationships get results."

I listened to Madeline's spiel, and trying not to be too hard on her, didn't cross examine the woman. "That's all well and good, but do you think you'd be able to get any traction in Olivia's case?" Without embellishment, I explained that I was up for confirmation. Precision and stealth were what was needed to save my daughter and my career.

"Judge, I came recommended by Peyton Bennett because I'm the best you can hire," Madeline said. "In this kind of case, the earlier you lawyer up, the better. You've waited almost too long now. I could start on this right away." Madeline handed me a card after scribbling something on the back. "Here's my cell phone number. Give me a call anytime." The lawyer gathered up her various bags. "I'll make this case my priority."

I walked her from chambers to the deserted stone hallway. Once the lawyer was gone, I leaned into a defunct pay phone alcove, stripped bare in the new mobile phone era. But when I lifted my heavy head, I realized the lawyer hadn't left the courthouse yet. Madeline's voice echoed from the nearby stairs.

"Yeah, hon, this one's in the bag. Mm-hm. I think I'll ask for a retainer of fifteen or twenty grand. What? No, I didn't tell her that no one gets their kids out of the system. She'll burn through money in juvenile court." Madeline paused a long time. "I know I don't practice there anymore. But a big-name client and a fat retainer would be a feather in my cap. Judy Bartlett *always* gets the big cases." A shorter pause this time. "Yes, I'll pick up the boys from school this afternoon. Talk to you later." The click of the lawyer's heels, the snap of the closing phone, the jostling of her bags were the last sounds I heard before I got to my feet.

Damned naiveté was going to defeat me. For a few minutes, I'd been taken in. But now I was back at square one. If I called in whatever favors I had left—and they weren't many, considering how many people I'd alienated along the way up the career ladder—I could kiss the confirmation goodbye. On the other hand, I could fight. I would not lose Olivia to the system like so many other black mothers.

Muffling a scream, I deliberately emptied my head of the images sensational news shows used for shock value.

I pulled back the wooden doors and lifted myself from the hard bench. I stumbled toward the federal marshal I'd just noticed standing in the hall.

"Ma'am, can I help you? Are you looking for a courtroom?"

When I didn't answer right away, he continued, "Is your lawyer here yet? Maybe he can help you check in with your judge." Motioning to the papers in my hand, he said, "If you let me see those, maybe I can help you figure out where you need to be."

I snatched the papers back. Peering closely at his name tag and badge number, I finally spoke.

"Excuse me, Deputy Marshall Bruty? I assume we haven't met. I'm *Judge* Sheila Harrison Grant." I extended my right hand. Deputy Marshall Bruty did not offer his in return. Dropping my hand, I said, “Today, I’m not a litigant in this court, nor am I just an attorney. I’m the judge.”

Deputy Marshall Bruty’s ruddy face turned an even deeper crimson, and he stumbled away without an apology.

I needed to find someone on my own. Someone young and eager whom I could intimidate and control to get me out of this tangle.

The name Casey Cort came from an unlikely source.

In spite of her resume, I had hired Claire Henshaw. Claire was not one of the typical applicants. She wasn’t white, male, nor a graduate of the Ivy League. Claire had what could be called kindly a *unique* resume. Not hired straight out of school by a firm, Claire had bounced around in a series of temporary jobs for the few large law firms in town. Temporary, perhaps, being a euphemism, because she had spent two years each at two different firms, and a year at yet another doing nothing but reviewing documents.

When looking for law clerks in the rush of getting my commission and fitting my robes, I had flipped through a lot of resumes and had all but tossed Claire on the reject pile. When I saw that Claire had gone to an historically black college, and then to Northwestern Law, a top school, I was intrigued and invited her in. When I called Claire for an interview, I could tell Claire was surprised, but she’d dropped everything and come in immediately.

The young woman was bright, intelligent, and reminded me of myself when I’d graduated from school. Why this woman’s career had been floundering, I didn’t know, but I’d hired her on the spot—for a two-year clerkship.

Claire was smart but needed help getting her legal skills up to par. As yet, I hadn’t given her complete autonomy, but I was hoping to get her there. I called the clerk to my office.

"Close the door," I directed. Claire did what she was told and promptly sat in one of my leather and cherry wood chairs. "I need to talk to you, but I need you to keep what I'm going to say in the strictest confidence."

Claire wilted in the chair, clearly intimidated by my tone.

"Look, I need your help," I said, lowering her voice with each sentence—until Claire had to lean in to hear better. "I'm in the midst of a personal crisis involving my daughter and a case in juvenile court. I've gotten the names of several reputable attorneys, but my meetings have not inspired confidence. I'd like to know if you can refer me to any smart, young attorneys, contemporaries of yours, who have experience in juvenile court. Someone who isn't looking to bill hours without rolling up their sleeves. If you know anyone, please give me the name. Two things: time is of the essence, and confidentiality is paramount."

I wasn't privy to what Claire had done after she left my office. But by the end of the day, I had a name, vitals, and a phone number of one attorney–Casey Cort.

20

Initial Consultation

Casey

October 26, 2001

It was late afternoon by the time I returned to my office. It had been another unproductive day in Juvenile. I'd been there four hours waiting for my case to be called—only to have the matter continued.

Tired, I wanted nothing more than home. But the wasted time wouldn't earn me a dime. I needed to sit down and bill on my paying cases. Two hundred an hour was nothing to sneeze at. Knowing I was going to be around for a while, I dumped my briefcase and overcoat in the empty reception area.

Picking up my messages from the front desk, I shuffled through them mindlessly until one message jumped out at me. Leticia had made an appointment for five-thirty. I looked at my watch. Only forty minutes until the prospective client came.

The caller must have been compelling. I had specifically directed Leticia not to schedule appointments after everyone had left the office. One run-in with an angry gun-toting cop had been enough to cut my appointment times short. Letty's handwriting was neater than mine, and reading the name on the message slip was easy: Sheila Harrison Grant. Something about the name niggled my memory, but she couldn't place it.

After clearing away confidential information, I had a few minutes to spare. Rolling my leather chair over to my credenza, I turned on my computers. In a matter of seconds, I was on the internet. Bringing up my favorite search engine, I typed in the potential client's name.

Results appeared quickly, but there were few. I clicked on the link to the Michigan law alumni section and there it was. Ah, I thought. Grant had recently been appointed to the federal district court bench. Now I remembered my mom pointing out the story in the paper. My parents showed me every law-related article, no matter how much disinterest I showed. my mom had asked what a recess appointee was.

Looking at Sheila's official photo jogged something loose in my memory. For some reason she thought she'd seen the well-dressed black woman in Juvenile court the other day. Unanswered questions started popping in my mind. Why had Grant been there? And what could she want from Casey? Having a judge come to my humble little office was nothing short of intimidating. Most of my clients were poor or lower middle class and impressed by my modest downtown digs.

Short on time, I tried to pretty up my office. I turned on lamps, extinguishing the greenish fluorescent lights above. Throwing open the curtains, I put my admittedly gorgeous view of Lake Erie on display. I picked up my discarded items from the reception area and tidied up the loose newspapers there. With everything in place, I looked down at my clothes.

Dowdy about described them. I was wearing one of those Chico's ensembles that look great on the mannequin, but sloppy in person. The gold three-piece wasn't exactly a power suit, but I'd wanted to be comfortable through the afternoon's court call. I was glad to have used up my nervous energy when the door opened. Poking my head into the reception area, I saw the judge.

"Sorry, there's no receptionist. I don't normally accept after-hours appointments. You must have been quite persuasive," I said while showing her in.

Judge Grant made herself comfortable in a chair facing the desk. Her knowing smile was disarming. "Trust me. I understand. Now that I'm a government worker, my staff promptly leave when the court closes at four-thirty."

I closed the door then sat on the edge of my leather executive chair.

"Your Honor, how can I help you?"

"Ms. Cort, I think we can dispense with the formalities," the judge said. Then she explained her predicament.

"Do you have a copy of the prosecutor's complaint?"

Sheila pulled a thin folder from her briefcase. I scanned the complaint, nodding. "Typical. Let me ask you some questions, then we can get to the case.

"What's your daughter's name?"

"Olivia Keziah Grant." The judge didn't bat an eye. Most clients started crying at the mere mention of their children.

"What's her father's name and address?"

"I don't know. If it's necessary, I can probably get that information out of his relatives. Keith's been out of the picture for years."

I was surprised by the typical client behavior from Judge Grant, holding back information. "We'll put that on hold for now. Have you been married to anyone else?"

"No."

"Do you have any other children?"

"No," Sheila said, unable to keep a smile from creeping on her face.

"You laugh, but sometimes people lie to me about small things that they think don't matter. Sometimes people lie to me about the big things—the things they know *do* matter. I just like to be up front. I need all the information that I ask about you, your ex-husband, and your daughter because I never like to be taken by surprise. I never want to be lied to. It's my only rule."

Sheila didn't blink.

I continued. "Who's your official employer?"

"I work for the U.S. Government under the auspices of the Administrative Office of the United States Courts. My title is U.S. District Judge for the Northern District of Ohio. But," Sheila hesitated, "I'm a recess appointee."

"Does your job have an expiration date?"

"I can only serve to the end of the year unless I'm confirmed by the full senate before then."

I squinted at the calendar on my far wall. "That doesn't leave a lot of time. How are you going to juggle this case and your confirmation process?"

"My daughter is more important than my job."

I nodded my head. Right answer.

"That doesn't mean I won't be working to make sure things come to a positive conclusion in Washington."

"Not to be indelicate, but you're not the typical juvenile court litigant. Most people with education, money or connections don't ever come under the county's scrutiny. What's going on here?"

"For some reason, my daughter thinks I drink too much, though she's never said a thing to me. I really think an overzealous young counselor at her school got it in her mind that she was going to *help* Olivia. And here we are."

I dropped my pen and sat forward. "It doesn't really matter why a child gets into the system. It's a matter of getting them out. I don't know if alcohol is the problem or not, but before this case is over, the county will try to find some *other* reason to keep your daughter out of your custody. Even if that reason is the time they wasted on the case or a great foster family."

The judge nodded. "From what little time I spent over there, I didn't get the feeling family unity was a top priority."

The judge spoke for a long time, instructing me on how she wanted the case handled. All the talking boiled down to: fight at all costs unless there was a less antagonistic alternative that would bring Olivia home. I reclined my chair and studied the judge. This was interesting. I'd had dozens upon dozens of cases just like this one over the five years or so I'd been practicing. But across the board, my clients had been poor and had probably gotten the level of service they paid for. I had never been paid my full rate to work on a juvenile case. The potential earnings and scope of visibility were enormous. I thought of myself as a good attorney, but I didn't know if I was up to the task. Nagging at me was a fear of failure or fear of success. I didn't know which.

I had been quiet too long. "I'm very intrigued by your case. But I don't want you to think because I spend a lot of time in juvenile court, I can work miracles. Juvie has an entrenched process. Even if we put up a real fight, try to push them, there is no guarantee that we can resolve this quickly."

"What else?" Judge Grant asked. I was amazed she hadn't walked out.

"I also think that it's important the case be kept confidential. On my end, I can promise you this. Under Ohio law, all cases concerning minors are secret. But the walls talk. You have to be prepared for the possibility of publicity and figure out how you're going to handle it."

"How much is this going to cost?" Grant was all cool professionalism. Most clients were knee deep in tissues at this point in a consultation.

I explained my rates to the judge, how the molasses-like juvenile process usually worked, and requested a retainer of twenty-five hundred dollars. I refrained from giving the judge one of my 'Your Rights' folders which were popular with most of my *other* clients, knowing it would make me look amateurish. Instead I rose, calmly shook the judge's hand, and escorted her out the door.

Back in my office, I looked through the window at Lake Erie. The sun had long since set, and I could see the lights of the cargo ships reflected on the smooth-as-glass water. Despite my tight budget and low-on-the-food-chain cases, I half prayed the judge wouldn't hire me. The pressure to perform could overwhelm me. There was a lot at stake for my future, the judge's career, and a child's future.

21

A More Permanent Placement

Olivia

November 1, 2001

I was struggling to hear the English lesson when a wadded-up ball of paper flew over my head. Mr. Cooper, the young teacher in charge, couldn't keep the class quiet. Every time he tried to open a discussion about the book we were reading, *I Heard the Owl Call My Name*, the class clown disrupted with fart noises or dirty jokes.

First, I was at Bethune with the kids I'd grown up with. Then there was Shaker with kids I couldn't ever hope to be friends with. And now this. *This* was Hough. The neighborhood whose name rhymed with and was synonymous with all its problems: tough, rough. School was chaos.

Dozens of kids acted like fools in every single class. Between the craziness and the overcrowding, I hated it. There weren't even any books left over for kids like me who'd started in the middle of the year. Instead the other new kids and I had to share books during class. There was no taking them home, either.

When I'd told my foster mom, she'd come through, buying copies of the books I needed. Her baby wasn't doin' no book sharin' program, she'd said. Regret flooded my veins. When I had been living with my mom, I'd taken school for granted.

Now that I was away from home for a little while, I feared falling behind my white classmates at Shaker. A month ago, I hadn't given a crap about that school with its pretty brick outside and its well-meaning teachers. Now, I'd give anything to get back there. This time I'd apply myself. This time, I'd make friends.

Clanging bells meant it was all over for today. I gathered my stuff and kind of grimaced at Mr. Cooper on my way out the door. Boy, I felt sorry for him. Quickly, I was swept up in the crowded hallway. Despite the press of teenage bodies, yelling at and preening for one another, I was alone. The rule was the same across all schools: no one talked to the new girl. Didn't matter though, I wasn't going to be here long.

When I got home to Sadie's house, things didn't seem quite right. Though I'd only been here a week, the two of us and the baby had fallen into an easy routine. Too quiet, that was the problem. The TV wasn't blaring. An unfamiliar car squatted in the driveway. Walking through the small vestibule, I followed my usual path to the dining room. I laid my book bag on the floor and knocked over some shopping bags. The neatly packed Aldi bags were full with the few clothes and books I'd come to the foster home with.

"C'mon in here, chile," Sadie called.

I walked into the silent living room. The TV was on, but muted. On the couch next to Sadie was a woman I'd never seen before. The badge on her lanyard was a dead giveaway: another social worker. The appetite I'd worked up for Sadie's dinner disappeared. No one looked like they had good news.

Like I was three or something, the social worker got to her knees in front of me. "I'm Jacqueline Foley, your ongoing worker."

"What happened to Miss Johnson?"

She spoke slowly, enunciating each word carefully. "Well, Olivia, Bernice Johnson only handles emergencies. Her job is to bring kids like you to people like Miss Sadie. My job is to help you and your mom." With growing earnestness, she continued. "But first, we have to get you in a regular foster home. Miss Sadie packed up all your stuff. So, we can get going as soon as I tie up some loose ends. Why don't you get some Kool-Aid or something before we go?"

My bottom lip trembled so much, I had to push hard to get the words out. "Why can't I stay here?"

"Oh, Olivia, I thought you understood. Mrs. Watkins only takes kids in when they need a home right away. I'm going to take you to a family where you can settle in. You'll be right at home in a jiffy," the worker said.

My vocal cords were strangling me. "But if I can't stay here, why can't I go home?"

The new social worker gripped my quivering chin in her cold, dry hand. "You can't go home until your mom gets better. There's a family waiting. You're going to love it. Get your stuff now." She let go of my jaw and strode to the vestibule, not looking to see if I followed.

"Mrs. Watkins," the worker called over her shoulder, "I'll call you later to discuss your county reimbursement."

Jacqueline reached back and her hand only met air. She turned impatient eyes on me, and shook her hand and arm with impatience.

I stood my ground. I didn't want to go somewhere new. Miss Sadie was just fine. I already had a family and didn't need another one. I would stay here until my mom got me. They couldn't make her go anywhere.

Miss Sadie's warmth was near. I looked up at the woman, pleading with my eyes.

"Ah, girl. I'm too old to take care of kids these days. You need some young'uns who can keep up with you. Go on now." Miss Sadie's push was gentle, but it was enough. Jacqueline reached back, and this time, I was within reach. The worker grabbed me with one hand, the bags with another, and pulled me out the door.

During the ten-minute drive to my next foster home, my head was full of questions, but I only asked Jacqueline one of them.

"What about my school books? I got new books. What's going to happen to them?"

The worker barely glanced at me. The car jerked to a stop at a red light. "Leave them in the back seat. I'll make sure to get them over to the school."

I didn't bother explaining that Miss Sadie had bought some of the books for me. Instead, I unzipped my backpack and took out all the books except one. I hadn't yet finished the Owl book and wanted to see how it would end. Since Miss Sadie had bought that too, I didn't think it would be missed.

By the time we arrived at the house on Hathaway Avenue, darkness was falling. Like all the houses where I'd grown up on Cleveland's east side, this was a simple two-story wood framed place in desperate need of a coat of paint. Lights blazed in the house, casting a warm glow through an otherwise bleak-looking neighborhood. I looked around at the motley assortment of dwellings on the street. Some looked lived in, others unoccupied, and then there were the vacant lots.

The social worker stepped from the car and popped open the trunk. "Get your stuff, Olivia," she said, looking meaningfully at her watch. "It's time to meet the Williams family."

Stumbling up the broken walkway, I held tight to my shopping bags. My stomach roiled with every step. Before Jacqueline could ring the doorbell, she grabbed my forearm in a tight grip.

"Ow, that hurts."

Jacqueline apologized but didn't loosen her hold. "Listen to me. This is a nice family. But you need to make sure that you lock your bedroom door when you're changing or sleeping. Do you understand?"

I nodded, but before I could ask why, the front door was opened by a light-skinned boy who looked about fourteen. A medium-skinned woman with a stocky build followed close behind.

"Jermaine, don't stand there and stare. Step out of the way and help this girl in with her bags," the woman said. "Hi, I'm Linda Williams. That there is Jermaine. He's another child we're fostering. Come on inside and meet my husband Geoffrey." Jacqueline let go of me to shake the woman's hand. "Nice to meet you, too. You must be Miss

Foley. The agency mentioned you'd be Olivia's ongoing worker. Do you know Jennifer Tannenbaum?" Jacqueline extracted her hand and shook her head. Mrs. Williams continued, "That's too bad. She's Jermaine's worker. You all should have one worker for both kids. Wouldn't that lighten the caseloads some? You could kill two birds with one stone. Oh, well." Mrs. Williams wound down and finally looked at me. Her gaze traveled up and down my body, making me uncomfortable. Something in Mrs. Williams' look made me feel lacking. "Let's get you settled in."

I shuffled inside and looked around this new place. It was clean. The furniture looked old, as did the part of the kitchen I could see from where I was standing, but there wasn't a speck of dust or a single object that looked out of place.

Someone on the couch hid behind a newspaper. The reader, probably Mr. Williams, never acknowledged the eddy of people swirling around the living room. The room was quiet as a page turned.

"Geoff," Mrs. Williams prompted. "Meet Olivia." Finally, the newspaper folded and rested in the lap of a stern-looking man.

"Nice to meet you, girl," he said.

"You'll have to excuse my husband," Mrs. Williams said. "He's been working double shifts at Birmingham. The last few weeks have been a struggle, but we can always use the money. Every little bit helps, you know." Into the silence, Mrs. Williams snapped, "Jermaine! Show Olivia to her room. I've got a few things to go over with Miss Foley."

Gamely, Jermaine hefted all my bags and led me up the dark, creaking stairs to get me settled into my new room in my new home. Thinking of the social worker's advice, I was gratified to see the door had a lock.

22

Change of Heart

Sheila

November 6, 2001

The peacefulness of the cold November rain I looked at through the window was at odds with the anxiety in my heart as I waited for Peyton. Earlier, I'd called and demanded that he come see me. I looked out the window while I waited. The cold November rain made me shiver. Though I couldn't feel the cold, wet drops on my face, or down my neck, I knew it was the kind of rain that would turn to snow with a single gust of Canadian wind. I was dreading this meeting only slightly less than I was dreading the cold, empty apartment that awaited my return.

A knock sounded at the outer door of my chambers. I took a few deep breaths to calm my beating heart. Moving at a deliberate pace, I rose, smoothed my skirt and padded through the anteroom—normally populated with my secretary, bailiff, and courtroom deputy—and opened the door.

Peyton stood on the other side, dripping. His London Fog was as soggy as his umbrella and galoshes. I brushed the rain from his shoulders but resisted touching him in the way I would have liked. Taking the umbrella from his hand, I placed it in the brass stand. The overcoat, I hung on the rack by the door. Unable to resist, my hand made contact with his chest as I laid flat his crooked lapel.

"Sheila…stop," Peyton said. He grasped my hand and removed it from his sport coat.

"Come…back," I said with forced casualness. "Let me give you the tour." I showed him the reception area, the cold marble fireplace mocking our intimacy long gone. I showed him the rest and finally we were in my chambers. I took a seat in my high-backed leather chair. Peyton sat stiffly in one of the hardwood chairs before my imposing desk.

"Why am I here?" Peyton asked, resting his crossed fingers in his lap.

Composure regained, I eyed him levelly. "For the first time, Peyton, I asked you for a favor—"

Peyton crossed his leather shod foot over his knee. "That's not exactly true, now is it?"

I continued. "I was very surprised that you turned me down. I asked you here tonight to clarify a few issues, and ask you again, to get the firm—especially Holman—behind my nomination.

"I think I have the juvenile court part of this crisis under control, but I need this confirmation to go flawlessly. You, more than anyone, understand, I *need* this job. But without your help, without the firm's backing, without Holman's help, I can't do this." I pleaded with my eyes. My gaze held his.

Peyton uncrossed his legs, hunching forward. "Sheila, I—"

"I don't want to play dirty. I don't want to have to drag the firm and Holman down with me, kicking and screaming. We've known each other too long for that. The bottom line is that I need the firm's support, but yours also. We used to care a lot for each other."

It was as if he didn't hear the last. His look was wary. "Are you threatening me? Bennett Friehof?"

"Peyton," I began, changing tactic. "The firm has meant a lot to me over the years. Was I angry at being passed over for partner more than once? Yes. But I'm still grateful the firm was willing to give me a chance when many other firms wouldn't even consider hiring a black woman. It's in that spirit of generosity and fair play that I'm calling on when I ask this."

"Fair?" Peyton face became a mask of hurt for a single second. It was quickly replaced by a coldness I'd never known him to possess. "Fair would have been a future for us."

Why did he always bring this up? Our affair had started off innocent enough but could never have lasted. "I was married, Peyton."

"I asked you twice, Sheila. The second time was after your divorce. Fair would have been giving us a chance."

"Like you gave the loft a chance? You never did anything to break out of your dad's orbit."

"I would have done it for you, Sheila." He'd said that time and again. But I didn't believe him. Sure, he'd moved out of his parents' Eastside mansion, buying and renovating lofts west of downtown. But he'd never struck out on his own. He'd never worked anyplace but his daddy's firm.

"Your dad handpicked your wife," I said, everything laid bare for once. "He would never have accepted me."

"You never gave me a chance. I would have gone to the mat for us." Would he? I would never know. Once I'd left Keith, becoming a partner and solidifying my place at the firm had been my only priority. Without a husband, I had no fallback plan. It was all on me.

"What would I have become? A stay-at-home mom in the heights making babies and volunteering at school?"

"My parents would have come around. They're not bad people. Just from a different era," he argued.

"Why are we talking about this? It's all in the past. You have Kimberleigh and your kids. I danced at your wedding, drank a toast to you. Us, whatever there was—"

"Four years, Sheila. That's what we had. Four of the best years of our lives."

I all but raised my hands to block my ears and trilled 'la-la-la-la.' "If you ever loved me Peyton, do this for me. I can't save whatever it was we had, but I have to do what I can to save Olivia."

Peyton rested his nose and lips on tented fingers. Silence stretched. "I'll see what I can do," he said, checking his watch, standing abruptly. Without acknowledgement he prepared to leave. I watched him slip on his galoshes, raincoat and hat. I stopped him with a hand on his arm.

"Peyton...there's something I need you to know." I slid my hand up to his roughened jaw and forced him to do something he hadn't done in a long time—look me directly in the eye. "Olivia is not Keith's daughter."

His blink was slow and involuntary. "What are you saying?"

Abruptly, I dropped my hand. "Nothing, I'm saying nothing. Go home to your wife. Think about what I said about the confirmation." I turned my back. I knew I was alone when I heard the chambers doors close behind him.

Why had I said that last thing? The issue had been dead and buried years ago. Why did he need to constantly bring up the past?

In no rush to go home, I sat before the cold hearth, remembering the day my daughter had come into the world.

"Where do you think she got those light eyes from?" my sister Deidre had said. "I don't think we have anyone with hazel eyes in Mommy and Daddy's family. Do we, sis?"

"When Momma and Auntie Cora get here, I'll ask them about our family history," Keith said. I propped up the uncomfortable, adjustable hospital bed, Olivia cradled in my arms. Keith and Deidre sat in the room's other bed—empty of another new mother—talking about the newborn girl in my arms. Flowers, cards and balloons filled the rest of the empty space.

With my free hand, I alternated between stroking Olivia's silky baby curls and the petals of the flowers Bonnie had sent. Deidre and Keith stopped talking when the large hospital room door swung open. Peyton Bennett strode in with a stuffed panda bigger than Olivia in one hand and flowers in the other.

Handing the gifts to Deidre, Peyton grasped both of Keith's hands in his. "Hey, man. Congratulations on your daughter." To me, he said, "How are you holding up? Ready to get back to work yet?"

Keith laughed. “Who knows? Maybe Sheila will be so busy with this little one, she’ll quit the firm.”

Swallowing past the lump that formed in my throat when my lover and my husband shook hands, I handed Olivia to Peyton. He awkwardly cradled her in his cupped hands. While he gazed at Olivia, Keith and Deidre picked up their conversation where they’d left off. “Peyton,” I said softly, “I’d like you to meet our daughter, Olivia.” The baby’s eyes blinked open, squinting in the bright fluorescence, staring unfocused at her father.

Blinking away the memories, I stood, gathered my things and got ready to greet my empty apartment for the fourteenth night in a row.

23

Puppy Love

Olivia

November 3, 2001

For a few disconcerting minutes, I had no idea where I was when I woke. Then the pink room, ruffles everywhere, came into focus. It was Saturday morning, and instead of a lazy morning of pancakes and Disney Channel sitcoms, I was in foster care. And I wasn't at Miss Sadie's house anymore. Nope, now I was at the Williamses—and they had rules.

The minute Jacqueline had closed her door and started her car, I'd gotten wind of the house rules.

The first rule: quiet. Mr. Williams worked hard at the steel mill. He didn't want to hear any girly giggling or have his phone line tied up with long phone calls to friends. It wasn't like I had any girlfriends to call, so quiet wouldn't be a problem.

The second through fifth rules followed in quick succession. At home being treated like this would have been punishment. I didn't know why I was being penalized when I'd done nothing wrong.

The room smelled like the roses on the bedspread. It was giving me a headache. But I didn't move for fear of making too much noise. Even though my stomach was growling, helping myself to food from the kitchen was a no-no—rule three. Rather than face possible new weekend rules, I let the cloying smell of fabric softener permeate me.

Pondering how long I was going to have to stay here, I was startled by a knock on the door. The two hands pointing to the bottom of the clock meant it was only six-thirty. Surely, they'd let me sleep in on a weekend. Before I could extend an invitation, Jermaine poked his head in the door.

"Are you awake?"

"No," I lied. "I was trying to catch a few more winks."

"Well," Jermaine said, suddenly acting shy. "Can I give you this card anyway? I made it for you." He tiptoed over the threshold and dropped the card on the end of the bed. When he got back to the door, he giggled and waved. "See you later, Olivia," he finished in a sing-song voice.

He was fifteen, but he acted really immature. But what did I know? Maybe teen-agers weren't as mature as they acted on those TV soaps. Avoiding it wouldn't make it go away, so I sat up and reached for the card.

It was made from red construction paper, embellished with crayon. I frowned, elementary school valentines crowding my memory. I'd thought it was going to be some corny 'welcome' card. Instead the front had a big heart. In it were the words 'I Love You.' The jangling alarm clock startled me, and I dropped the card on the scarred hardwood floor as she scrambled to hit the snooze button. Bells were not quiet. I fell back into the scented pillow. Another day away from home had officially begun.

24

Retained Counsel

Casey

October 26, 2001

Turning left into my six-unit building, a weight lifted from my shoulders: home. Seconds after I inserted my key into the front door lock of my apartment, the smells assailed me. Greg and Jason were home.

"Dinner. Ten minutes," my neighbor Greg yelled into the hall.

My cat, long ignored, swiped at my leg. Sweating now in my haste to satisfy the neglected, I bent down, opened a lower cabinet and put a handful of Cat Chow in the bowl. Simba untangled himself from my legs and ran toward the food. I threw my coat toward the couch and went across the hall where readymade food was waiting.

The smell of the warm whisky-laden punch Greg poured when she entered the apartment unjangled my nerves so wound up by the judge. I took a large sip of the drink—definitely a heavy pour.

"How are you?" Jason asked, settling next to me as she made myself comfortable on a kitchen stool. Greg adjusted his apron strings and got back to cooking whatever was responsible for the delicious smell. "We were just talking about how we haven't seen you in days," Jason continued.

Another sip of punch and all the tension had fled. Greg and Jason's apartment was a mirror image of mine, only warmer and cozier. They'd painted their stark white walls and added honey hued furniture. Hand woven rugs from their travels lay on the refinished hardwood floors. My apartment still had the vanilla walls and industrial Berber carpet that came with the lease. Every time I visited their apartment, I left with renewed energy for my own decoration project, until lack of time and money intervened.

"Casey, taste this," Greg said, extending a nicked wooden spoon my way. I had no idea what in the hell it was—but it was good.

"What is that?" I asked.

Greg patted his stomach as he answered. "First, I promise it's low fat." I repressed the urge to pat my own expanding waistline. "It's Thai chicken and coconut soup." I nodded like I had a clue. The food they made always had some exotic name or ingredients she'd never heard of. "It's Asian fusion night," Greg finished.

Jason rolled his eyes dramatically. "As much as you can have in *Cleveland.*"

I sipped my hot toddy and sat with Greg and Jason in companionable silence. At times, I envied them. I longed to find someone to share my life. Though Greg and Jason bickered and argued, they had a palpable love and affection for each other. It was great having friends like them, but when I went home at the end of the night, I was alone.

Placing a bowl of bright green pea pods in front of me, Jason said, "We had to buy these frozen, but they're still good. Have you ever had soy beans before?"

I wrinkled my nose when Jason demonstrated pulling the beans from the fuzzy pods with his teeth. Nervously I tasted one. They weren't half bad. Greg added salt and I had another. Now they were downright good. Jason had moved back to the stove. He was emptying the contents of a cutting board into the sizzling wok.

"What else are we having?"

Above the hot fat, I barely heard Greg. "Sesame beef, hot jasmine rice."

I put my empty mug on the counter and walked into the large dining room. Without being asked, I started setting the table, only stopping to run to my own apartment to get two bottles of wine, one red, the other white—my usual contribution to dinner. After we sat down to dinner, and I'd poured us all glasses of Shiraz, I got serious.

"I know I ask you guys for advice all the time, and only take it half the time, but I *really* need your help." Before I had a chance to continue, Greg and Jason interrupted with their usual suggestions.

"Get paying clients!"

"Work smarter, not harder!"

"Seriously, guys," I said, silencing their laughter. "You've got to keep this in confidence."

"Don't we always?" Greg's tone was sober.

"I had the weirdest day. A judge came to me for advice. Her child was removed by the county. She wants to get her daughter back home, of course, but she needs to keep it a secret to protect her job."

"Shit," Jason said.

"I know. I handle cases in Juvenile all the time, but this." I shook my head. "This is big time. I mean, I think I could do this case with one hand behind my back. But what if I fuck it up? I could ruin a girl's life. The mom's career."

"At least the judge will pay," Greg said.

I closed my eyes in shame. "That's true. I hate to say it, but that's a real factor in taking the case if she wants to hire me. The rent is due. I'm tired of looking at my anemic bank balance while my clients find excuse after excuse for not paying."

"Money is good. Really good," Jason said. "But you have to decide if you can live with her second guessing every decision you make. You need to make sure she doesn't want a marionette. Working with professionals can suck." He was interning with a family doctor in Beachwood. "When we get doctors in, they've already self-diagnosed. They treat us like a treatment center. 'Write the scripts. Order the tests.' Puts us in a precarious position."

"I need to get out of this hole."

"You're always so damned vague about your past. What in the hell happened?"

"I got blackballed."

"How? The law isn't some private club," Jason said.

"But it kind of is. At least in Cleveland," I said.

Greg topped off all three wine glasses. "Now that we're sufficiently lubed up, spill. It can't be as bad as you say."

I hadn't told anyone, other than my parents, my sordid tale of woe. And my parents still didn't get it to this day. As far as they were concerned, graduating from college and law school made me a success. If only parental pride paid the bills. "I crossed the Strohmeyer family."

"Strohmeyer as in Meyer Beer?" Jason asked.

"*'You'll be a high flyer when drink Strohmeyer'* Beer?" Greg sang the jingle as familiar to me as the Alphabet song.

"The very one," I said.

"How?" Greg asked. The boys had both leaned forward, dinner all but forgotten.

"Ted Strohmeyer—heir apparent—was a year ahead of me in law school," I started. I took a deep breath. I'd trained myself not to think about, and definitely not to talk about what had happened. "I was on the law review."

When I stopped talking, Greg prompted. "That's a good thing, right?"

"In theory. So, I was looking for stuff to publish, right? And I saw Ted's article. I mean, maybe his name stood out and I picked that one up. Anyway, it was pretty good. A new area of the law and all that. So, I stayed late, started vetting it to make sure no one else had covered the same ground. Legal journals pride themselves on being on the cutting edge."

"And?" Jason asked.

"And this school in Indiana, Valparaiso had already gotten there before us. I was reading the other article and it seemed the same. But I didn't trust myself. So, I went home and did a copy and paste of each article into Word, then did a doc compare." I took one large gulp of wine. Then another. "Turns out Ted wasn't so original after all. He'd copied whole paragraphs, footnotes, everything."

"Rich guys always think they can put one over," Greg said.

I nodded. "Yep. And I went down in flames. The school trumped up charges against me, stripped me of my place on the law review. My job at Morrell Gates mysteriously disappeared. Boyfriend too."

Greg's next comment was a statement, not a question. "Nothing happened to Ted."

"Not after his family single-handedly brought the Browns back to Cleveland. Not after building that brand-new stadium. He worked at a big law firm for a few years, then went in house with dear old Dad." I was loathe to admit that I'd followed Ted's upward trajectory, the polar opposite of mine.

"You couldn't get another job?"

"This is Cleveland, not New York or L.A. What damage the Strohmeyers didn't inflict, the Brodys did."

"Brody? As in a senator or something like that?" Greg asked.

"Attorney General," I corrected. "And judge and prosecutor. The Brody family's got the whole justice system covered."

"Your boyfriend was a Brody?"

"Tom. Dumped me ten seconds after the school offered me up as sacrifice."

"I never knew," Jason said. "Damn, I'm really sorry that happened to you."

"Not your fault. I wish the others were as sorry as you. I was disposable and I was disposed of."

"And there's no way—"

I shook my head forcefully. "Nope. I've tried all the avenues, and unless I leave the state and try my luck elsewhere, I'm dead to the Cleveland legal community."

"But you work for yourself, right?" Greg shrugged a single hopeful shoulder.

"Yeah, and I'm left with the cases no one else wants. I'm maxed out at a few hundred from the county."

"So, to do well, you have to do volume. Sounds like the medical racket," Jason said.

"Yeah, but I can't squeeze child custody matters into a ten-minute visit."

"You need more money per hour then with no maximum," Greg computed.

"And that's where this potential client comes in..."

"She's willing to pay through the nose, right?" Greg asked.

"Probably. And I handle cases in Juvenile all the time. I just worry about what you said earlier. Can I work for a professional? Will she be scrutinizing every damn step I take? Am I good enough to work a miracle and save her daughter and her job?"

"Whoa, pull back on that God complex there, Casey," Greg admonished. "You didn't get her into the situation she's in. You'd only be one player in what sounds like a very complex system."

"That's true," I said. We ate for a while without speaking. "I hate to say it, but the money's the main factor in maybe taking the case. I mean, the rent for this place is due on the first. I'm tired of giving temporary shots to my anemic bank balance."

When I got back to my apartment, Simba was nowhere to be seen, but my answering machine's insistent red beacon pulsated in the hallway's telephone alcove. Playing the single message, I was surprised to hear Judge Grant's disembodied voice. I suppressed a shiver that the judge had somehow gleaned who was the subject at tonight's dinner conversation.

"Ms. Cort. Judge Grant. I would appreciate a call back regarding the matter we discussed today. Though you're the youngest and least experienced attorney I consulted with, you were the only honest one. I'd like to retain your services. Call me when you get this message so that we can set up a strategy meeting and get my daughter home."

I pressed a button on the machine, saving the message. I'd sleep on it. That passive-aggressive message made my Spidey senses tingle. As I got further into this law thing, I was learning not to take every client who walked in the door. Judge Grant could be more trouble than she was worth.

The summons forgotten, I woke from a fitful sleep the next morning. I was a crusader, wasn't I? As a lawyer, I was in the perfect position to go against the status quo. Most of my cases were lost because of broke and recalcitrant clients. I could do more if the county would pay more. My witnesses would be better prepared, my investigations more thorough. I'd seen too many children snatched from their homes without solid evidence, and here staring me in the face was a chance to challenge the system.

Back and forth I seesawed on the tram ride to work. At One Hundred Sixteenth Street, I was going to take the case. By Fifty-fifth, I'd talked myself out of it. At Tower City, I decided that I was done with fear ruling my life.

Immediately upon arriving at my office, I whipped off my coat and picked up the phone before I could change my mind again.

"Judge Grant." My potential client answered the phone after I made it through the screening.

"Casey Cort. I'll be happy to handle your case." I could have cursed myself. 'Happy?' Having your child removed by the county wasn't happy. But for once, I didn't try to fill up the silence on the phone line.

"Good. I'll messenger over a signed retainer agreement and the check." A dial tone let me know that the judge was done.

When Letty walked in to show me the check before it was deposited into my trust account, I savored the moment. Twenty-five hundred bucks was the largest retainer I'd ever asked for. Finally, I was going to get paid.

25

Special Needs

Olivia

November 6, 2001

I hitched my nearly empty backpack higher as I stepped off the bus and walked toward the office. This was my fourth school in nearly as many months. The kids at Harry E. Davis Middle School looked anything but friendly. In their dress code-adhered white oxford shirts and navy-blue pants, they marched toward the school like little soldiers.

I was dutifully dressed like the other kids. The Williamses had bought three of each, shirt and pants. The stiff clothes hung in my closet alongside the few items I had: the clothes from my last day in Shaker, and a few cast offs from other girls who'd stayed there. Not a single item fit me right.

Butt numb, I shifted in my seat. Jackie Foley was supposed to meet me and get me enrolled. My social worker had only been ten minutes late. But since she'd arrived, the second hand had swept around the clock face about forty times.

It was because I was a 'county' kid, I knew. When they thought I was out of earshot, that phrase was used plenty. They said it like I had a disease or something. The office door in front of me opened and closed, Jackie emerging. She bent down to address me face to face, like I was a little kid in need of calming down.

"Olivia, before you get to class, we're going to have you tested to make sure you're in the right grade. The counselor and I have been reviewing your records, and something doesn't match up."

I looked at Jackie's face. "I'm not going to school now?"

The social worker shook her head. "We don't think it's a good idea to put you in school until we're sure the class is the right one." It's not that I wanted to go to Harry E. Davis, but I didn't want to go back to the Williamses either. My disappointment must have shown on my face.

Jackie countered with a smile. "Look at it as a surprise vacation!"

For three whole days, I pulled weeds till my fingers were numb. Then I burned the same fingers in scalding water washing floors, walls, and everything in between. If I never smelled lemon furniture polish again, it would be okay with me. Television was out, even as a treat for all the work I did. Reading, too. I tried that as an excuse from chores.

I was never so happy to see anyone when Jackie came to the house to take me to the county psychiatrist's office for testing. Even dressing in uncomfortable jeans was a price worth paying. Sitting in a chilly office, filling in bubble forms was a more welcome vacation than time with Aunt Linda and her endless tasks.

I took three tests. One asked me about my feelings, another asked weird questions and expected me to memorize lots of lists, and the last seemed like the same kind of test I'd taken dozens of times in school. The rest of the week passed before Jackie came again.

This time, the social worker talked with Mrs. Williams a long time before she came to me. I'd been told to wait in 'my' room. I was up like a shot to unlock the door when Jackie's knock finally came.

The worker's smile wasn't real. "Okay! We've got your test results," she enthused. "You're going to be starting at Davis on Monday. We're really happy with your results." Jackie tweaked my nose. I tried not to shudder. I wasn't a puppy.

"Am I still in the seventh grade?"

"Yep. You're one smart cookie. We think we've figured out why your grades don't reflect your aptitude scores." The worker paused a long time. I tried not to panic. I wasn't crazy or anything, right? The doctor had been a psychiatrist. Maybe there was something wrong in my head. I felt my bottom lip tremble involuntarily. Pressure built behind my eyes. I blinked back tears.

"Oh, honey," Jackie soothed. "This is nothing to worry about. You've got something called Attention Deficit Disorder." The woman smoothed the Pepto Bismol-pink covers and joined me on the bed. "Do you sometimes have difficulty focusing in school? Like, do you daydream during class?"

I nodded. "Sometimes...when I get bored."

"There you go. Your mom missed this. But we're going to give you medication that will make school much easier for you."

Mrs. Williams had crept up the stairs silently. I hadn't noticed Aunt Linda was leaning against the doorjamb until she spoke. "I have the prescription right here. I'll make sure you take your pills every day. Jackie says they'll make you as right as rain." To Jackie, she said, "Olivia's been a bit out of sorts since she got here. But we'll have her in tip-top shape before you know it."

Before dinner that night, Mrs. Williams gave me two pills. When Aunt Linda turned her back to fill a glass of water, I looked at the white labels. Below my name and the Williamses' address were the words Adderall on one and Zoloft on the other. When Mrs. Williams turned back around, I took the proffered water and swallowed the pills whole.

26

Euclid Hospital

Sheila

November 10, 2001

Without Olivia, the apartment was always dark and cold. Given the mess I'd made of my life, I deserved a little rum with my cola to take the edge off. They couldn't take my daughter away twice. Sipping my drink, I sank into the couch and surveyed the mail.

I tossed the flyers and catalogs on the floor without a second glance. Bills, I set aside for later. I put my drink on the table and looked at the Explanation of Benefits envelope from my health insurance plan. Just what I needed right now, some bureaucratic insurance nightmare.

I hadn't been to the doctor in over a year. Olivia hadn't since I'd enrolled her in Shaker. Ah, maybe that was it. Resigned, I tore at the envelope and slipped a blue page from its confines. It was Olivia, but the letter was about her recent visit to Cleveland Clinic's Euclid Hospital.

The paper fluttered to the floor as my hands lost their will to hold it. I felt around the side table for the cordless phone. I needed to call Casey. Olivia was sick and no one had told me. Visions of my baby in the hospital emerged before my eyes. Instead of dialing the inexperienced attorney, I picked up the paper and called the Records Department phone number listed.

I might not have had my daughter in my custody, but being a mother still trumped everyone else's right to treat my daughter. Claiming to need a second opinion on my daughter's diagnosis, I had them fax Olivia's recent medical records to me. Before they closed, I called Billing as well and spun another tale to get those records.

In two days, I had assembled a file on Olivia's so-called illness. Immediately after I put two and two together, I called Casey.

"They've diagnosed Olivia with Attention Deficit Disorder," I said to Casey without preamble or introduction.

I heard Casey shuffling through papers. "That's not in any discovery. How did you find out?"

"Health insurance records. We've been to the Clinic before. Who hasn't? They probably put in her social security number and it linked up. But why didn't the county—the people supposedly caring for my daughter—tell me anything about this?" Despite my attempts to modulate my voice, I could hear it rising. "We need a second opinion, our own physical examination. ADD and ADHD are diagnoses that a bunch of people throw around, an excuse to move black kids to remedial classes, get them hooked on drugs. Adderall, Zoloft, she's already taking these things."

"Judge Grant, the diagnosis itself is not the only problem. The bigger issue is that the court will take it seriously. It will impact your ability to get your daughter back."

"I would want my daughter back no matter what kind of disability she may have." Did people give up their children if they were damaged goods?

"Of course. I wasn't suggesting otherwise. I'm saying that you'll need to learn all you can about these disorders so we can prove to the judge that you can care for Olivia. If the trial were held today, the court might conclude from your attitude that you don't take her medical needs seriously."

I was thankful the eye-rolling, neck-rolling *hmpf* that came from my mouth would be held in strict confidence. Dismissing my petulant inner teenager, I disconnected the call, telling Casey I'd see what I could do.

What I did was call to find out if there were classes or support groups I could join. It was pure coincidence that Olivia was enrolled in a patient education class starting the very next morning. I cleared my docket and made my way to the hospital first thing.

It didn't take long to find the education center in the pediatric wing of the hospital. I signed myself in next to Olivia's name on the list, introduced myself to the nurse/instructor and took a seat in the windowless room. The empty chairs filled up quickly with parents and children. A severely dressed black woman and Olivia were two of the last two enter. My heart sped up as adrenaline flooded my veins. With monumental effort, I held back the tears that nearly leaked from my eyes. If I hadn't cried the day Peyton got married, I wasn't going to cry now. My daughter ran to my arms as soon as she saw me.

"Mom! What are you doing here?" Olivia asked.

"I'm here to see you, Poppet," I said, hugging my daughter. The feel of her flesh and bones was as familiar as my own. Even under some awful perfumed soap, my daughter's smell was unique. "It's good to see you," I whispered into my daughter's hair, thick with Afro Sheen.

"I hate swallowing pills. It's so hard, but Aunt Linda says it's supposed to make me do better in school."

I was taken aback. My sister was Deidre. Keith had no siblings. "Linda?" I purposefully omitted the term of address.

Our brief reunion was cut short by a firm hand on my upper arm and a voice of steel. "Excuse me, ma'am," the instructor said to me. "I need to talk with you in the hall."

"Are you speaking with me?" I asked. Hugging my own child wasn't against the law.

"Are you Sheila Grant?" the nurse asked. When I nodded, another hospital employee took Olivia by the shoulder and walked her to the woman she had come in with, the putative Aunt Linda. While the instructor led me to the hall, then disappeared back into the classroom, an orderly with a fistful of noisy keys locked the door, barring my readmittance. This time the person who joined us was in a pantsuit and pearls.

"What's this about?" I asked.

"Ma'am, I don't want to get in the middle of anything here. We got a call from the county social worker saying that you don't have custody of your daughter. The woman your daughter came here with today is her foster parent and legal guardian."

"There's been a huge mistake. I'm fighting with the court right now to get my daughter back. I'm her mother. It's my right to come down here and see what medications she's taking. See for myself what kind of behavior modification you're using on her."

"Ma'am, I understand your concern. But we're a public hospital. We must abide by the county's request."

The burly orderly crossed his arms and barred the door like a bouncer at an over twenty-one club. My next question was superfluous, but I asked it anyway. "Are you saying I can't go back in there?" I asked.

"No, ma'am, you can't. This is a hospital, and we don't deal with child abuse cases. I suggest you talk to your daughter's social worker. And if we get the okay from her, you can come to our other education sessions."

"All right with *her*," I said, my voice rising. "That's my daughter in there."

"You need to keep your voice down. This is a hospital," Pantsuit and pearls said.

"Keep my voice down? You're sending letters telling me my daughter is sick, but you won't let me participate in her care? Are you crazy?" The echo of my voice off the sterile walls and the furtive glances of everyone around us alerted me that I'd gotten too loud.

"Ma'am, you're going to have to leave voluntarily, or I'm going to have to call hospital security. If you have a problem, I suggest you take it up with the social worker or the court."

All at once, the fight went out of me. As a lawyer, and now a judge, I knew having a confrontation with anyone here could damage my credibility during the upcoming hearing.

"I'll go," I heard my rational self say. But before I left, I banged hard on the locked door and waved to my daughter when our eyes met.

27

Client Interview

Casey

November 13, 2001

"What do most people do? I know my heart, and I know my daughter belongs at home. But you know juvenile court. What's your advice?"

I had to remind myself that the judge was a person, like Dean Condit was a person, and even Ted Strohmeyer was a person. And people were sometimes vulnerable, like Judge Grant seemed now.

Honesty first, advice second. "Juvenile court at its core is no different from the criminal system. The prosecutor's win rate is around ninety-five percent," I said, using my hands to illustrate quotes around the word 'win.' "Most cases don't go to trial because most of the parents are unsophisticated and agree to disposition and temporary custody."

Judge Grant sat back hard in the chair. "They just give up their children?"

"It's not that simple. They think they're fighting. The social worker, who talks to them all the time, convinces them that if the parents just follow the case plan, then when conditions are right, they'll get their kids back. And that may have been true in the seventies, even in the eighties. And maybe the social workers even believe what they say. But I've sat with these parents, and it's damn near impossible to keep a full-time job, rent a place to live, and go to parenting classes or drug rehab or whatever."

"Does anyone fight temporary custody?" Bewilderment was the only word I could think of to describe Judge Grant's expression. White shoe lawyers were always surprised by what happened outside the castle walls.

"Not really. Juvenile court is like a schizophrenic. On the one hand, everyone talks about reunification and hope for the family and promise for the kids' future. On the other hand, the judges, magistrates and GALs all think the parents are awful, how foster care or even adoption is better for the kids. How children need a permanent placement—and that's never with the parents."

Judge Grant was silent for a few moments, her look thoughtful. I stood and looked at the ships sailing on Lake Erie. Even when devastation wrought your life asunder, everyone else kept going.

"I'm going to fight," Judge Grant said. I turned back to scrutinize the mother. "I hear what you're saying. Because what I'm reading between the lines is that if I don't get out of the system now, I'll never get Olivia out. Even if I do all they ask."

"The court likes a redemption story. *I was wrong. I sinned. I'm here for forgiveness.* You'll be coming in saying, I'm not going to fit in your little box. It's going to be an uphill battle."

"What do we need to do?" Grant asked, looking for pen and paper.

I leaned against the window ledge, crossing my arms in defiance. "Are you an alcoholic?"

Judge Grant smiled. "You're something else. I don't think most lawyers would have had the guts to ask that question."

The judge hadn't answered the question, and I raised my eyebrows. "Okay, we've established that I'm gutsy—which is good because my job is to be your advocate —but you didn't answer the question. Do you have a drinking problem?"

"I'll admit to you that I do drink. When I worked at the firm, I'd go out for drinks with other lawyers, and often with clients. At home, when I need to unwind, I occasionally have a drink—but do I drink more than other people? I don't think so. Am I an alcoholic? No."

Good answer. I prodded a bit more, looking for volatility if not answers. "Do you think you're a good parent?"

"You don't pull your punches, do you?"

"The prosecutor certainly won't. Answer my question, please," I said, softening my statement.

"I've made my share of mistakes. I sometimes lose my temper—raising an adolescent who's starting puberty is hard—I don't think any parent would tell you differently.

But I've provided a good home for Olivia. She's well taken care of, and I love her dearly—which is most important."

Letty brought us coffee and pastries from Au Bon Pain. While Sheila and I sipped, I started pulling papers from Judge Grant's file and then lifted a new legal pad from the stack in my credenza.

"Let's start at the beginning. Now, I got some of the preliminary stuff out of the way from our consultation." I clicked my pen and filled in my picture of Judge Grant, Olivia, and their life in Shaker Heights. After scribbling for a few minutes, my rise from my desk was abrupt. My mind whirled with ideas and approaches on winning this case. I paced back and forth, then realized I needed to be alone to think.

"I think I have enough information to begin work on the case. I need you to do a couple of things, though."

Judge Grant nodded, pulling her own legal pad and gold pen from her slim briefcase.

"First, I'll need a list of people we can call on your behalf—character witnesses. Second, you'll need to set up a meeting with the guardian *ad Litem.*"

"How much influence will the guardian have on the case?"

"Depends. Not all judges weigh the information the same way. Typically, the guardians come in, say the kid is fine in foster care, and the judge does whatever they were going to do in the first place." Judge Grant's face looked pained. Maybe federal court evaluations were more than a rubber stamp of the prosecutor's desires. I wouldn't know.

I continued. "Sherry Otis was assigned to your case. She's more careful than most. She actually follows the rules and prepares written reports in all of her cases. Do I know the weight Judge MacKinnon will give to her report in your case? No.

"My advice: call Otis. Make an appointment. Maybe have her come to your chambers—for the intimidation factor. If you feel that's inappropriate or she insists, then I'd see her in your home."

"When will we meet again?"

"I'm going to get discovery and do some interviews. Then I'll call you to see where we are and where we need to go." I paused. I'd been burned before. "Is there anything you're not telling me?"

The judge's hesitation was so slight, I wasn't sure there'd been one. Judge Grant stood to put on her coat, put her hand on the door knob, and she looked at me over her shoulder.

"No, Casey. You know everything. This is in your hands now."

28

Metzenbaum

Sheila

November 14, 2001

No one had prepared me for the county's idea of a visiting room. I had fully expected a thickly carpeted, child-oriented room, with sturdy furniture and functional toys.

Instead I was smack dab in the middle of a cafeteria. Then I remembered, the building had been used as a juvenile detention center most of its life. From my walk through the front doors and down the corridor, nothing more than the name had changed. Round Formica tables, vending machines, and unforgiving fluorescent lighting dominated the room.

Despite the garish lighting bouncing off the plastic, the room was subdued. Few parents played with listless children. Others were opening flagrant foil wrapped pouches for the children, or worse, buying them junk from the vending machines. The parents spoke in earnest. County employees with their ever-present badges yoking their necks were watching the parents watching the children—taking notes.

I took a seat at an empty table and set my purse on the linoleum floor. A group of black and brown children spilled into the room, noticeable for their absence of noise and ebullience. Among them was Olivia, being led to me by another badge wearer. The county employee looked around the room, appearing to take in the anxious faced mothers, their impatience palpable, until Olivia pointed in my direction.

I stood, pulling Olivia into an awkward hug. "Poppet, I'm working on getting you home," I urgently whispered in the girl's ear.

Almost hesitantly it seemed, Olivia sat down at the table with the woman who had escorted her.

"Miss Grant?" The familiarity of the address galled me. But maybe I should be grateful they hadn't called me Sheila. "I'm Dawn Palomo, the visiting coordinator today. I'm here to observe your visit." There was no question, so I didn't respond. "Um, so I've been looking at your file and see that you haven't signed the case plan." Palomo paused again, and when I said nothing, continued. "Well, maybe you have your reasons for that. One of the case plan's requirements is for you to successfully visit with your daughter two hours every two weeks."

Another long moment of silence stretched. Finally, I asked, "Do you have a copy of that case plan?"

Palomo brightened.

"Yes ma'am, I do." She wet her finger and paged through a slim file, finally pulling out some papers and pushing them in front of me. "Now if you'll sign here next to your name...."

I took the stapled stack without signing. "I'm sure I was supposed to receive a copy. I'll keep this one."

"Well, that's okay, I guess. I need to talk to these other families. I'll see you before the end of your visit." Palomo moved to another table.

I looked at Olivia—really looked at her—for the first time since we sat down. "Poppet, how are you? They treating you okay?"

"When can I come home?" Olivia's question nearly squeezed the blood from my heart.

With that one simple question, the wind left my sails. All the bluster and bravado I'd relied on until this moment was gone. I looked out the barred window, blinking back tears. It was the least I could do for my daughter. Squaring my shoulders, I took a deep breath.

"I'm working hard on that right now. I've talked to Peyton. Hired a lawyer. We're going to get you home as soon as we can," I said, glad my voice didn't betray my emotions.

"I hate it here. You have to get me out. They make us do chores all day, cook, clean, and morning calis— calis— I don't know what you call it. Some kind of exercise. They don't even have cable."

"Who is 'us'?" I was immediately suspicious.

"Jermaine and I. He's the other kid there," Olivia answered.

"Jermaine's in foster care?" I tried to pull my mind from the brink. Maybe mixing sexes was standard in foster care.

"Yeah. He's kind of weird."

"How old is he?"

"Fifteen? I don't know."

"Why is he there?"

"I don't know, Mom," Olivia whined. "Why are you asking about him? I'm telling you, it's awful there. And the school is bad too. The kids act up in class. The work is about two years behind."

I set aside my unease. Olivia was right. Jermaine wasn't the issue. Getting the girl home was. I couldn't think of what to ask my daughter. How could I pick one thing when I wanted to know everything? For more than a decade I'd known everything there was to know about Olivia.

For a single instant I knew what it was like to be Keith, having only glimpses of my daughter's life. Olivia was looking at me, expecting more. She always expected more. I sat up straighter and tried to engage.

"Are you getting enough sleep? The calisthenics," I sounded out each syllable of the word that had tripped my daughter up, "should make you tired. At least you lost some weight."

"Oh Mom." Olivia looked disappointed somehow, though I couldn't see where I'd failed. "Do you know when I can come home?"

"Poppet—"

In earnest, Olivia leaned forward. "I promise I won't talk to any more counselors. I'm not stupid. I think Alison—Ms. Feingold, I mean, got me put here. I was just upset, okay? My grades weren't good and I complained. If you'll let me come home, I'll be better. I won't eat so much. I'll watch less TV. I'll even clean up more around the house," Olivia paused, breathless.

I didn't have any words to mollify my daughter. What more could I say? During the remainder of the two hours, I talked to Olivia about work, the weather, anything I could think of to fill the silence. Too soon, the visiting coordinator cum driver was taking her away.

29

The Case Plan

Sheila

November 15, 2001

Easing my brown leather pumps from my feet, I tilted my expensive chair and rested my feet on the leather desk pad.

"Nancy! Chris!" I called out. No answer.

I had sent everyone home early, but I didn't care for surprises from my more diligent workers. When no one responded, I opened my pencil drawer and pulled out the little brass key. The flat shiny metal fit smoothly into the lock of my middle right drawer. Easing open the antique wood, I pulled out a small accordion file.

I pulled a cord on the desk lamp to chase away dusk. It was easier spending my evenings in my chambers. The apartment was preternaturally quiet without Olivia. I'd hated the constant drone of all those cable channels Olivia so loved, but without my daughter there, it wasn't a home. It was merely a place to shower and sleep.

Placing the small accordion file on my desk, I pulled out every piece of paper I'd collected on Olivia's case. Just as I knew that the Juvenile court action was unfair, I also knew from my years of practicing law that burying my head in the sand was never an adequate solution.

Silently, I reread the complaint. Then I paged through the rest of the file, making sure I hadn't missed anything my first, emotionally wrought, time around. Finally, I pulled out the case plan I'd gotten at Metzenbaum.

Seven landscape-oriented pages of text stared back at me. The first page had all the usual information: Olivia's name, the county and court's case numbers. Next was a list of people with relationships to the child. I, as the mother, was first. My ex-husband Keith was listed as father PNE. PNE? I pulled a yellow legal pad from my desk and made a note to ask Casey what that meant. Also listed was Sherry Otis as GAL. I thought for a second. Wait, GAL had to be guardian *ad Litem*. Unbidden, Sherry Otis's face came to me. She was the woman the magistrate had pulled from the hallway. I wasn't looking forward to dealing with her.

I turned to page two of the case plan and looked at the list of county 'recommendations' for action that would bring about family reunification. I shook my head. The county had reduced thirteen years of parenting to a form, and a bad one at that.

The boxes on the left addressed the so-called problems with my little family. 'Mom has parenting issues,' and 'Mom has alcohol issue,' it read. To address their fabricated issues, the county proposed solutions. The boxes on the right outlined what steps I was supposed to take—all under the county's supervision. They'd have me enroll in a thirty-day inpatient drug and alcohol treatment program, enroll in a sixteen-week parenting class, and of course keep my house suitable, and my job on an even keel. These looked like the aspirations of a twenty-something with little time on the job and middle-class ideals.

I shook my head. If I agreed to do all of this, Olivia wouldn't even be eligible to come home for four months. How could any social worker, prosecutor, or judge think this was a good idea?

Pulling Casey's card from a paper clip on the front of the file, I dialed Casey's office number on the off chance that the young attorney would be working late. The phone was answered before the first ring was completed.

"Casey Cort."

"Sheila Harrison Grant," I announced. There was a pause on the line. Casey didn't rush to fill in the silence. I had to hand it to the girl, she was a quick study. She'd make a really excellent lawyer someday. "I was just reviewing the documents in my case. Did I mention I got a case plan? I'll fax it over when I hang up," I paused. "I know my posture had been to fight this case, but I'm thinking of doing what the social workers want. I want this done, over with. If that would work, Olivia and I could survive the four months."

I gave my declaration a moment to sink in. I took the tiniest sip of the rum on my desk. Without ice, the drink should be silent.

"Realistically, if I stopped fighting—promised to do everything asked of me—could Olivia be home by Christmas?"

"Judge Grant, the parenting classes themselves are at least sixteen weeks. Maybe we could get you into a twelve-week class, that's the shortest I've seen. But they have to be completed before the county or the court will consider reunification," Casey said.

I threw the papers on my desk in frustration. "How in the hell do parents do this?" I asked. "This process doesn't seem geared toward keeping families together, but toward pulling families apart."

"Many of my clients have felt that frustration," Casey said diplomatically.

"Level with me. How many cases have you been involved with in juvenile court—even where you were the Guardian *ad Litem?*" I asked.

"About two hundred-fifty, more or less," Casey answered.

"In all of those cases where the county was seeking temporary custody and the parents were making an honest effort at it—in how many of those cases have you seen reunification?"

Casey didn't respond right away. I could hear breathing in the receiver, the squeak of an office chair as Casey leaned forward or back. Then Casey spoke. Her voice seemed far away, though the girl was less than a mile away.

"Truthfully...none. I've never seen a child go home."

30

Daddy's Little Girl

November 21, 2001

The black and white sheriff's car pulled in front of the blue wood framed house on East Ninetieth Street. There was one difference between this and other official vehicles. The side panel had the added words: Civil Process.

Cuyahoga County sheriffs served all subpoenas, warrants, and writs in the county. The two sheriff's deputies who emerged from the vehicle, looked at each other in silent communication.

"Between you and me," the older deputy said to the younger, "this is probably the mom's house. These guys make babies. The moms never see them again. This—" He paused as he looked at the subpoena. "Keith Grant isn't here. He's out in the wind."

The deputies adjusted their holsters and walked to the door. The younger one rang the bell, and someone shuffled to the door inside. And elderly black woman opened it a crack.

"Can I help.... Oh dear," she said when she took in the uniforms, badges, and guns.

"Mrs. Grant?" the older deputy asked.

"No. I'm Mrs. Bigham."

"Are you Keith Grant's mother?" the younger deputy asked.

"No. That's my sister Mildred's boy. She passed on a couple of years back," Mrs. Bigham said.

"We have a subpoena for Keith Grant. Does he live here?"

"Oh, no. That boy moved over to the west side after he divorced that Sheila. She was the death of him, you know...with her bourgeoisie ways. What's that you got there?" She gestured to the papers in the deputy's hand. "Is Keith in trouble? That can't be," she said more to herself than them. "He was always a good boy. I can't imagine he's in any kind of trouble...."

"Ma'am, we're here to serve a subpoena from the Cuyahoga County Juvenile Court. We either need to leave this with you for Keith Grant or get his current address."

"I don't have no current address for him. But he does come around to pick up his mail." Mrs. Bigham reached out a hand—the other remained fixed on the knob, to brace herself or to make a quick getaway, it was hard to tell. "I'll give it to him when he stops by."

The deputies looked at each other. Shrugged. They gave the documents to the older woman. She was a competent adult, this was the respondent's last known address. They had done their part.

❧❧❧

Keith

I watched the drizzle outside my nondescript Ohio City apartment. The views weren't as pretty as the east side, but life on the west side of the Cuyahoga River gave me the sense of a fresh start without leaving the city.

I glanced at the time displayed in the lower right-hand corner of the television screen. It was already afternoon, and I hadn't gotten much done during my one day off from rounding up graffiti-spraying hooligans. Even MetroHealth Hospital wasn't free from urban blight, hence my job there as a security guard. I muted the afternoon news, as depressing as the rain, and picked up a copy of the Plain Dealer. The city's newspaper wasn't a beacon of sunshine, either. Folks couldn't catch a break in Cleveland.

USX looked like they were moving from three shifts to two, one headline proclaimed. Another announced that LTV was planning to turn off its main burner—a sure sign the steel mill was shutting down. Birmingham Steel was closing. Cheap steel was the reason cited. Ohio firms couldn't produce steel at the cheap prices of European and Japanese firms. Why the paper harped on this bad news, I didn't know. If no one in Cleveland had a job, no one would buy the ever-thinning newspaper.

Snapping the broadsheet closed, I momentarily closed my eyes in silent prayer, grateful that I had a job. It might have only been enough to pay for an apartment—near the Norfolk Southern—an active railroad line, nonetheless. But

I was off the court's radar. The independent company that had hired me to work security for the hospital was letting me work under the table. They saved on payroll taxes, and I could keep the court from reaching into my pocket for child support.

I wanted to care for my daughter in my own way. I was not a deadbeat dad. But Ohio required child support be deducted from every paycheck. Essentially, the courts were saying I wasn't trustworthy. And I couldn't turn a blind eye to the huge bureaucracy that had sprung up to squeeze blood from turnips. All that money for all that 'enforcement' that could go to help kids who really needed it. And while I took care of Olivia as best I could, Sheila didn't really need any help from me.

My ex-wife had always been highfalutin. My mother, God rest her soul, had been right on the money about Sheila. She wasn't content to live a life like my parents—buying a house in Glenville, working regular jobs, building a family.

When I'd dated Sheila in high school, then when she went to college, I knew she wanted more. And that had been part of the attraction. I'd sit with her while she studied, and we'd have those kinds of big intellectual discussions that hadn't been part of my own family life. I'd been so proud when she flipped her tassel at college graduation, I'd proposed to her that night at her parent's house.

In what seemed like minutes after we'd walked down the aisle, Sheila announced that she wanted to go to law school. I'd mistakenly thought she'd be happy with college—be happy with the good paying office job she'd landed. But, no, law school was her ambition. I'd tried to convince Sheila that we were fine the way we were. I even tried to get her pregnant. But I never knocked her up and wasn't too surprised to find birth control pills in her dresser drawer near our first anniversary.

Before I followed her to Michigan for three years, my mother warned me that giving in to this kind of whim would be the end of my marriage. And I might've listened to my mother if I'd had time to think. But law school was a roller coaster that never stopped. During the year, we were always going to one mixer or another. Her 'summer' jobs—nothing like the ice cream scooping we'd done in high school—were all consuming. I dropped out of her social life halfway through law school.

There was nothing worse than going to all those lunches, dinners, and parties at the big houses on Fairmount or North Park Boulevard. Her colleagues and I were as different as night and day. The attorneys she worked for were all white men whose wives didn't work.

Brad or Chet or Chip were always shaking my hand and asking me what I did for a living. Was I a golf man? Did I belong to the skating club? When I said that I worked for RTA, they started asking me about the big bosses. When I didn't know them or when they looked at my hands and realized I didn't work in the upper offices, they wrote me off.

It didn't take glasses to see that I didn't fit into her world. All of the law school friends told jokes where the punch lines were in Latin. They talked about making money and buying expensive things. No one seemed interested in starting a family and living a modest life.

When I stopped going to her parties, the moot court competitions, and dinners with her employer, Bennett Friehof, Sheila didn't complain. Instead she talked about getting out of Glenville and moving on up to Cleveland Heights or

Shaker. We could be the first blacks in these once white enclaves, and she wanted to be on the vanguard. Sheila talked about me going back to school.

"You're really smart," she would say. "Smarter than a lot of these white guys I go to school with."

Live up to your potential became her favorite line of advice.

But I didn't want to go to school. I'd barely gotten through high school with teachers who thought I was dumb. I couldn't imagine showing my mug in college where I'd be older than everyone else. Besides, I was making more than Sheila and most of my friends from my job—even with occasional lay-offs.

The best surprise of our marriage was when Sheila got pregnant with Olivia. Then, I was sure, things would change. My wife could give up practicing law. I was making more than enough at Birmingham Steel by then. Sure, Sheila's paycheck was bigger than mine, but we didn't really need her money.

I paid the mortgage on the Glenville House. I paid most of the bills. Her money went for the extras—the new Buicks in the driveway—house repairs. Like most of my co-workers whose wives stayed home, I thought Sheila could make friends with the women in our neighborhood, push swings, make dinner. Motherhood would change her, I expected.

But Olivia's delivery into the world didn't make a damned bit of difference. After a few short weeks of what couldn't even be called maternity leave, she was back to the long hours working toward the elusive partnership. Olivia couldn't derail her, she said, as if our daughter was a nuisance. It was clear that Sheila didn't need my income, so I stopped pulling double shifts and working overtime.

When my mother wasn't caring for Olivia, my daughter was with me. I couldn't believe how much I loved Olivia when she was born. A female carbon copy of me, my little girl was feisty, smart and opinionated. I hoped my mother could steer Olivia in the right direction. She'd stayed home while my dad worked. We hadn't been rich with material things, but I had grown up well loved. I wanted Olivia to have the same values I'd been taught.

My mom's sudden death was a blow. Olivia was in school by then, and Sheila wanted more. Get a better job, she insisted. We needed to get the hell out of Cleveland before Olivia's schooling got serious, she'd said. Up like a hot air balloon Sheila's career went, and I wasn't going anywhere. So, it wasn't a surprise when the county sheriff served me with divorce papers. For years, I had suspected Sheila was having an affair with one of those white lawyers she worked with. At first, I'd threatened to stay and fight, but lawyers cost money, and with my mom gone, I was without resources.

Quickly I learned that she was good at her job. Papers were coming in the mail nearly every day accusing me of this and that, requesting income and property information, and probing every aspect of my life. Even though it nearly broke my heart to abandon Olivia, I decided to leave. Crossing the Cuyahoga River and settling first near West Twenty-fifth Street, then Ohio City, was easier than I thought it would be.

I didn't show up for the divorce. It was a foregone conclusion Sheila would get what she wanted—with the help of her high-powered lawyer friends. And what would happen to a black man like me if he did show up, without a lawyer, without means to pay child support? It wouldn't be good. I'd heard from my friends in the old neighborhood that the county would take me straight to jail from the court room. And if I was in jail, I'd lose everything. It was better if I stayed away.

The door opened, and Valene bustled in. She was the kind of woman I should have had in my life all along.

"What are you doing?" she asked. She hung her coat by the door and came over to give me a kiss on the cheek. Her warmth and bulk made this sterile apartment home.

"Thinking."

"About Olivia." Her statement wasn't a question.

I turned and watched while she opened the fridge and cupboards, pulling out ingredients for a meal. "How'd you know?"

"I can see it written all over your face." She turned on the burner under a cast iron pan. "Call her."

"She'll have Child Support after me faster than you can say, 'jump,' I said.

"Not your ex. Call your daughter. You know Sheila works twenty-four seven. That girl is probably alone after school. Try calling her. That girl would love to hear from her daddy."

Valene somehow stared me down and peeled onions at the same time. As fast as the knife flew, she didn't even cut a finger. Snapping the newspaper into a careful fold, I walked to the wall phone in the kitchen.

He dialed the seven digits my auntie Cora had given me when she'd heard Sheila'd moved.

With each ring my heart sped up, then it stopped with each pause. After six rings, the answering machine picked up. I hung on Sheila's voice.

"Not home," I said guilty that I felt nothing but relief.

"She's at that age. Probably with some friends. Try again tomorrow."

I nodded and walked back to my chair. I'd give it a couple of weeks, work up my courage. What if my daughter hated me, wanted nothing to do with me? That rejection would be nothing but my own damned fault.

31

Behind the Closed Door

Olivia

November 17-18, 2001

Exhausted, I laid in my borrowed bed. Saturday at the Williamses was not a day of rest. That was reserved for Sunday, the Sabbath. No one in the house on Hathaway Avenue lay around, watched TV, or snacked all day like a normal family.

Mr. Williams ran the house like he was still a Navy lieutenant and the rest of us were seamen. This morning had begun with the usual calisthenics in the backyard. My complaints about the cold, damp weather had fallen on deaf ears. I'd huffed and puffed through jumping jacks, squats, and the single pushup I could manage. All the while, Mr. Williams muttered disappointment under his breath.

Through his cupped hands, he yelled, "Olivia, you're not keeping up! A strong body is essential for a clear mind!"

My mother had taught me better than to talk back. Rather I tried, halfheartedly, to push my body up with noodle-like arms, but my shaking muscles had refused to cooperate. Jermaine had come to my rescue.

"Watch this," he whispered before breaking formation and running a lap around the yard. When Mr. Williams' eyes were no longer on me, Jermaine had done one-arm pushups that had both distracted and wowed my taskmaster.

After all that at six a.m., I was ready to go lie down on the couch, remote in hand, and watch a couple hours of children's programming. Even without cable, I'd have been willing to settle for whatever the local networks had to offer. But even that meager desire went unsatisfied. Where Mr. Williams had left off, his wife took over.

Aunt Linda said that foster kids should work for their keep, so I had taken up a rag and dusted. Last week, I'd vacuumed, scrubbed the floors, washed the walls, and ironed the clothes. And the weekend before, my hands had been rubbed raw from bleach and ammonia.

This week Jermaine took on the tasks I hated, saying his hands were used to it. Grateful, I gave him the bucket and rags. I stayed as quiet as possible, making sure every surface gleamed with furniture polish. Before dinner, Jermaine had pulled me into the corner of the dining room and given me a hug. During the embrace, he'd whispered in my ear, "See, we got to stick together. That's the only way to get through this here."

Having an ally should have lessened my fear of this unfamiliar house. Despite bone deep exhaustion, I couldn't sleep. Gray shadows filled the darkened room. Mind racing, my heart was doing its best to keep up. Blood pulsed between my ears.

Falling asleep and staying that way had always been easy. But in a strange house, all bets were off. The green numbers on the clock glowed nine-thirty. All I wanted was the oblivion to come so I could stay awake during the two-hour church service tomorrow.

My body jolted like someone was walking across my grave. The small Strawberry Shortcake night light flickered on, bathing the room in an odd pinkish-yellow glow. I'd forgotten to lock the door like I'd been told. What was there to fear? My mother had long ago told me that monsters weren't real.

"Aunt Linda, is that you?" I asked. My eyes tried to adjust to the faint illumination.

"No, it's Jermaine," the visitor whispered in response.

Relief flooded my body. Breath escaped my burning lungs. He was at least one person in this mess on my side. The way he took up for me this morning, first with the exercise, then with the cleaning was cool. But I didn't want to buddy up now; sleep and its companion, oblivion, was what I craved.

"Why aren't you in bed, Jermaine? We have to get up early again tomorrow. Church, remember?" I whispered, hoping our voices didn't disturb the quiet the Williamses required.

"Did you read my card?"

I squinted at the figure filling the doorframe. He'd left it right on my bed. How could I have missed it? "Yeah."

"I wanted to come in here and tell you how much I love you."

He'd been a big help today. But he was a strange boy. "Okay, well...thanks. I'm ready to sleep now. Good night," I said, turning away from the door and pulling the covers to my chin. Now I could get some sleep.

I heard the door close, so I was surprised when Jermaine's heavy weight depressed the mattress. I didn't mind so much when he started kissing me. It was kind of disgusting that his tongue tasted like the cigarettes he must have smoked in secret, but it felt good having someone touch me. It was difficult trying to be cool and sophisticated—wasn't that how I was supposed to act—when he took off my t-shirt, then my training bra.

With surprisingly strong hands for a boy, Jermaine grabbed my upper arms and pulled me out of bed, and up to the full-length mirror on the closet door. We stood immobile, side-by-side for a long moment. I only had on knit shorts. His pajama bottoms tented in the front. I looked away from our shadowy figures, embarrassed.

With probing fingers, Jermaine turned my face back to the mirror. "Don't, baby. You're looking good." He moved behind me, and I could feel him pressing into my back. With clumsy hands, he squeezed my newly forming breasts and pinched at my nipples. God, that felt good. I saw my reflection squeezing my legs together. His hand slipped down, probing at the space between my legs. Dinner churned in my gut. I wanted to pull him closer and push him away at the same time.

It wasn't right. This shouldn't be happening. How could I stop him, though? On all of my favorite teen dramas, and the weekday soaps I watched re-runs of on SoapNet, the girls liked this kind of attention from boys. They dated one boy then kissed another, without feeling guilty or bad like I did now.

Jermaine's breathing changed. With a hard push, I was back down on the bed. One arm pinned my chest, while the other pushed down my shorts. My nearly naked body was his to use. Pushing against his chest did nothing. With a single hand, he held my wrists above my head, thrusting his smoky tongue into my mouth. The two hands that had done pushups and taken over my cleaning chores had turned into an octopus' eight.

So many thoughts.... Images of Jon Heath, my Shaker crush, giggling hallway chatter of teenage television vixens talking about making out and bases. I'd probably passed from first to second tonight.

I struggled a little when Jermaine's hands probed in my underwear between my legs. This was getting worse and worse. I hoped he would just go away already, satisfied with kissing and touching me. Relieved when his weight lifted from me, I took a deep breath, ready to say good night. But my reprieve was short lived when Jermaine pulled his swollen penis from his pajama bottoms.

All thoughts of first, second, and third bases ceased. *No!* I screamed in my head, but I was determined to stay quiet. I didn't want to think of what would happen if either of the Williamses came up here. They'd told me to be quiet time and again. Now if they found out the noise was from the foster kids making out, who knew where I'd end up. Still, I wanted him to stop.

I began to struggle in earnest. The words finally moved from my brain to mouth.

“No!” I whispered loudly. “You can’t do that. I have a boyfriend, and Jon...wouldn’t.... His name is Jon,” I stammered. “He’s not going to like this.”

Jermaine put one of his many hands over my mouth and whispered. “I love you, girl. I won’t hurt you. You know this feels good.” Assuming my acquiescence, he rubbed his penis against my thigh and stomach.

My heart nearly broke my ribs with its pounding when I realized he wanted to have sex with me. Remembering his ease with the morning’s exercises, I knew he could overpower me. And true to my realization, Jermaine held both my wrists in a viselike grip, continuing to thrust his thick, smoky tongue into my mouth, blocking all speech.

When I started to kick, he lay his entire heavy weight on me, covering my mouth even more thoroughly.

The pain was a shock. I went as still as a statute. Minutes later, when I again became aware of my surroundings, one of his hands was over my mouth, and he was thrusting into me, tearing me apart. I moved my head from side to side, and his grip loosened. But I didn’t scream. What would be the point now? It was already done.

Jermaine rose up, thrusting harder. “Girl, I love you so much. I want to make a baby with you.”

I didn’t know what to say, had lost my will to scream. Instead, I felt the wetness of silent tears coursing down my cheeks. The taste of salt on my tongue accompanied the realization that I was no longer a virgin.

When he was done, Jermaine left me. I was never so happy to be alone. I put the borrowed t-shirt and shorts back on and tried to sleep with the disgusting taste of stale tobacco in my mouth and the stickiness between my thighs. I wanted nothing more than to brush the taste from my mouth, wash his nastiness from between my legs, scrub the smell of his sweat from my body, but leaving my room was against the rules.

Aunt Linda would be furious if she discovered I had strayed from the room during the night. We weren't supposed to leave our rooms, disturb Mr. Williams' rest, unless there was an emergency. This didn't qualify.

It took what seemed like hours to finally drift off again, then the door opened a second time. Jermaine came back in, pulled down the covers, and got into bed with me, pushing his hard penis against my butt once again. It was all my fault for not listening to Jackie. It was all my fault for not locking the door like I'd been told. My mother had always said I was hard-headed, didn't listen.

I was grateful when I woke up in time to get ready for church, and he was gone.

32

Shattered Glass

Casey

November 16, 2001

I watched the winds whip up white caps on Lake Erie as I inserted a jazz CD Jason had burned for me into my boom box. The sound of a woman singing in French filled my office, and I sat down at my desk. Everything was set up for a work filled morning. My coffee was on my right, my time slips on my left. In front of me was Sheila Harrison Grant's very thin file. Jenny Nolan in the juvenile court clerk's office liked me. Maybe I could ask for a small favor. Thank goodness the clerk answered on the first ring.

"Are you looking for more cases? I have a ton to get off my desk today."

Knowing I'd have to scratch Jenny's back, I agreed to take ten of them—having no idea of the commitment involved, but knowing they'd all be limited to the standard two hundred fifty in compensation. Ten percent of my work done in an instant, Jenny said, "So what can I help you with this fine morning?"

After having Jenny search through the aged computer system and dredge up a case number, I made the big ask.

"Can you fax me all the documents in the case?"

There was a long pause as Jenny no doubt saw her morning, cleared by me taking a handful of cases, suddenly filled with the task of battling an ancient fax. I held my breath.

"That would take too long," she said. I knew it. But before I could go on a self-pitying rant, Jenny spoke again. "I'll make a copy. Come pick it up in twenty minutes."

The sun was smiling for me, both literally and figuratively. I wouldn't have to badger the prosecutor any longer. Case information I should have had was in my hot little hands thanks to Jenny. I took the witness list to my car and planned out my day.

The list was typical. It included nearly everyone who'd ever stepped a foot in Cuyahoga County. After a cursory glance, I scrutinized the list more carefully. All the social workers who'd come into contact with Olivia were there, of course, as well as someone from child support, and a few doctors who were practically on the county's payroll. But there were a few surprises. The first was Alison Feingold with a far east Shaker Heights address.

I pulled my Cleveland map from the glove compartment and flipped to the east side. Sliding my index finger along the thin line of Shaker Boulevard, I was able to guess that the address likely belonged to the middle school. A quick call on my cell revealed that Feingold was a new school counselor. I made an appointment to see her in an hour.

Walking into any school always took me back. Even in school districts with a lot of money, there was a certain sameness to schools—generic sea foam green paint, cinderblock walls, linoleum floors. Shaker Heights Middle was no different. The warm air coupled with the smell of fried food and chlorine made her a little nauseous. I was happy to check in at the administration area where potpourri from nearly every desk was a godsend.

"Good morning. Are you Casey Cort?" Alison asked.

"Yes," I said, following the woman to her office. Without invitation, I sat in one of the counselor's chairs, and cleared off a space on the desk for my legal pad. Looking unsettled at my boldness, Alison nonetheless closed the office door and sat in her chair.

"Can I call you Casey?" When I nodded, she continued. "And you can call me Alison. From your call, I wasn't really sure what you wanted from me."

I considered the counselor, dressed like she was fresh from an episode of Ally McBeal. Weren't her legs cold in that skirt? My own skirt reached nearly to my ankles. "I'm an attorney. I usually serve as a guardian *ad Litem*. Today, though, I'm here on Olivia Grant's case. I'm representing—"

"Oh, my goodness. I'm so glad you're here. I've been trying to reach Olivia's social worker, but I keep getting voicemail and the runaround. I'm really worried about Olivia. How is she?"

I set my pen down for a second and caught the young woman's eye. Had she mistaken me for Olivia's attorney? Rather than correct the apparent misunderstanding, I let Alison go on.

"I want to tell you about myself. I've only started here this year. I graduated from Baldwin Wallace last year. The principal here has let me be pretty innovative. I started this after-school club, you know?" Alison went on to describe how she'd felt marginalized as a junior high and high school girl. I had a hard time believing that, with her blonde hair and model slim body, but didn't interrupt.

The counselor had wanted to create a group where girls from different cliques could get to know each other. If the kids discussed school and family problems in a nurturing environment, she'd hoped to eliminate some of the bullying and mean girl behavior that was so prevalent nowadays. So, she'd put the subject of her graduate thesis in action.

"And I was so glad when Olivia Grant moved here," she continued. "She added needed diversity to the group, you know. Most of the girls here come from comfortable backgrounds. I knew Olivia could really mix it up, being from Cleveland. But she needed a lot of help. She was so down all the time, you know. It's sad about her mom drinking all the time at home. So many of the minority students I've counseled have substance abuse issues in the home. Such a shame." Alison shook her pretty head.

"First, let me give you my card," I said. "If you have any questions or think of anything after I leave, give me a call."

Alison looked at the card. "Oh, it says here you work downtown. You're not with the county?"

"Many private attorneys work at Juvenile court. Some parents are represented by the public defender, but the rest of the gap is filled by private attorneys." Alison nodded. I picked up my pad, clicked my pen. "I'd like to ask a few questions."

Olivia had started in Shaker at the end of last year, March to be exact. She'd fared well in standardized testing. The girl had a higher than average IQ and had always scored above the ninety-five percentile.

"What made you think something was wrong at home?"

"It started with her grades," Alison said. "Her team teachers said she wasn't engaged in class. In college, we learned that was a sure sign something wasn't right at home. Then when I got her involved in the club, I saw that she was afraid of her mother. She submitted this note." Alison took the creased sticky note from her file and handed it to me.

"Did you confront Olivia about this?"

"That's when she told me about her mother's drinking. All the pieces clicked. Poor school performance, depression, no friends. I called the hotline right away."

I gave her as hard a stare as I could muster. "I'm a statutory reporter. I had to follow the law."

I asked a few more questions, got a copy of Olivia's file, and left the school. Checking my map, I realized I was close to the home of Lyn Byers, another name on the witness list. A quick call to Grant revealed Byers to be a mother of one of Olivia's friends. My client had said she wasn't sure she'd ever met the woman, and if so, it had only been in passing. Intrigued, I drove the short distance to the Byers' home. It was an intimidating three-story Tudor set far back on tree lined Kingsley Road.

I called the mother from her cell and introduced myself as Judge Grant's attorney.

"Casey? This isn't a really good time—"

It was nine-thirty, a time I thought of as a golden mommy hour. Done with morning drop off, there were at least three hours, maybe five before pickup. "I'm here at your front door. I only need a few minutes." The curtains twitched. I turned off my Honda, which sputtered to a stop. I gathered my briefcase and made the long walk to the front door. Life on this side of the river was a far cry from where I'd grown up.

Before I could knock, the front door opened. A tall thin woman stood, with watery blue eyes and dishwater blonde hair not much different from my own. I extended my hand. Byers' grip was reluctant. She stepped back and allowed me into a large oak paneled entryway. Despite her reticence at her guest, her manners didn't fail. I was asked for and handed over my coat. Following Byers to a sunny kitchen in the back of the house, I took a seat at the granite island.

"Would you like some coffee?" Byers asked, refilling her own mug.

While I would have loved a cup, this wasn't a social call. I got down to business. "Children and Family Services has taken custody of Olivia Grant—for neglect—based upon allegations of alcohol problems. You've been identified as a witness by the county."

"I'm supposed to testify?" Byers looked taken aback. This is what I hated about Juvenile. Everyone loved to get down and dirty when it came to talking about other people's parenting, but they didn't want to go public. "No one said anything about this to me."

"Who have you talked to about the case?"

Byers set her mug on the granite counter. "A couple of weeks ago, I got a call from Alison Feingold, the girls—Cate and Olivia's counselor. She was concerned about Olivia. Asked if I knew anything."

"And did you?"

"I only told her what I knew. That Olivia and Cate haven't been friends very long. The girl's new to Shaker. Two times Olivia's mom Sheila was supposed to pick her up. And she didn't. I mean it's no big deal, but among moms it's a common courtesy. Olivia always seemed nervous when I asked about her mom or having some girls over to her house. Sheila never reciprocated. And on the night of my daughter's birthday, I saw her break into her own house. So, when Alison called me, I put two and two together."

And came up with five, I thought.

"When I put together what Alison told me about the drinking and Olivia breaking in, what else could I think? Sheila must have passed out. How else could she forget to pick up her daughter, and not hear the doorbell that night?"

Byers' phone rang, and she talked briefly to the caller, making no attempt to put him or her on hold. Placing her hand over the receiver, she said, "Can you show yourself out?"

I gathered my things, got the London Fog from the closet and walked to the car. Byers would be easy to destroy on cross. Speculation was not evidence. I sat in my car a while, puzzling out the case and knew where I needed to go next. Fortunately, Vera Rhinehardt, Sheila's landlord and neighbor, was home.

After accepting a glass of water and taking a seat on the couch in the small but beautifully restored apartment, I got down to it. What exactly, I asked Rhinehardt, had she seen?

"I thought there was a burglar," Rhinehardt started. "Glass broke and I woke my husband Josh. He took a bat from the closet and went to investigate. When he came back, he said the girl from upstairs had broken in."

I slipped into interrogator mode. "What happened next?"

"I got some cardboard from the basement, fit it to the pane, and swept up the shattered glass."

"Did you confront Olivia or Judge Grant?"

"Not that night, it was late. But the next morning when Sheila was leaving, I asked her about it. She was obviously embarrassed, and promised to drop a check in the mail."

"Did she say why it had happened?"

"Olivia had forgotten her key and Sheila, thinking it was going to be a late-night teen party, didn't wait up for her."

I was unimpressed with the prosecutor's case so far. There must be something else, I surmised. I pushed on.

"Anything else happen upstairs that got your attention?"

"Maybe a couple of weeks after that, I heard yelling." Vera looked a little sheepish. I guessed she was more than a casual observer of her tenant's lives.

"Could you make out what was being said or was it just yelling in general?"

"Nothing distinct, but it wasn't the first time."

"Did it worry you enough to call the authorities?"

"No," Rhinehardt laughed, a little uncomfortable. "I was a teenager once. I got on the wrong side of my mother a lot. If we'd been renters, the landlord would have heard me being chewed out a time or twelve."

"Anything else?"

Rhinehardt was quiet a long time. "I haven't told anyone, not even Josh, but sometimes the yelling was accompanied by bumping, like the girl was being hit or had fallen. And once, this summer when the window was open, Sheila called Olivia names I thought were bad."

"Like what?"

"Like the girl was fat, and lazy. But it was a holiday weekend, and everyone in America had probably been drinking, so I put it out of my mind."

"Have you told any of this to a social worker or prosecutor?"

"No. Should I?"

I wasn't going to answer that one. I deflected. "I'm trying to get Olivia home."

"Where is she, with her dad or something?"

"In foster care."

Rhinehardt gasped, her hand covering her mouth in surprise. "Why?"

"There's smoke here, but no fire. The school counselor is new, a little zealous. I'm trying to bring her home." I said.

The witness list looked like a shot in the dark, but the prosecutor neither had the time nor resources to investigate. I'd have a hard-enough time winning the case without speculation and innuendo muddying the waters.

33

Washington Murmurs

November 16, 2001

Senator Tommy Franklin sat in his small Capitol Hill studio sipping his third—make that fourth brandy of the night. He pulled stacks of papers from his briefcase and laid them on the small wooden side table. Although he'd been in Washington for over a decade, he hadn't made it his permanent residence like so many of the other senators. Still a bachelor at the ripe old age of forty-eight, many colleagues assumed he was gay.

Lonely, was more like it. His career, first as an attorney with the Justice Department, then as the junior senator from Ohio, had kept him from seriously pursuing any one woman. So here he was approaching fifty, a warm drink and endless position papers his only company.

None of the papers would keep him from inevitable slumber. He sat back in his leather club chair and debated which would accompany him to bed, the latest research from a lobbyist, or a pending legislation. Then he came across a thick folder—the file of one Sheila Harrison Grant.

As he leaned forward in the leather chair, he quickly paged through the folder, found Grant's grades from law school, her publications, the results of her FBI investigation, the same they did for all judicial candidates, and information about her time of Bennett Friehof. It was mildly interesting reading. This one didn't look like she'd be a judicial activist.

He pulled out the background information. That was the kind of thing you could make a lengthy speech about during hearings. And her background was the stuff of gold. Working class background would resonate with his constituents and voters around the country. Her father had been a shipyard worker, her mother a part-time domestic. Grant had been the first in her family to go to college. An unfortunate marriage and divorce from a neighborhood guy who turned her into a single mom. The media would eat this up. Black single mom makes partner at white shoe firm. A variation of that headline would play out across dozens of different newspapers.

When Tommy went to put down the file, a thin sheaf of unstapled pages slipped out. They appeared to be an update to the FBI investigation. Some credit card summaries and bank statements slipped through his fingers. He flipped through the pages, not noticing anything at first. Grant lived pretty close to the edge of her budget, but with a secure job, that wasn't too risky a move. Her new car and Shaker Heights rent put a pretty big dent in her earnings. Then

Tommy looked at the credit card summaries. Her yearly spending was broken out in several categories, travel, dining, and others. It was the expenditures under the government category which caught his eye.

The beverage control approved store on Chagrin Boulevard had gotten seventeen hundred dollars of her hard-earned money. Liquor laws in Ohio required potent alcoholic beverages be sold in licensed, pre-approved locations. Some beers and wines were sold at supermarkets, but anything stronger was heavily regulated.

Tommy closed the file, removed his reading glasses and rubbed at his nose with his thumb and forefinger. He downed the contents of his own drink. The last thing the Democratic Party needed was some alcoholic fucking up the confirmation process. It was difficult enough as it was, getting the flawless candidates confirmed.

He retrieved his cordless phone from the kitchenette wall. Looked down at his watch, ten o'clock. It was too damn late to call anyone, but he pushed common courtesy aside. He wanted answers now. Clicking through his Palm Pilot, he pulled up the phone number he wanted.

"Peyton Bennett," the disembodied voice answered.

"Tommy Franklin." Without preamble, he continued, "What's going on with Sheila Harrison Grant?" He heard Bennett murmuring to someone, then walking to another room. "You said she didn't have any skeletons. I don't need Dale Hodges up my ass. Finished her dossier, and she reads like an alcoholic. Either that or she's one hell of a hostess. Tell me she hosts weekly neighborhood progressives." Tommy knew his voice was impatient.

Bennett hesitated.

"Tell me. Now."

"I have some bad news," Bennett said. "The county's taken Sheila's kid. The girl revealed her mom's drinking to a school counselor. The counselor took her role a little seriously. She seems a little overzealous."

"Bottom line this." Tommy didn't need details. Big pictures were his thing.

"The kid's in foster care and Mom's fighting in juvenile court to get her back. I've set her up with a lawyer who's got the inside track."

"Shit. A call would have been nice, Bennett." Tommy hoped his yelling didn't rouse his neighbors. They could be a persnickety bunch about noise.

"Juvenile hearings are completely secret. The files are sealed. Sheila should be out of this before anything could leak out."

"Bullshit and you know it. Dale Hodges collects information from every person he's ever gotten a job. That man's more connected than a mobster. The minute the papers were filed, a clerk whispered something in his ear. Now I'm a step behind. Is she going to step aside, tend to her family issues?"

"She can't." Bennett said no more. There was something more, but his dad's firm would likely keep that secret. Firms were better at confidentiality than courts.

Tommy's head spun. "We need a solid minority appointment to liven up the base. The first black district judge and all that. It would get the black community out to vote. The Democrats are losing Ohio. I thought Grant was our ticket. Shit, shit, shit. I'll look into whether or not this can be saved."

"Thank you," Bennett said.

Tommy disconnected the call.

34

She's not my mother

Olivia

November 21, 2001

Daydreaming was more fun than being stone cold bored out of your mind. I hated the pills. Sure, it made it easier to pay attention in class. My formerly wandering mind was firmly focused on the teacher. But school lessons hadn't gotten any more interesting.

Math was my last class of the day. I'd already started algebra at Shaker. This teacher was taking more than a week to teach the metric system. Some of the other students were frantic note takers, while others goofed off. How many days would I be subject to multiplication and division by ten, I wondered.

To keep myself occupied, I started writing down what the teacher was saying about millimeters, centimeters and the like. Mercifully, the end of the day bell rang.

I walked down the still unfamiliar hallway, hating school, but dreading *home*. Grateful my rusted locker opened on the first try, I took out the books I'd been given this week. As I picked up my Civics book, the pages broke away from the spine. Crap, these were some of the oldest books I'd ever seen.

I bent down to pick up the scattered pages. Another student came to my aid. I nearly cried when the girl helped her, rather than kick the book down the hall. I'd seen that more than once in my few days here.

"I'm Vickie," the girl said while our faces were pointed at the floor. "Where you from? You just move here?"

My face grew tight. I'd never met any other kid in foster care before I'd landed there myself. Facing other kids with my messed-up situation had never crossed my mind. Warm with embarrassment, I answered the girl anyway.

"I just moved in with the Williamses. They're my foster parents." When Vickie's face changed, I hastened to add, "I won't be there long. I'm going home really soon. My mom is straightening things out."

Vickie didn't exactly recoil but stepped back nonetheless. She thrust glossy textbook pages at me. "Foster care? That's messed up. Foster kids can become crazy folks. Your mom on crack? Your dad in jail?"

My eyes smarted. I purposely dropped a few more papers so I wouldn't have to look at Vickie. "No, there's nothing wrong with my mom," I said, looking at the floor. "It's a mistake from Shaker."

"You a Shaker girl. Oh, that's why you talk like that. Don't go gettin' all uppity in here." Vickie walked away. I released my breath, glad I'd survived my first encounter. No sooner than relief flooded my body, I noticed Vickie'd joined a group of girls who were looking at me and laughing.

Head down, I shuffled the remaining stretch of hallway. I was already late. Aunt Linda liked to keep Jermaine and me on a tight schedule. There were only two cars left in front of the school when I finally got there, a beat-up Ford and Aunt Linda's Cadillac—shiny from Jermaine's and my weekend chores.

A couple of boys were hanging by the front door. A chill went up my spine as they approached. They wouldn't dare touch her out here in public.

"You Olivia?" one asked. Before I could answer, the other said, "Your mom's been waitin' fo' you."

A dull ache accompanied the full feeling behind my eyes. I pulled away from the tight circle the boys had made around me and yelled, "She's not my God damned mother!" Then I snatched open the Cadillac's car door, threw my backpack in, plopped down, slammed the door, and crossed my arms violently.

Because I was staring forward, trying not to cry, the slap on the left side of my face was unexpected.

35

Relative Placement

Keith

November 26, 2001

I was reclining in my green easy chair, waffling between the Plain Dealer and U.S. News when my girlfriend slash fiancé, Valene Winstead interrupted my thoughts.

"Keith, honey, your aunt is on the phone." She cupped the mouthpiece between her hands. "She says it's important. Something to do with the county sheriff," she whispered, then handed me the phone.

"Auntie Cora," I said. "How are you?"

"Boy, don't how you do me. Get your black ass over here. Some deputies came by with some court papers for you. I didn't have no address to give them, but I sure could call you to come get these papers. You know I don't like no *po-*

lice coming round my house. Here in Cleveland, them *po*-lice ain't nothin' but trouble."

Under the gruff exterior, my auntie was a marshmallow. "I'll be over later tonight to pick it up with my mail," I said, ending the call.

Valene cocked her head. "What's the problem?"

"Auntie Cora said the police dropped off some papers for me," I repeated.

"You ain't in trouble, is you? I ain't never heard of no one getting any papers delivered like that. Are these more divorce papers? I bet them child support folks is after you. They really crackin' down on brothers, you know. A lot of guys I know are going to jail behind this child support mess. I always said that you should try to get custody of Olivia. Sounds to me like your ex-wife's downtown job is more important than raising that girl."

Though I no longer communicated with Sheila, I'd read about her appointment to judge. Secretly, I was proud of her. Against all the odds, she'd made it. And there wasn't a day that went by that I didn't think about Olivia. She was and would always be my heart. But I knew with an ex-wife who was now a judge, and me not having paid more than a few hundred dollars of child support, I was in a mess of trouble if I tried to exercise my rights.

Despite the promise to my mom's sister, I didn't pick up the papers waiting for me that day or the next. Until I couldn't put off picking up my bills any longer, and after some persistent nagging by Valene—only then did I swing by Cora's house and pick up my mail.

While riding the red line home and after looking through and discarding my junk mail, and glancing at my credit card bills, I opened the envelope from Juvenile court.

The summons was stamped in large black ink with the words PERSONAL SERVICE. It was addressed to me with a case number typed on the cover. It stated:

A motion for Temporary Custody has been filed in this court, a copy of which is attached concerning the child or children named on the attached complaint. If the court grants temporary custody of the child(ren), the parents and other relatives will lose rights, and privileges. See Box 3 reverse side for additional rights. YOU ARE HEREBY COMMANDED TO APPEAR BEFORE THIS COURT AT 2163 East 22nd Street, Cleveland, Ohio on December 18, 2000 at 1:00 P.M.

This matter has been assigned to the docket of Judge Dorthea MacKinnon.

The next paragraph said:

The Party/Parties herein required to appear may lose valuable rights or be subject to court sanction if such party/parties fail(s) to appear at the time and place stated in this summons.

I couldn't make immediate sense of what I was reading, but the name at the top of the letter got my attention: Olivia Grant. I looked over the papers again, but didn't think I was being sued for child support. I flipped to the next page headed COMPLAINT.

It stated:

CELESTE YOUNG, Social Worker, Cuyahoga County Department of Children and Family Services, first being duly sworn, states upon information and belief that a child in Cuyahoga County Ohio is NEGLECTED and DEPENDENT as defined in Section 2151.031(B) & 2151.04(C) of the Ohio Revised Code in the following particulars:

1. The child was removed on October _, 2001 pursuant to an ex-parte order granted by Magistrate Chambers.

2. On October _, 2001, CCDCFS was contacted through the hotline. The caller stated that Mother was unable to care for daughter due to alcohol problems.

3. Mother has been uncooperative with CCDCFS

4. Alleged Father has never established paternity and had minimal contact with the child.

5. Alleged Father provides no care or support for his child.

Reasonable efforts were made by Cuyahoga County Department of Children and Family Services to prevent the removal of the child from the home, and removal is in the best interest of the child.

Olivia was...gone? I looked at the paper again. There were no dates, just blank lines. So, October? My mind racing, I missed the Madison stop on the train, and had to get off and turn around at Triskett to get home. I was relieved to find Valene busy in my kitchen.

I laid the mail and my newspaper on the table. "I picked up the court papers from Auntie Cora's house today," I said without preamble.

"'Bout time." Valene didn't turn away from the stove.

"I think Olivia's in foster care."

Steak and onions forgotten, Valene whipped around from the stove. "I knew you should have gotten that child before now. That woman you were married to sounds like she wasn't giving that baby what she needs."

"What do I do?"

"We get a lawyer and sue for custody. There's no reason that child should be in foster care. She needs to be here with us." Smoke caught Valene's attention, and she turned back to the blackening food.

I walked from the small kitchen to the bedroom, where I sat down and made a series of phone calls.

I dialed the number I'd kept in the back of my wallet. Wishing I'd tried harder to get in contact with Olivia, I listened to the phone ring, wondering if Sheila would even pick up. Sheila's home number had been unlisted for years.

Seeing the folks from her old neighborhood when she visited there was one thing, but getting phone calls from wayward relatives who wanted money—because they thought she and all lawyers were rich; or free legal advice—because that's what family was for; or favors like fixing parking tickets—because they didn't know the difference between a lawyer and a court clerk had been trying on her nerves.

I knew the diatribe backwards and forwards. But Olivia always kept Auntie Cora apprised of their phone number. Today was not a day for social niceties.

"Sheila, what in the hell is going on over there? I just got some papers from Auntie Cora's house talking about Olivia being in foster care."

"Good evening Keith," Sheila said. "It's so nice to hear your voice. You haven't seen your daughter in what, three or four years? Do you have a job yet?"

"Cut the bull—acting like your shit don't stink. How in the hell did Olivia end up in foster care?" I didn't wait for an answer. "Are you planning to get her back or drink yourself into oblivion?"

"How dare you? Who in the hell gave you the right to pass judgment? Didn't want to leave your momma's house. Didn't want to keep a job. Then when I left your lazy ass, didn't step up and do the manly thing and take care of your daughter.

"Don't start talking to me about how to raise a child. You aren't here day in and day out to deal with the everyday stresses. Is she fitting in? Does she have enough friends? Is she eating too much junk food? What to tell her when she cries that dear dad doesn't love her. So, don't come in here like you're father of the year," Sheila said.

I took several deep breaths then glanced at the bedroom door. It was closed. Though the walls were paper thin, I hoped Valene wouldn't hear most of this; she hated anger. But I needed to ask this next question even if it resulted in a full-blown argument.

"Are you drinking?"

"Hell yes, I'm drinking," Sheila answered blithely. "I need a little rest and relaxation at the end of the day. Maybe I have a cocktail or a night cap, but I'm no drunk. This whole mess in Juvenile court is a mistake. You know they don't like to see black people make it in Cleveland."

I couldn't fault her logic. The daily newspaper was filled with black leaders taken down by extramarital affairs or unpaid taxes. Look at what the FBI tried to do to Martin Luther King.

"What happened?" I asked, conciliation in my tone.

Sheila's voice lost its impatience.

"Olivia's guidance counselor got a little overzealous. She's one of those young white girls out of school—you know the type—gonna save black folks from themselves."

I did know the type. I'd met them when Sheila had been in college and in law school. I'd have preferred a life without those people. But Sheila had sought it out. And this was the result. I tuned back in to what my ex-wife was saying.

"She called the county and told them some crap. But I've got it handled. I *am* a judge, you know. And before that I was one of the best trial lawyers in this town. Give me a couple of weeks."

"I'm not here to pass judgment. I have no idea whether you and your high-powered friends can get you out of this mess, but I know I'm not going to leave my daughter in foster care. There are all sorts of nasty folks who take kids in.

You remember Mrs. Embertson always had some raggedy ass foster kids running through the neighborhood. You know she wasn't treating those kids right. She didn't give a lick about what happened to them. Just collected her checks and went right on. I don't want Olivia living with a Mrs. Embertson," I finished. I'd probably said more words in these last few minutes than I'd done in the last few days. I wasn't a talker, but Olivia needed me.

"Look, Keith," Sheila said, her tone softening. "Even though you haven't been around and haven't paid a dime, I know that you love your daughter."

I gripped the phone, hard. My knuckles strained against the molded plastic. Why she had to always get a dig in, I didn't know.

"I'll never forget how you were when she came home from the hospital. Look, I'm going to do what I have to do. And you do the same," she said, ending the call. Even though I hadn't called asking for permission, I'd gotten it.

After pushing food around my plate for twenty minutes, I filled in Valene on the call to Sheila.

"I haven't been able to save much money since I've been here. There was the time I was out of work for a while." I ducked my head. Even if layoffs were as common in Cleveland as lake effect snowflakes, it was still hard to put my failure into words. Thinking about Olivia, I soldiered on. "I'm just getting those credit cards and payday loans down. I can't figure how I'm gonna be able to afford a lawyer."

"Now, you know as long as we've been seeing each other, we've kept our stuff separate. I've never asked to move in, or messed with your money or anything." Valene paused. Her substantial bosom heaved with a heavy sigh. "I'm not one to be all up in your business, but let me have my say. I think it's very important that you get custody of your daughter." She held up a hand to stop my response. "I know I been sayin' this all along. And it weren't no big thang when she was with her mother, 'cuz I know how that is. I raised all my kids without the help of no man, but this here is serious.

"I've seen this happen to a lot of women at my church. Once the county gets a hold to them, Family Services never gets out of your life. They always stoppin' by, checkin' the fridge, countin' the bedrooms, wantin' to see your light and heat bills. I know a couple of folks. Let me call around and try to set up some appointments with some lawyers."

Glad I wasn't going it alone like last time, I grasped Valene's hand in mine. "Thanks," I muttered.

"Honey, this is important. Just be sure that you can get some days off work. You're going to need them."

First thing the next morning, I called the phone number on the back of the summons. After working my way through a seemingly endless touch tone menu, finally I connected with a live person.

"I need to speak with the social worker handling my daughter's case," I said.

"Do you know who's assigned to it?" the voice asked.

"No, ma'am. My daughter's named Olivia Grant."

The sigh from the other end of the line was heavy. "Unfortunately, sir, we can't look up children that way. Do you have her case number?" Happy I could provide at least that, I recited the number from the summons in my hand. Her sigh went from weary to exasperation. "Sir, I can't look up cases by juvenile court case number. Do you have the CFS case number by any chance?"

"Ma'am," I said, trying not let my own exasperation show, "I don't have any of that information. I just got some papers in the mail saying that my daughter's in foster care. My ex-wife didn't even tell me that anything was going on. I can take care of my daughter, I just need her social worker to know that I can take custody."

"Okay, hold on, sir. What did you say your daughter's name was again?"

"Olivia Keziah Grant."

I was put on hold for ten minutes. The line was so quiet, I thought several times that I'd been hung up on. Just as I was about to give up, the operator came back.

"Look sir, we're not supposed to look up stuff for the clients, but I feel for you and your little girl, so in between calls, I found your social worker. Do you have a pencil? You should write this down." I clicked my ball point, poised to take notes. I wrote down the social worker's extension first. "Her name is Jacqueline Foley. If she's not in, leave a voice mail, and she'll return your call."

"Thank you, thank you, thank you," I said, sending up a silent prayer.

"I'll connect your call," the operator said.

Dutifully I left a message then went to work on the night shift.

When I returned home nine hours later, there was a message from Foley. She'd gone ahead and made an appointment for ten that morning. So, with no sleep or time to spare, I showered, changed, and walked to the RTA stop.

At ten A.M. exactly, I stepped off the bus and walked into the Jane Edna Hunter building's cavernous lobby. Avoiding a collision with two rambunctious boys, I made his way to the reception desk.

When the young, heavyset Puerto Rican woman approached me, I felt every year my age. She was so youthful, I wondered if I were old enough to be her father. Even if I wasn't, she probably wasn't old enough to care for my daughter. I pushed that aside and extended my hand.

"Keith Grant," Foley said. "It's not often we see fathers in here." She gestured around the room, where indeed only women sat. "Why don't you come back to the conference room? I need you to sign some papers, and we can talk."

Before Foley could close the door, I started talking. "Miss Foley, what can I do to get my daughter to live with me? I only just found out she was taken from my ex-wife. There's no reason for her to be in foster care. She can live with me."

"Of course, we prefer that children live with a non-custodial parent or relative. But because your ex-wife has been uncooperative, we didn't *know* there *were* any available relatives. Olivia can be placed with you while this case is open as long as you have sufficient room and can pass a background check." Her eyes pierced mine. "You can't have a felony record. And no one living with you can have an open case with the county."

I might have been guilty of a lot of things, but crimes weren't among them. Before getting my hopes up, I decided to be upfront. "I know that I'm behind on my child support. And I haven't kept up on my visitation. But I love my daughter. She can have my room. I can sleep on the pull-out couch, if that's okay. I want her with me—whatever it takes."

"If all checks out, I don't see any reason why Olivia can't stay with you," Foley said. The weight that had been centered near my heart became as light as a helium balloon. After she asked about my schooling, my job, and my marriage to Sheila, she pushed some papers toward me. "Before we get the ball rolling, I'll need you to sign this."

I took in the thick stack. "What's this?"

She turned the papers to a landscape orientation. "This case plan is a list of what you and your ex-wife need to do to regain custody of Olivia."

Confused, I laid my hands on the papers. "If she lives with me, won't I have custody?"

"Not exactly," Foley said. "Your wife had legal custody. Now Olivia's in the county's custody. Although we can place your daughter with you, she'll still be our responsibility."

"How can I get full custody?"

"You'll have to talk to a lawyer and go to the divorce court. But for now, I'll need you to sign this." Foley pushed the papers closer and handed me a pen.

"What does this say I have to do?" I wanted Olivia home, but being the husband of a lawyer had taught me one important thing: not to sign anything without understanding it first.

Foley flipped the pages open. "All the services are for the mom: alcohol treatment, parenting classes and other stuff.

The only thing you have to do," she pointed a finger at the last line, "is take a paternity test. But since you were married, that's a technicality."

Screw it. This was Sheila's problem. I wanted Olivia home. So, without reading I signed next to the initials PNE and my name.

Foley pulled a slip of paper from her folder and pushed it toward me. "Here's the info on paternity testing. Call this number."

I didn't like needles.

"Is it a blood test?"

"A cheek swab, that's it." Foley gathered up the case plan and opened the door, signaling the meeting was over.

"Is she okay? When can she come live with me?" I didn't want to leave without something tangible I could share with Valene.

Foley looked at me, and her features softened a little.

"I'll order the criminal check today. As soon as I get the results, I'll make an appointment to meet you at your home."

Satisfied that I was making progress, I wound through a maze of cubicles back to the reception area and made my way out onto Euclid Avenue. Catching the number six bus westbound, I got out near Sixteenth Street.

Wrapping my coat more securely around me, I fought a yawn and leaned against the wind, walking the two blocks north to Superior. I entered at the address on the slip Foley had given me and made my appointment for paternity testing.

I may have failed my daughter in a number of ways, but it was time to step up.

36

The Visit

Olivia

November 27, 2001

"Is your hair dry?"

I followed Aunt Linda's voice and came into the kitchen, towel around my neck. The minute we'd gotten home from school, I'd been ordered to wash my hair and put on clean underwear. "Good, you have your bathrobe over your clothes. Sit here," Aunt Linda said, gesturing to a tall wooden stool.

"What are you going to do?" I gingerly touched my curls, soft from conditioner.

"Someone important's comin' over. Need you to look your best," she said, laying a heavy brass comb directly on the fire of the gas stove.

"Who's coming?" I asked.

"Who did your hair before? Your mom?"

My mom didn't 'do hair.' I shook her head. "I got it done at the beauty parlor," I answered.

"You should get your money back," she said, slathering a thick layer of the blue green Afro Sheen through a section of her hair.

I didn't answer. I didn't want to talk about my hair. On the one hand, everyone praised me on having 'good hair.' But my mom wouldn't let me get a perm like the other girls in Glenville, and she wouldn't do it herself.

So, my hair looked good only on the weeks when my mom remembered to take me to the shop. The rest of the time, I pulled it back into a low ponytail. I'd been planning to ask for a flat iron for Christmas so that I could do it myself.

My thoughts were arrested when the comb sizzled through my hair and hot grease bubbled near my scalp. Every time the hot metal came from the fire to my hair, I tried not to flinch. But it was so hot that I moved, and the searing pain from metal on skin made me yelp out in pain.

Aunt Linda jerked me still. "Don't move. That's why you got burned. I'm almost done. Don't move again," she admonished.

Despite the smell of burning flesh in the air, I sat stock still. When my hair was done, I took the pink turtleneck sweater and maroon corduroy jumper Aunt Linda had laid out on the kitchen table, and ran upstairs to put a cold washcloth on my neck.

At the appointed hour, I unlocked her bedroom door and came back down. The raw flesh on my neck was throbbing like the dickens, but I took my place on the couch, not saying anything about the burn or the spring poking into the back of her right thigh.

When Aunt Linda went to the vestibule, I looked over her shoulder through the window behind her. An older white woman with bright red hair got out of the blue Ford, tiptoeing through the slick wet leaves to the front door. Damn, when had those leaves blown there? No doubt I'd have to scoop those up when this woman was gone. Aunt Linda had pulled open the door even before the bell rang.

"You must be Linda Williams. Sherry Otis. We spoke on the phone." The woman came in without a spoken invitation and scanned the room. "You've got a nice place here. How long have you been fostering?"

"Couple of years. Geoffrey, my husband, has more time for the kids now that there's less overtime at the mill."

Otis had barely looked at Olivia. Wasn't the red-haired woman there to see her? Mindful of Aunt Linda's admonition, I didn't say a word.

"How nice of you to help these children in need. I've been a guardian *ad Litem* for the last twelve years and have represented hundreds of children. Some of these parents..." Otis shook her head, leaving the sentence unfinished. "Anyway, I'm here to meet," she looked down at some papers she'd removed from her purse, "Olivia Grant."

Both women looked toward the couch as if only now remembering I was sitting there. "We're only fostering two now. Come meet her."

They walked toward the couch from the vestibule. "Olivia, this is Sherry Otis. She's your lawyer. Come stand up and shake her hand." As directed, I stood and somberly greeted Otis.

"Hello."

"As Linda said, I'm your lawyer."

Along with all the other crimes my mother was accused of, I didn't want them to think I didn't have manners. I cleared my throat, and ignored the pain radiating from my hairline. "Nice to meet you."

"Well, don't you speak well and look nice," Otis said. "Linda must take good care of you here."

Since it wasn't a direct question, I didn't supply an answer. Instead, catching Aunt Linda's ever watchful eye, I sat back on the couch and folded my hands on my primly crossed legs. Aunt Linda perched on Mr. Williams' easy chair, and Otis sat at the far end of the couch.

"How do you like it here with the Williamses?"

Aunt Linda's eyes pinned Olivia to the couch. "It's okay," I answered.

"Do you know why you're not with your mother?" the redhead asked.

Despite my best effort to show no emotion that would incur Aunt Linda's wrath, I could feel my lower lip trembling. In an effort to disguise that, I shook her head.

"You told your school counselor that your mom yelled at you, called you names, and drank every night. Do you remember that?"

Trusting Alison had gotten my mom and me into this mess. I wasn't about to trust another adult.

"Olivia, Mrs. Otis asked you a question."

I didn't say a word. I'd watched enough court shows to know that now was the time to exercise my right to remain silent.

"Mrs. Otis," Aunt Linda started, "Olivia has been difficult. But that's what happens with these kids from bad homes." Before Aunt Linda could make me look worse,

Jermaine bounded into the room. I could feel every part of my body become rigid when he hugged me tight, then planted himself on the couch between my lawyer and me.

"I'm Jermaine. Who are you?"

"Jermaine, please. Go to your room. You're being rude. This woman is here to meet with Olivia." At Jermaine's pout, Aunt Linda's tone softened a little. "You know how Jennifer comes to see you?" When he nodded, she continued. "Mrs. Otis is here to talk to Olivia about her mom. Why don't you go pick up the leaves on the walkway?"

Jermaine kissed me smack on the lips before he ran out of the room, probably to get his coat. He always did whatever they asked, without complaints. Even with him gone, my jaw clenched so tight, I thought my teeth were going to break.

"Why don't you go to your room too, Olivia? I need to discuss some stuff with Mrs. Otis."

"It was nice meeting you," the red-haired woman said.

That was it? My mom had always said a lawyer kept a client's secrets. Didn't Otis want to know mine? Jermaine and I weren't boyfriend and girlfriend. Otis had to know that I hadn't wanted him to do what he'd done.

I shuffled out of the room, throwing a baleful glance over my shoulder at Otis. The woman's eyes didn't meet mine. Nothing more could happen when Otis was there, so I kept my bedroom door wide open. I heard Aunt Linda offer the woman some peach cobbler. There was a lot of whispering between them, but no one ever came back to talk to me.

More than an hour later, they both took a tour through the house, both sipping from mugs of coffee. When I heard them laughing below my window, right outside the front door, I got up and locked the door and undressed for bed.

37

Confirmation

Sheila

December 4, 2001

I squared my shoulders then pushed my way into Bennett Friehof. There were no squeals in the hallway accompanying my arrival this time. The receptionist appeared too busy to chat. Even Bonnie, my longtime secretary, was lukewarm when I passed the woman's desk.

None of that mattered. When I was finally directed to Troy Holman's office, I didn't hesitate in making my knock strong and loud. Holman was his usual gregarious self, his greeting effusive. Grasping my outstretched hand into his, he shook vigorously.

"Good to see you. Good to see you, Sheila. Sorry to hear about your troubles," he said. Heat rushed to my face and for once I was glad my skin was dark. Closing my eyes briefly, I put aside my embarrassment and focused on the goal. "Let me cut to the chase. I met with Tommy Franklin and Dale Hodges. Good 'ol Dale. Good 'ol Dale gave me a hell of a time. Hell of a time."

I didn't have the energy to bow and scrape today. Time was running out for my daughter and me. "What do I need to do?"

"Bottom line then," he said, all warmth going from his face. "When you meet with the senators next week, you are to characterize your situation with your daughter as a *custody* problem. That's something people can wrap their head around. If anyone presses you for detail...which they shouldn't—they hate personal problems—mention that you were divorced and you're dealing with a deadbeat dad who's trying to get custody rather than pay child support. *Capisce*?"

I swallowed the bitter pill. "I understand." I'd swallowed the same bitter pill when Peyton took over the Arron Medical case.

When Peyton had come to Sheila's office a year and a half ago and I had explained the situation, he'd exploded, "Shit, Sheila, you've fucked this one up. This is malpractice, you know." He had paused, clearly thinking. "Get my secretary a copy of the file. I don't know what we're going to do, but let me try to figure something out, before we get the ethics partner involved."

I had wanted to argue that it wasn't malpractice. The client had given me only half the facts. No sound legal advice could come of that. But the client had gone to school with partner Dennis Traxson. So when Peyton came back a couple of days later with a possible solution, I went along.

Peyton's idea was dead simple. We would try to get Arron's insurer to pay the claim. Peyton had discovered upon reading the complaint that in addition to suing for discrimination, David Park had also sued for defamation. Arron had given bad references to several companies where Park had applied for a job. Predictably, Arron's insurer didn't cover intentional discrimination by the company's employees – no insurance policy would cover something like that. But what the insurance policy did cover was defamation, which included dishonest references.

Peyton gave me a list of tasks. First, I was to get the client to authorize the hiring of a mock jury so that the firm could get an idea of how the facts would play before real people. Second, I was to sit in while Peyton and Traxson tried the case to a jury, with an actor playing the role of Park. Then I was assigned the task of setting up a meeting with the insurance company and obtaining a number the plaintiff was willing to settle for.

When Peyton and I were setting up the conference room for the meeting with the plaintiff, Peyton admonished me not to utter a single word. He was in charge. At any other time, I would have been incensed at the idea that I take a back seat to anyone, but as a party to the situation, I held my tongue.

Peyton and I had introduced ourselves to the attorneys for the insurance company as they came into the conference room.

"So, Peyton, why am I here?" Howard Grossman, the insurer's attorney asked. "From what I can see, this is your typical discrimination case. *Your client,* made a huge blunder and they're probably going to pay David Park a lot of money—but we don't really have a role here—you know our policy doesn't cover the discrimination claim."

Peyton listened, looking thoughtful before he spoke. I knew it was an act.

"Normally, Howard, I'd agree with you. But if you look more closely at the complaint, *our client* was sued for defamation, a loss you *do* cover." More self-assured now, Peyton continued, "Now, as a matter of course, in our representation of clients, we test out these matters before a mock jury to see how they're gonna play. When we tested this case, we came upon something very interesting."

Peyton pressed some buttons and a screen at the end of the conference room filled with images of the mock jury's deliberation.

Luz Dalangin was wiping away her earlier tears. "You know what the real clincher is for me?"

"What? The e-mails to the new guy?" someone asked.

"No, the fact that Staszak gave him bad references. Arron just out and out lied—for no reason. It was spiteful through and through. Who knows if he'll ever be able to get another job?"

The others nodded in agreement.

Luz continued, as the self-appointed leader. "Let's talk about damages. Do you think ten million is enough?"

Seeing the deliberation for the first time, I was surprised at how vehemently they'd reacted to Arron's bad references on Park's behalf. Peyton stopped the tape. When I looked at Howard, he seemed as surprised as I was. He quickly excused himself to make a phone call. While Howard paced and talked in the hallway outside the conference room, I spoke.

"Peyton, where is the part of the tape where they deliberate on the discrimination matter?"

Peyton's clear blue eyes narrowed. "We can talk about this *after* Howard leaves."

Howard shuffled back into the room. "I've talked to my adjuster. The best we can do is the policy limit of five million—for an absolute release of the claim."

Peyton reached across the heavy wooden conference table and grasped Howard's hand. "Thanks, Howard, I'm glad I was able to bring this to your attention. I'll talk to the plaintiff's lawyer, and be in touch."

After Howard gathered his papers and left, Peyton tapped the keys on the speakerphone in the middle of the conference table, making a call. "Vernon Dinwiddie? Glad I reached you. Talked to my client, and we can meet your three-million-dollar demand, but the case must be settled today with a complete release or the offer is off the table. Get back to me in an hour."

His next call was to the general counsel at Arron. "Gene, Peyton Bennett. Good news," Peyton practically boomed over the speakerphone. "I've settled the Park case at no cost to you."

"No way," Gene said, surprised.

"That's right. We got the plaintiff down to three million. The case is done today. I'll get the dismissal papers and release over to you for signature by tomorrow, close of business."

When the next round of calls was completed, Peyton looked me in the eye for the first time that day. "All done, crisis averted. I saved the client seven million, the insurance company two million, and the plaintiff gets his payday—everybody's happy."

"But," I stammered. "Wasn't that unethical? Shouldn't you have shown the insurance company the entire tape?"

"What can I say?" Peyton smiled, but it didn't reach his eyes. "I'm my father's child."

"I remember a time that would have been a curse."

"Cut the holier than thou crap. We are not lawyers for the insurance company. We represent Arron, and we just got them out of this case for nothing, nada, zip. What you did was possibly malpractice.

"I don't care who the client is. You never take their word for it. But we're past the point of worrying about ethics, aren't we? You and I know happy clients don't sue for malpractice. We'll put this one to bed today, but I can't do any more favors for you. I don't know how the management committee is going to view this. I'll speak on your behalf, of course."

Despite the way our relationship had ended, Peyton had still spoken up for me when it came to the confirmation. I turned my attention back to the former congressman.

"Good. Good. Now let's talk about who you're meeting," Holman said, having reduced my problems to a footnote in my confirmation process.

When I entered room two hundred twenty-six, nearly two weeks after my meeting with Holman, I took a minute to appreciate what it had taken for a woman like me to be before the Senate. The sacrifice of thousands of slaves, and all those who came before me rested on my shoulders. The absence of my daughter sat like a pit in my stomach. The twin burdens of past and present nearly stopped me in my tracks.

A senator's aide jostled me, apologized, and propelled me into the room. The chamber's thirty-foot ceilings soared above wood paneled walls. The rain pelting the leaded windows was silenced as if in reverence to what was about to happen.

I was offered and accepted a beige leather chair, joining two other nominees at a long mahogany table. The two lawyers beside me were discussing the election and how the outcome could affect the judiciary. I looked past the seal that represented the country I'd pledged to protect, toward the nineteen leather chairs arranged in a semicircle behind a wood rostrum. They were empty, aides testing the microphones before them.

Behind me, she could hear fidgeting children being shushed by stoic spouses. An acute sense of loss washed over me without Olivia on this important occasion. At least I had my elbow clerks and staff from my chambers, and I tossed them a smile, strained with remorse.

At precisely two-thirty, the senators filed in, taking their seats behind their name tags. The Judiciary committee chairman, Owen Hewitt, a Republican from Colorado opened the hearing.

"Good afternoon. First, I want to welcome Judge Grant, Judge McEnry. Mr. Overback, and Ms. Jandreau.

"I know Judge Grant, her family, and the fine citizens of the northern district of Ohio are glad we're having these hearings today. As my colleagues know, Judge Grant was appointed as a recess judge to fill a vacancy in the district. Her nomination was especially historic because she was the first black female to serve on that court. In order for Judge Grant to remain on the bench, she needs to be confirmed before the end of this congressional session. It's only fitting and appropriate that she's here today. Mr. Franklin, would you like to say a few words to introduce Judge Grant?"

Senator Franklin angled the shared microphone and spoke. “Judge Grant, your Horatio Alger story is exceptional. I’d like to inform the committee, if I may, of a little about your background.” The senator pulled his small half-moon glasses from his pocket and perched them on the end of his nose. He pulled a paper from a stack before him and spoke again. “Judge Grant was the first person in her family to graduate from high school, college, and law school. After school, she started working at Bennett Friehof and Baker, the prestigious Ohio firm. While there, Judge Grant did exceptional work and became the first black woman partner in the firm.

“Judge Grant, before you take the oath, please introduce those people who came to support you today.”

I stood, partially turned, and swept out my arm in a gesture to indicate the row of expectant faces looking at me. “I’d like to introduce my chambers family, who I’ve come to know and rely upon in these past months. First, my clerks, Claire Henshaw, Liza Salzano, and Adam Hirsh. Also, I’d like to introduce my deputy who keeps my courtroom running, Nancy McFadden.”

Senator Hewitt gestured for my group to stand. “Please, please, I just want you to stand, and get your names on the record. You’ll be entered into the record and become part of history.”

After my chambers staff and I sat, Chairman Hewitt continued. “Judge Grant, if you would stand and please raise your right hand.” I stood again, and raised my right hand as so many did in my courtroom. “Do you solemnly swear that the testimony you give before this senate committee shall be the truth, the whole truth, and nothing but the truth, so help you God?”

"I do," I said and sat.

"Judge Grant, please begin with any statement you have before we start with our questions."

I sat up straighter, pushed my shoulders back, and looked down at my prepared remarks. "Thank you. Members of the committee, and the distinguished senators from Ohio Mr. Franklin and Mr. Hodges, I'd like to thank you for bringing my nomination up for hearing. It is both an honor and a privilege to be here before you today. This is truly the high point of my legal career.

"Before I continue, I'd like to acknowledge two people without whom I wouldn't be here. My parents, Herbert and Keziah Harrison. My mother was a domestic, and my father was a shipyard worker. Though they weren't formally educated, they instilled in me the importance of education. Without their support and devotion, I would not be sitting before you today.

"I am pleased to be here and look forward to answering your questions. Thank you."

After my introduction, similar introductions occurred for the other nominees.

Chairman Hewitt looked at me again. "Judge Grant, we have your written answers to our earlier questions, but we'd like you to clarify a couple of issues for us today. What is the principle of *stare decisis*?"

I explained that it required judges follow established principles of law and that I wouldn't be an activist judge. My answers to every other question the senators lobbed were clear and concise. I had not worked, cajoled, and arm twisted to get to the goal line, only to fumble. In the end, I was proud of my performance to be as neutral a judge as was ever appointed.

"Thank you, Judge Grant. You've been doing a good job and we've only heard good things from your colleagues." Chairman Hewitt asked similar questions of the other nominees, and the senators, rather than ask questions or give speeches, put their written statements into the record. "This will conclude the hearings for today. The senators and I could ask you many more questions, but I think all four of you are stellar candidates, and you should be proud to be here today. Federal judges are appointed for life, so you have an awesome responsibility to uphold the Constitution of this great nation. You will be the backbone of the American justice system. I salute the President for presenting these nominees, and I urge the full senate to vote on confirmation as expeditiously as possible."

I'd been told this morning by Hewitt's chief of staff that the democratically controlled senate would push these nominations through. The contentious election was leading to sweeping changes, and it was in everyone's best interest that all open nominations such as hers be confirmed before another Republican logjam gummed up government works. If only juvenile court could be greased as easily.

38

Doth Protest too Much

Sheila

December 6, 2001

I held the cordless receiver to my ear as I made one final pass across the wood floors with a dust mop. "Bottom line this for me, Casey. What can I expect from this meeting?"

"I don't know what Sherry Otis' approach will be, but I can tell you what I do when I interview parents as the child's guardian," Casey said.

"Go on."

"By the time I visit their house, I've talked to them on the phone at least once. I've also talked to the child, the social worker, the foster parents."

"What are you looking for?"

"I'm trying to figure out if the parents are as crazy, or neglectful, or whatever the heck the social worker has said.

Then I try to assess whether they want their children back. Can they fix the problems that caused them to lose their kids in the first place? I have to also separate poverty issues—like having no lights and gas, from other issues like limited abilities or substance abuse."

"But you're not a social worker or psychologist, so—"

"I'm not trying to solve the problem, just getting a sense of whether there is a problem, and if it can be solved."

"That sounds all well and good, but you're still at the stage of your practice where you think the best of people and have good intentions. What's Sherry Otis' angle, do you think?"

"Okay, look. I think everyone in juvenile court knows that Otis plans to run for the next opening on the bench. Since you're where she wants to be, in a manner of speaking, you may be able to play that up. I don't know what kinds of recommendations she makes. All cases are confidential. But she's known as a good guardian *ad Litem*. She always turns in written recommendations, and last year the GAL project recognized her for her dedication to the county's children."

"Ah. Gotcha," I said. This woman was going to be one of those morally superior people resentful of my hard-earned position. It wouldn't be the first I'd encountered. "The bell rang," I lied. "I have to go. I'll let you know how it went."

The butter yellow suit that was one of my favorites, hit the bedroom floor seconds after the call. It would probably be the equivalent of wearing judges' robes in front of a woman who aspired to have the same. I quickly changed into white Juicy Couture sweats. Casual elegance. A grieving mother at home, I'd telegraph.

The doorbell rang for real this time, and I jammed on navy flats and clattered down to the front door. Despite the day, Otis was dressed not much differently than the last time I had seen her. The suit today was turquoise, the jewelry gold, the lipstick maroon.

The red-haired woman looked me up and down, judgment on her face. “Judge Grant?” Otis questioned. When I nodded, she continued. “I'm Sherry Otis, Olivia's guardian *ad Litem*. Nice to meet you.”

I gripped the proffered hand in a firm shake, not mentioning our meeting at that first hearing weeks ago. Instead I said only, “Thanks. Please come in. I'm up the stairs.” I turned and led Otis up the dark wooden staircase and through the open living room door. “Please sit,” I said, offering the guardian a seat on the white upholstered couch. “Can I get you anything to drink?”

“I'm a bit of a teetotaler,” Otis said.

Taken aback, I tried not to show how much the comment had stung. “I have water, coffee, tea,” I said like the last hadn't passed between us.

“A glass of water, please,” Otis said prissily.

I took my time walking to the kitchen, opening the cupboard, pouring the water from the filter pitcher. By the time I came back, ice cold drinks in hand, my emotions were in check.

I pulled out two coasters and lifted the glasses to slide them under. “What can I tell you about myself and Olivia that will help you make a decision?”

Otis pulled a lined white legal pad from her briefcase. “I have some questions here,” she said before flipping some pages. “Has being a judge affected your ability to parent?”

"Can I call you Sherry?" When the woman nodded, I continued, "Being a judge has been a pleasant challenge, on the one hand. Managing a docket is different than managing a case load. But what's far better than logging long hours at a firm is the amount of time I have now to deal with Olivia. I work an eight-hour day, so I can dedicate more time to my daughter."

"That's good to know," Otis said neutrally. "Have you started on the case plan?"

"No, I haven't." Otis looked up from scratching on the pad, her eyes wide with surprise. "The county, the social workers, that counselor have gotten it all wrong. I'm a hard-working, single mother. It has taken a lot of sacrifice to get where I am today. I'll admit I haven't been home as much as I could have been, but working for a big firm, making partner. That took a big commitment. I think men," I lowered my voice conspiratorially, "are always looking for a reason to deny you the big case, the better office, the promotion to partner. I had to work really hard to get to that point. In the meantime, my marriage crumbled, and Olivia's father disappeared. So Olivia may have suffered.

"She was a latch-key kid. I didn't do the whole 'mommies and muffins' thing. But I've done the best I can and Olivia having to think and fend for herself some of the time is stronger because of it." It wasn't an answer, exactly. I hadn't practiced law this many years to be unaware I was avoiding the question. But I had no intentions of starting down the slippery slope the case plan presented. I'd bided my time. Done things the right way. It was time to get my daughter out.

Otis' necklace strands jangled as she bent to her briefcase again. "I've finally gotten a copy of the complaint from the court. There are some serious allegations here. How do you respond to these?" She waved the papers.

"These specious allegations are completely untrue." I sighed. "Look, you know how this goes. We're in a profession where drinking is its own specialty. The nightly get-togethers at the Lincoln Inn are the biggest parties in town.

"When I was an associate, I had to prove I could hang with the boys. As partner, I was constantly entertaining clients. Social drinking was expected. I don't keep much alcohol in the house but do have an occasional drink at night to relax."

"Got it," Otis said. "Us career women have all the pressures. It's the same in juvenile court. When hearings go late, the men just roll with it. While the women are scrambling to make child care arrangements. And the judges, they just continue on through the late afternoon, no child care worries of their own."

Otis was coming over to my side. I nodded my head in sympathy. "It's hard being a woman in this profession."

Fostering their newfound camaraderie, I offered Otis a tour of the two-floor apartment, showing off some of the historical features, like the original fireplace, the leaded glass cabinets in the dining room, the quirky milk chute. As I showed her out, I put a firm hand on Otis' upper arm.

"I'm probably not supposed to ask you this, but have you seen Olivia? How is she holding up?"

"She seems to be doing well in her placement." Otis' eyes shifted away from me.

"Sorry to put you in an awkward position. Thanks," I said and closed the door behind the guardian.

I trudged up the stairs, rubbing my face with my hands. It was overwhelming, convincing the well-meaning folks in the Cuyahoga County juvenile system that I could do what I'd already done for years, raise my daughter. I poured out the water we hadn't drank, put the coasters back in the drawer, then got my keys and drove to Chagrin Wine and Beverage.

39

The Civil Rights Lawyer

Keith

December 6, 2001

"You're not wearing that are you, Keith? You look like a security guard," Valene said, smoothing her own hair and checking her teeth in a saucepan's reflection.

"I *am* a security guard," I said, brushing stray lint from my pants. "What's wrong with this?"

"Your work uniform? I got us an appointment with the best black lawyer in Cleveland. We need to dress like we're going to church," she said. "I heard he picks which cases he takes. We don't want to give him a reason not to take us."

"We're not going to fool him into thinking we're rich because I have on a suit," I said.

"Change," she said.

Valene drove us—with me in my good suit— to Vernon Dinwiddie's office in Buckeye, an Eastside neighborhood.

Looking around the cracking pavement in the parking lot, I wondered aloud, "If this Dinwiddie is so good, why doesn't he have an office in Key Tower? Sheila always said the important lawyers practice downtown."

"Hmpf, *Sheila said.* If it wasn't for her...." Valene muttered under her breath. Out loud she said, "From what I hear over at Antioch, he owns this building he's in. He gets so many clients, he doesn't need a downtown address."

Valene settled her Chrysler into a space close to the front door. While it wasn't a downtown skyscraper, the building looked to be maintained, but its sixties architecture didn't inspire confidence in me.

According to the building directory in the empty lobby, Dinwiddie's office was on the third and top floor of the building. The gold carpeted, shiny brass fitted elevator took them to the top floor, absent of sound.

Dinwiddie's receptionist held her palm like a stop sign, in a sort of greeting. "Law Offices," she said, answering the call. "Mm-hm," she paused. "Ma'am, I appreciate your son's predicament, but Mr. Dinwiddie's not in right now." She paused again. "As soon as he gets back in, he'll give you a call." She dropped the phone in the cradle. "Now, how can I help you?"

Valene hesitated, "Um, my fiancé and I have an appointment to see Mr. Dinwiddie at ten, but if he's not in..."

"No, no he's here," the receptionist said, contradicting her words of a minute ago. "He isn't taking calls right now. He needed time to prepare for your meeting."

"Okay. Let him know that Keith Grant and Valene Winstead are here to see him." We sat down on cracked vinyl chairs. I shook out that morning's paper. I hadn't had a chance to read it over our rushed breakfast.

After thirty minutes of alternating between reading the news and watching Valene fidget, the receptionist directed us to an office. A man dressed head to toe like a reject from a western movie offered us a seat.

I looked away from the bolo tie, snap front shirt, and cowboy boots toward the large windows of the office that looked out on bustling Buckeye Avenue. As I sat next to Valene on a gold brocade couch, I took in the green shag carpet and wood veneer furniture. It was like being caught in a time warp.

Dinwiddie perched himself on a wingback chair. "Sister Valene, one of the church members told me to expect a call from you. I hope that we can help you in your time of need."

Valene nodded like the man was preaching. "My fiancé Keith is the one who needs your help today. His daughter Olivia was taken from his ex-wife by the county." She handed over the summons and complaint I had picked up at my aunt's house.

Pushing up his large glasses, Dinwiddie took the papers for examination. He slowly read each page, nodding. Valene leaned forward in anticipation the entire time he read. The documents had barely hit the desk before she spoke. "Do we have a case?"

Dinwiddie left his perch, and sat more fully in the chair. "These cases aren't easy. But I'm sure I can get your daughter out of foster care and into your custody," he said. Valene sat back, her relief visible. "I've been practicing a lot of years in Cleveland, and I've handled some of the hardest cases out there.

"I knew Doctor King and represented the likes of Andrew Young and Stokley Carmichael. Those were the hard cases back then." He leaned forward, done with reminiscing. "I don't take every case, but you look like good people, so I'll help you out. I require a retainer of at least five thousand."

I tried not to let the shock show on my face. I could never afford that. It was time to get out gracefully. I tried to catch Valene's eye. When I did, she put a restraining hand on my arm. Instead of standing, she reached into her voluminous purse and pulled out a green plastic covered checkbook I'd never seen before. Dinwiddie handed her a pen and she wrote out a check.

"That was my Christmas Club money. But your daughter is more important than nice gifts," Valene said, then enveloped my hand in hers.

"That's good," Dinwiddie said, slipping the check into his desk drawer. "It takes a village."

"So what do we need to do?" Valene asked.

"I'll handle everything." He stood, they mimicked his movements, and he escorted them to the lobby doors. "I'll call you if I have any questions."

40

Home is More than Four Walls

Olivia

December 3, 2001

The smell of the soiled and sticky red vinyl seats combined with the constant jostling of the Red Line train was making me sick to my stomach. Combine that with nerves, and I just wanted the earth to open up and swallow me whole. My dad had picked me up from the social worker's office. After sharing an awkward hug, and him thanking Jackie for letting me stay before some kind of test was done, we'd headed out to his apartment.

When he was looking out the window, I looked at my dad. He hadn't said much during the ride. It had been a really long time since we'd seen each other—probably not since I was a little kid. He smelled and looked like I remembered. Yet he was a stranger.

My dad caught me staring, so I asked the questions that were swirling in my brain. "Where am I going to sleep? Do you have room for me? Can I get my stuff from my room at home?" The train slammed to a stop.

I couldn't read the look on his face. "I only have the one bedroom. You can have it, or sleep on the couch. Whatever you want," my dad said. When the train started, he looked away then picked up the Plain Dealer.

When we got to my dad's apartment, I walked behind him through the front door, passing what I assumed were a bathroom and a bedroom. Looking to my dad for cues and getting none, I dropped my shopping bags of belongings on the only clear space I could find on the floor, near the living room's daybed.

Stepping over to the vertical blinds, I pulled them back to look past the sagging porch to the drizzle beyond. It had been a long time since I'd lived with both my parents. But I couldn't miss the contrast between my mom's pristine looking apartment with white couches and coasters everywhere and my dad's stacks of junk mail, newspapers, and magazines.

My dad started opening even more mail, and I watched as he separated papers from envelopes. At least there wouldn't be any school progress reports in the stacks, prompting him to kick me back to foster care.

A key scraped in the lock and a heavyset woman walked in. The woman gave me a warm smile. "You're here. Praise the Lord," she said, closing the door.

My dad looked up from the two stacks he'd been making on the dining table. "This is my fiancé, Valene. She's going to help you get settled in."

"When are you getting married?" I asked. In my mind, I wondered what other huge things I didn't know about my dad's life. The minute the words left my mouth, I knew I'd asked the wrong question.

Valene fixed her faltering smile. "Come on over here. Let me help you get your stuff situated."

I picked up my bags and followed the woman down the hall toward the bedroom doors. I couldn't help comparing this woman to my mother. How could my dad like two girls who were so different? I didn't say a word when Valene pointed out the space made for me in the closet, next to my father's short sleeved white dress shirts and his black cotton Dockers.

"So, girl, you unpack now. I'm going to make dinner." Then evaluating my face, she asked. "You eat soul food?"

I nodded. After the meager rations at the Williamses, I'd be happy for anything filling. Valene left, and I hung my few pants on wire hangers next to my father's, and stuck my shirts in an empty drawer.

Restless, I followed the smell of frying chicken to the combined kitchen and dining area and watched Valene cook. My dad's head was buried behind Time magazine. The headline shouted "The Supreme Showdown."

One of my teachers had talked a lot about the election in Current Events. "When am I going back to school?" I asked no one in particular.

"We'll go down to register at Emerson Middle School tomorrow," my dad said. He looked at me long and hard for a second, his brown eyes scanning my face as if looking for something familiar.

Valene was piling chicken on a platter. "Girl, come help me." Glad of something to do, I stood and moved to the kitchen. Once Valene showed me where everything was kept, I set three places on the table. Like I'd been taught at the Williams' house, I folded the flowered paper napkin into a small pocket, tucking the fork and knife in its paper confines. I got three tumblers from another cabinet and watched my father fill each with Pepsi. Out of tasks, I sat down, watching Valene bring over bowls of mashed potatoes and green beans.

After Valene said grace, we all scooted closer to the table to eat.

"Tell me about yourself, girl." Valene said while dishing out chicken and potatoes.

Where did I start? How much did this woman know? "I'm in seventh grade now," I said.

"How was you treated in those foster homes? We was worried about you."

"They were okay," I lied. "The first lady cooked good, but her other foster kid was a baby, so it was hard to sleep at night." I paused, nerves twisting my belly. "I didn't like the Williamses. They had too many rules: when to get up, how to make the bed, everything. We hated it."

"Who's we?" My father squinted at me before putting a forkful of potatoes into his mouth.

I put down my fork as the twisting in my belly wound tighter. "It was me and this kid named Jermaine." Heat rushed to my face. Neither one of them seemed to notice, intent as they were on eating Valene's food.

I realized I'd been quiet a long time when Valene spoke. "Go on girl, tell Miss Valene what happened over there."

My appetite gone, I put down the chicken leg. I couldn't stop my bottom lip from trembling as I spoke. "Aunt Linda was mean. She hit my face, right here." I pointed at my left cheek. "All because I said to some kid that she wasn't my mama." The trembling got worse, arresting speech for a long moment. "But she *wasn't*," I insisted.

Valene's hand grasped mine across the table. "Oh, baby. That's too bad. You're here now. No one can take you from us. Our lawyer promised us that. Now eat up, baby."

Shame and hunger engulfed me. I tore through the first chicken leg, and grabbed another. More potatoes followed. And I swallowed and swallowed. The more I ate, the less I thought about Jermaine.

Though sleeping on the daybed wasn't as comfortable as the princess bed at the Williamses,' and my father's clutter overwhelmed me, I liked living with my dad. It wasn't the stuff of the fantasies I'd had when anger at my mother had flooded my mind with thoughts of running away.

He didn't talk much. What I knew about him, I was learning from watching. He didn't exactly invite questions, so I didn't ask him why he and my mom got divorced, or why he'd stopped coming to see me, or when he'd marry Valene.

On top of that, I was trying to put Jermaine out of my mind. For the first time ever, I was throwing my all into school work. I knew now that I didn't need friends, didn't need to fit in. It was fine being the lonely black girl in the big brick building. The other kids were immature anyway. My dad had bought me a ton of new clothes, bulky sweaters, and big sweat suits. I was able to tuck my head into the hoods, and the kangaroo pockets swallowed my hands. I felt invisible this way.

In contrast to my taciturn father, Miss Valene was really nice. She was teaching me how to cook, and never criticized me for eating too much. Just this week, I'd learned to make breakfast biscuits from scratch, and real macaroni and cheese. Even the vegetables Miss Valene made were tasty. She didn't force dressing free salads or steamed broccoli on me. The string beans and greens were good.

Every day I'd come home from school and take a bath. My dad was working, so he didn't ask questions. During one bath, I wasn't surprised to hear Miss Valene let herself in. The woman bustled about before knocking on the bathroom door.

"Baby girl, you in there?" she called out.

"I'm in here, Miss Valene," I said to the closed door. Without prompting, my dad's fiancé came in. I immediately pulled the washcloth up to my chest. But the sodden green cloth didn't cover much.

Miss Valene settled her sizable bulk on the toilet but turned her head toward the door. "I'm sorry. I should have knocked. You're not a little girl."

"It's okay," I whispered.

"You sure take a lot of baths," she said. Valene's observation was a surprise to me. I'd made an effort to keep the tub ring free and not use too much soap. "Good thing water's included with Keith's rent."

"Miss Valene?" I said. She could hear the hesitation in my own voice. The woman turned toward me.

"Yeah, girl?"

"I really didn't like Jermaine." Try as I might, I couldn't stop the words from tumbling from my mouth.

"That other foster kid?"

"He made me do things."

"What kind of things?"

"Things I didn't like."

Valene offered me a towel. She wrapped the thin terry cloth around my body. I couldn't stop my teeth from chattering. When I stood, Miss Valene stood also and pulled me into a fierce hug. I could do nothing to stop the sobs wracking my body, nor the tears streaming from my eyes. When I took one last shuddering breath, Miss Valene let me go.

"You're here now. You're safe," the woman said. "Go on, get dressed. No need for you to catch cold. I forgot I have to make a phone call. Then you can help me with dinner. Okay?"

I could only nod.

41

Under Oath

Casey

December 6, 2001

"What is your point, Ms. Cort?"

"I'm trying to get to the bottom of what's true, so I know what DCFS can prove once witnesses are on the stand." My voice sounded pathetic even to my own ears.

"Who do you think you are—questioning me?" Judge Grant was up and out of her chair. One long finger aimed straight at my chest.

"I'm your lawyer. My job is to defend you." The finger didn't move for long seconds and despite my best efforts, I shrank back into my leather executive chair. I certainly didn't feel like an *executive*.

This wasn't going at all like I had hoped. I'd planned this meeting, on my turf, down to the very last detail, giving me home court advantage. What little authority my office had lent was eroding quickly.

"Then why are you gathering evidence against me?" Judge Grant's voice rose, its tone accusatory. For a fleeting moment, I wondered how Olivia had survived her mother's withering gaze.

"I'm doing my job. I don't like surprises, and I don't like lies. I told you this during our very first meeting. Yet everyone I've talked to is giving me a different story than you gave me."

"You're going to crucify me on the stand based upon supposition and circumstantial evidence?"

"That would be malpractice," I said. Then mumbled under my breath, "but I've seen parental rights terminated for less...."

Judge Grant eased back into her chair, crossing her arms. "Tell me again about this so-called evidence." Nothing in her posture suggested she was receptive to my answers.

"Lyn B-byers," I said, pausing. Mortification at my stammer trickled down my spine. I sat taller. "I interviewed Gwendolyn Byers. She said you didn't show up as planned. Then she saw Olivia break into the house.

"Your landlord corroborates the broken window story. Plus, she claims to have heard you verbally abuse your daughter. Alison Feingold says she saw the same behavior on a different day. Further, the counselor says she's heard all of the above from Olivia."

"Is Olivia going to be called to the stand?"

"No," I acknowledged. I could see where Judge Grant was going with this. I was less surefooted than I'd been minutes ago.

"So what corroboration do you have for all this? Did any of these people see me drunk? Passed out?"

"No…."

"Then there's no reason that *my* version of events can't be plausible. Is there?"

I dropped my head like a chastised child. "I suppose not. I wanted to make sure you didn't perjure yourself. I needed to be comfortable before I put you on the stand."

"Do you know who I am?" Judge Grant said, steel in her voice. She was halfway out of the chair again. "I've been practicing law for over twenty years. I was litigating cases before you could tie your shoes. I may not know juvenile court, but I've had trials in nearly every court in Cleveland and across the country. I know what a lawyer can get away with and the boundaries a witness can push. Do you get what I'm putting down?"

The admonition came through loud and clear. "I get it."

"Anything else we need to discuss?"

I sifted through the thick folder clumsily. This meeting needed to be over. My head shake was imperceptible. I couldn't say I hadn't been forewarned. Jason had given me the lowdown on working with a professional in your same field.

"Here's a copy of the transcript of your emergency hearing." I pushed the thin stack across my desk. "I managed to twist the clerk's arm, and the judge is willing to give us consecutive days for the hearing." At the questioning tilt of the judge's head, I explained that hearings were mostly conducted one day at a time, and those days were often in different weeks if not different months. "I don't want there to be any reason Olivia's homecoming could be delayed."

Judge Grant thrust the papers in her briefcase. “I’m glad we understand each other,” she said before stalking from the office.

42

Temporary Custody

Casey

December 20, 2001

"What do you know about Judge MacKinnon?"

I had told Judge Grant everything I knew, time and again. But to placate Grant, I said, "She's better than most."

"Maybe another black woman will give me the break I need."

Our conversation was cut short when the clerk admonished everyone to rise. I looked at Judge Grant to make sure she hadn't gotten out of the habit of respecting the presiding judge.

"Cuyahoga County Court of Common Pleas, Juvenile Court is now in session. This is the temporary custody trial for Olivia Grant. If you're in the wrong room, please excuse yourself now. All hearings are confidential." The clerk waited a beat, and when no one left, continued. "In court today are the mother, Sheila Grant; the father, Keith Grant; the guardian, Ms. Otis; the prosecutor for Children and Family Services, Dick Foster; and Casey Cort for the mother."

Judge MacKinnon took her seat behind her high wooden bench when the clerk was done. She appeared to scan some paperwork then peered down at us all. "Good morning."

Like good elementary school students, we murmured "good morning" back.

"The guardian for the child, Ms. Otis? She had to run to another courtroom, but gave me a written report. She'll be back as soon as she can." Judge MacKinnon squinted above my head. I turned around to see what the judge was looking at.

"And who's that in the back?" the judge asked.

A woman brought her considerable bulk to full height. "Ma'am," the woman said. "I'm Keith's fiancé, Valene Winstead."

"Ms. Winstead, I'm very glad you're here to support the father and Olivia. Our county's children need as much support as they can get. But we have a rule here in juvenile court that non-related parties cannot stay in the courtroom."

Valene waved at Keith, grabbed her purse and left the courtroom. I faced forward again. "Mr. Grant," the judge continued. "You're the father." Keith nodded. "Where's your lawyer? I'm looking at the file here, and there's nothing about anyone making an appearance for you. Did you need the public defender? If we need to postpone this hearing so that you can get adequate representation—"

"If that man thinks..." I heard Sheila mutter.

Fortunately for Keith's bodily health, he spoke up quickly. "Ma'am…I mean, Your Honor, my lawyer is Vernon Dinwiddie. I don't know why he isn't here."

"Counselors, let's take a five-minute recess and find Mr. Dinwiddie. We can't continue this without the father represented." Judge MacKinnon rose from the bench and disappeared.

I watched Judge Grant make a beeline to her ex-husband and said a silent prayer for him.

"I can't believe this," Judge Grant hissed loud enough for everyone to hear. "Give me Dinwiddie's number."

I listened as Judge Grant used her authority to summon Dinwiddie to the courtroom immediately, if not sooner. I knew that the lawyer's secretary probably only heard the words, 'judge,' and 'sanctions.' It worked, because a scant quarter of an hour later, Dinwiddie swaggered into the courtroom in his customary western gear. The clerk informed the judge, and to my relief, court resumed.

"Thank you for joining us this morning, Mr. Dinwiddie," Judge MacKinnon's sarcasm broadcast her displeasure. "Preliminary matters for Mom or Dad?" I shook my head and glanced at the prosecutor whose movements mirrored mine. "We're getting a late start. Were the agency and the parents able to reach any kind of agreement?" The force of Judge Grant's hands gripping the wood in silent objection shook the table. "If there's nothing further, why don't we have our opening statements? Mr. Foster?"

Dick Foster stood, trying to smooth out the wrinkles of his light grey pinstriped suit. "I'll waive opening statement, Your Honor."

"Good morning, Judge MacKinnon," I said while standing. "At this time, I'd like to reserve my opening statement until the presentation of Judge Grant's case."

"And you, Mr. Dinwiddie," the judge inquired, her eyebrow raised.

"I'll waive, too, Your Honor," he said with a dismissive flick of his wrist.

The judge looked toward the prosecutor. "Okay, Mr. Foster, ball's in your court. Call your first witness."

"Your Honor, we call Agnes Wingfield."

An older woman in a navy coat dress made her way to the stand. Her reading glasses swung to and fro as she was first sworn in and then gave her name.

"For the record, can you tell us where you work?"

"I'm a support officer at CSEA, the Cuyahoga Support Enforcement Agency," Wingfield said.

"Are you familiar with the Grant case?"

The support officer opened a manila folder she'd brought to the bench. "Yes, I have reviewed the file."

"How long have the Grants been divorced?"

"Ten years, approximately."

"During that time, how much support has Mr. Grant paid?"

"Two hundred forty-two dollars."

"How much does he owe Olivia?" Foster's voice took on a dramatic tone. I tried not to roll my eyes. The prosecutors always did this to try to show how bad the parents were. Never did they point out that most parents were broke. No doubt coached on playing her part in the little drama, Wingfield straightened up.

"At your request, we did an arrearage calculation. Because there was never a modification upwards or any report of employment, Mr. Grant was only required to pay the state minimum of fifty dollars a month. Subtracting, of course, the amounts he has paid, by our calculation, he owes five thousand six hundred fifty-eight dollars."

I doodled on my pad as the prosecution lay down the basics. It was their case to win, and Foster was one of those lawyers who built it brick by boring brick. There'd be little cross examination this first day.

"Thank you, Mrs. Wingfield," Foster said. "Now, on November sixteenth your agency was also asked to administer a routine paternity test to Mr. Grant and Olivia. Is that correct?"

"Yes. At the request of CFS, we did a DNA test on Olivia and Keith Grant."

Judge Grant leaned forward, her body tensing, her pen nearly snapping in half in her hand. Alarm bells started going off in my head. Why was my client so tense? All this stuff was routine. I resisted the urge to look at or shake my client. I didn't want to tip off the judge that something might not be right. I put my own pen down and started paying close attention to the evidence being offered.

I took the papers Foster handed me. Identical sets went to Dinwiddie and Judge MacKinnon.

"Your Honor," he said, "I'll ask the attorneys for the parents to stipulate to the reliability of the DNA results."

The judge lifted her head and looked at each of us at the defense table in turn, expectant.

"I'll stipulate, Your Honor," I said.

Dinwiddie was close behind her with his, "I'll second that."

The judge slid the copy to the side, motioning for the prosecutor to continue with the witness.

"Mrs. Wingfield," Foster asked, "can you please read the results to the court?"

"When we compared the DNA of Keith Grant with that of the North American black population, the results show with a ninety-nine-point nine percent degree of accuracy that Keith Grant cannot be Olivia Grant's father."

Professionalism that kept me silent in court, no matter what happened, slipped. I couldn't control the audible gasp that escaped me. I looked over at my client. Despite the rigid posture and knuckles gripping the wood table, Judge Grant didn't blink. Keith Grant's anguish was obvious in his watery eyes and shaking hands. Judge MacKinnon, not willing to litter the transcript with family drama, called a ten-minute recess.

"What in the hell, Sheila?" Keith Grant said. "Did you know all along Olivia wasn't mine?"

Judge Grant didn't have a moment to answer. But the silent communication between her and her ex-husband told Keith and me the truth of the matter.

"Were you ever planning to tell me?" Then some kind of understanding dawned in the man's eyes. "Don't think I don't know who the father is. All those nights you spent working late. I always knew...something was going on. My mother always said—"

"You mother was the damned problem," Judge Grant snapped. She rose from the table and stalked from the courtroom. I breathed in deep to calm my heart. The worst had happened. I'd gotten an unexpected surprise. The world hadn't ended. The case wasn't lost. I rose from my wood chair on wobbly legs and joined Foster and Dinwiddie.

"... tell your client that CFS is going to have to remove Olivia from his house. We cannot have the minor child staying with a non-relative who's not certified by the county. I suggest you and your client coordinate with the ongoing worker to arrange placement."

Of course, Olivia couldn't stay with Keith Grant. I tried not to close my eyes and click my heels together. Judge Grant had created this hell for all of us, and the flames were licking at my ankles.

Foster's nod barely acknowledged her. "We're taking Keith Grant off the complaint and the case plan." When Foster finally laid his judgmental eyes on me, it was all I could do not to shrink back. "Ms. Cort, if your client wishes to name the father of her child, we can bring him in, have him waive notice and go on ahead since the allegations only concern the mother. Otherwise we'll have to adjourn until we can serve him and start this all over again with the real father."

I was shaking my head even before I realized it. I didn't give a damn who Olivia's father was. Adjournment wasn't an option. If I agreed to postpone the hearing, we'd never get this thing done. It would be six months before Olivia got out of foster care. That was too long.

I found my client on a bench in the deserted hallway. Judge Grant looked surprisingly composed when I sat next to her. But of course, she was the only person not surprised by what had happened.

"Lying has consequences. You've made an uphill battle into Mount Kilimanjaro. But you know that." I wasn't a nagger. But I wanted the truth. Now. "How long have you known?"

"Since she was born."

I held my breath, trying to calm my breathing. This was a client. I had to remember, betrayal had no place here.

Forging on was what I needed to do. "Do you want the father involved? Does he know?"

"He assisted me with the confirmation process. His wife, his kids...they only know us as acquaintances."

I realized I hadn't been clear. "Unless he comes here today and waives notice, your trial won't end today or tomorrow. You don't want to do that. She's already going to have to move to another foster home."

Judge Grant didn't blink. "The hearing will have to be postponed." I wanted to wring my client's neck. Who in the hell needed this kind of protection? Even the last president had been disgraced by an extramarital affair and had been elected anyway. Olivia's father couldn't be that prominent.

Ah, hell. None of this crap mattered. Taking the decision out of Judge Grant's hands, I spoke. "I am going in there and telling the prosecutor that the father is unknown."

The consequences would come from Judge MacKinnon soon enough. I rose and pushed open the double doors. I could hear the click of my client's heels behind me.

When everyone had reassembled, Judge MacKinnon came back to the bench. "Mr. Grant and Mr. Dinwiddie have been excused. Judge Grant, do wish to name Olivia's biological father?"

I stood and answered for my client. "Your Honor, at this time Olivia's father is unknown. We'd like to proceed with adjudication and disposition."

"If you have no questions for Mrs. Wingfield, I'll ask her to step down." After the CSEA officer left, Judge MacKinnon fixed her gaze on Judge Grant. "Understand, that when the father is unknown, we will have to give notice by publication delaying this hearing. Your daughter will remain in CFS custody during that time."

I looked at my client, my stomach cramping. It would only take two words and a single phone call from my client and the father would no doubt be here. Judge Grant remained steadfast.

Into the strained silence, Judge MacKinnon spoke. “We’re done for today. I’ll send the file to the clerk’s office for service by publication in the Legal News.”

43

You Can Never Go Home Again

Valene

December 21, 2001

By now, I was used to Olivia's daily baths. So I wasn't surprised when I opened the apartment door and found the bathroom door closed and heard the faint sound of water sloshing. Now that the girl and I had a rapport, I merely knocked once before taking up my usual perch on the toilet seat.

My sigh was deep, straining my bosom against the buttons of my flowered blouse. I lifted my head and looked at Olivia.

"I have something I need to tell you." But before I could say more, the girl peppered me with questions.

"Where's my dad? Did you go to court today? What happened? Am I going home? Staying here?"

"You know that social worker of yours, Jackie?"

"Did you see her?"

I nodded. "Yes, I saw her and your mom in court today." With a swift movement of my hand, I silenced Olivia. I needed to get this out before I lost my nerve. "The thing is, Olivia, you're going to have to go back to foster care."

All movement from Olivia stilled. Soap and washcloth drifted to the bottom of the tub. Bubbles swirled to a stop. "Valene," she whispered. "I can't go back to the Williamses. I don't want to see Jermaine."

"The other foster kid? I know you said he was fresh, but boys are like that. Even if you go back there, it won't be forever."

Tears streaked down the girl's cheeks. I wanted to wring that Sheila's neck. Cool, calm and collected that woman had looked, skinny in her perfect suit. Not blinking an eye when the truth was exposed for all the world to see, Keith had said.

I looked back at Olivia, the girl shaking. It was probably cold in there. Valene looked around for the towel.

"I *can't* go," Olivia whispered insistently.

"What's going on?"

Olivia's voice became so quiet, I had to lean close to hear the faint sound, the words puffs of breath against my ear.

"He did it to me."

I didn't have to ask what 'it' was. I closed my eyes and cursed God for making women's lives such nightmares. Olivia had joined the unfortunate club of women that I myself and nearly everyone I knew belonged. Pulling a towel from the back of the door, I half pulled, half lifted a crying, shaking Olivia from the tub and wrapped her in a towel and a hug.

"C'mere, baby. Why don't you go lay down in the big bed? I'll call Jackie and get this figured out."

After Olivia disappeared into the bedroom, I quieted my shaking hands. Plucking Jackie's card from the fridge, I dialed the phone. When the social worker answered, I said, "This is Valene Winstead, Keith Grant's fiancé. We have a problem."

"I'm sending someone there to pick her up in the morning like we all talked about. Will you have her stuff packed?"

Putting steel into my voice, I said, "You. Will. Do. No. Such. Thing. This girl isn't going anywhere right now. She needs her family. That Jermaine you stuck her with had sex with this girl."

The pause on the line was interminable. "Are you sure?" Foley finally asked. I wanted to stick my hand through the phone and strangle whoever it was at CFS who'd placed Olivia with this rapist. "I have a lot of experience with this, and sometimes these girls make up allegations so we won't change their placement."

I prayed silently to the Almighty to give me strength. "I've seen this child. She's not making this up."

"Don't do anything rash. I'll call you back."

Later, I brought Olivia a tray of food and tucked the girl in with some DVDs and the remote. When the phone rang, I answered it.

"I'm sorry," Jackie said, contrite. "I just spoke with Jennifer—that's Jermaine's worker—and it's possible something may have happened."

"What do you mean?" My voice rose again. "Did you know he was bent that way?"

"He came from an extremely abusive environment. The agency was waiting for a bed to open up at a therapeutic group home in Bainbridge."

"Waiting for a bed?" Incredulity filled me. I hung up on Jackie before I took the Lord's name in vain. It was quiet from the bedroom. Olivia was sleeping. It had been her favorite activity after bathing since she'd gotten here. I wrung my hands, drank some tea, then summoned Keith home, a move I hoped wouldn't get him fired. Bowing my head, I prayed.

Olivia was still asleep when Keith walked in the door.

"You know I can't up and leave work. I had to bribe Joe to come in and take over my shift. I'll be working Thanksgiving, Christmas, and New Years for the rest…" I knew my face had said it all. "Did they take her early? What did you say to her? Is she okay?"

"You need to sit down," I said. "Olivia was in the bath again when I got here after work. She looked so down. I talked to her a little bit about leaving." I paused, the tears I'd kept at bay all afternoon spilling down my face. "She was molested."

Keith didn't speak, instead dropping his head into his hands. His shoulders shook in silent misery. I let my own tears flow. Neither of us spoke for long minutes.

He pulled a handkerchief from his pocket and cleaned his face. "What are we going to tell her?" Keith asked. "She has to leave tomorrow. We're not a certified foster home. There's no way we can keep her here."

"Are you going to tell her that you're not her father?"

"No."

"Do you know who her father is?"

He looked away, his gaze shifting out the window. My eyes followed his. There wasn't much to see.

"I think so," Keith finally answered.

"Is he going to step up for his daughter?"

"Uh-uh." Keith shook his head forcefully. "This is a rich white man from a rich white family." No more needed to be said. It was an age-old problem. But Keith continued anyway. He spoke more than I'd heard from him in a long time. Lord knows how long he'd carried this burden.

"I wanted her home. I wanted a family, but Sheila disappeared. She worked twelve-hour days. But instead of being tired, she walked around with a smile that wasn't for me. Wasn't but a few words a day came out of her mouth and it was always 'Peyton this' and 'Peyton that.'"

Keith shut his eyes, no doubt unmanned by the tears welling in his eyes for the second time that hour. "I'm sure it's Peyton Bennett. That man—he used to look at Sheila like he owned her. Came to the hospital when my baby girl was born. How could I have been so stupid? All these years..."

We shared a quiet dinner, only waking Olivia to take her a small plate. The girl ate a few bites before going back to sleep.

I had a rule about not staying over at a man's house when I weren't married, but I knew God would forgive me this one indiscretion. I made Olivia the biggest breakfast I could, fried catfish, grits, biscuits, gravy. After the girl tucked into her meal, she looked up at me.

"I'm going to be late for school."

"Don't worry about it. You're going to miss school today. Your dad and I need to talk to you." I repeated what I'd told the girl yesterday, that she couldn't stay with us any longer.

"But why not?" Something dawned in the girl's eyes. "You don't want me here anymore, do you?"

"Oh, honey," I said. "Of course, we want you to stay. But the social worker said you'll need to go to a special foster home where you can get help." God wouldn't strike me down for this lie. He couldn't be that full of wrath.

"Can't you help me here?"

"You know your daddy works nights and me, early mornings. We can't take you to the special doctors you're going to need. Don't think we don't love you, but the county has the power to decide what's best for you right now. Your daddy and I have tried, but we can't fight that. We want you to get better, feel better, be better."

I watched the life leach from the girl's eyes. She pushed away from the table. "I guess I better get my stuff."

"I packed your stuff for you last night. I gave you one of my best suitcases, and I've got all your new clothes in there. I threw out that other stuff." I talked, trying to make up for what, I didn't know. "I also packed some of my Seven-up cake. I know you like that..." God damned life wasn't fair. I pulled a small cell phone from my pocket. "Olivia, I'm so sorry it has to be this way. I don't know if you're allowed to have this, but if you need anything, just call, and we'll do all in our power to help—"

A sharp honk outside cut off my good-bye. The harsh sound of the apartment's buzzer followed. Keith got up to let a woman with a badge into the vestibule.

"Olivia," the woman said. "Do you remember me? I'm the one who takes you to Metzenbaum to see your mom. Jackie's in court today. I'm here to drive you to your next placement."

“Where are we going?” Olivia asked, hefting her backpack and the suitcase.

“You’re going to be all by yourself this time. The woman’s name is Marcelle Wormwood. She’s one of our best foster parents. Even better, she lives in Shaker. You’ll be back at your old middle school.”

I turned a dishcloth over and over in my hands. I followed Dawn and Olivia out, down the front walk. I said a silent prayer. God needed to grant me this one wish.

“Dawn, did you say your name was? Let’s talk over here for a second.”

I watched Olivia shivering at the curb, her last silent entreaty leaving her lips and floating upward.

“Do you know what happened with that child? Maybe you could let her stay for a little while. Through Christmas vacation, at least.”

Palomo looked from me to Olivia and back again. “I could maybe lose the file for a couple of weeks—”

I gathered Palomo’s cold hands between mine for a long moment. “Thank you. God will smile down upon you for this.”

44

Temporary Custody [part 2]

Casey

January 16, 2002

If the weeks between the last aborted hearing and this day had passed slowly for me, I could only imagine what it had been like for Judge Grant. When the clerk opened the courtroom doors that morning, I quickly took my position at the counsel table along with my client.

Judge Grant was very conservatively dressed in a dark gray wool suit, white blouse, and dark hose. Her hair and nails were meticulous. I had to look very closely to see anything amiss. But Judge Grant's eyes were red and upon further inspection, the buffed nails and trimmed cuticles were on hands that trembled slightly.

Judge MacKinnon came to the bench and started without preamble. "Are we on the record?" she asked the clerk. The tape recorder was whirring, and the clerk nodded. The judge read the case number and Olivia's name. She peered about the file in her hand. "Who's missing?" The judge's gaze swept the room. "Where's Sherry Otis this morning?"

When no one answered, Judge MacKinnon sighed. Turning to her clerk, she said, "Can you call around and get Otis in here?" Turning back to the assembly, Judge MacKinnon said, "We're on the record. The court is planning to call Otis as the court's witness last. Unless there's an objection, in the interest of time, I'd like to go ahead." When no objection was forthcoming, she said, "Mr. Foster, please call your next witness."

Dick Foster moved toward the podium. "We'd like to call Celeste Young to the stand."

The youthful-looking social worker who came to the stand looked far more inexperienced than I had imagined. After the witness was sworn in, and she stated her occupation, Foster got to the meat of the matter.

"How did you come to be familiar with the Grant child?"

"It's my job to investigate allegations. I was assigned when Olivia was taken into custody."

"Did you meet with Sheila Grant?"

"Yes."

"What was the result of your first meeting with Mom?"

"I was unable to get information from the mother. She was too upset by her daughter's removal."

"Excuse me," Judge MacKinnon interrupted. "Have you completed an intake on the mother?"

Celeste shifted in her chair, turning to the judge. "No, Your Honor."

"Has Mom done anything on the case plan?" I tried not to close my eyes and rub my temples at the judge's tone of incredulity. I was so tired of a system that expected every parent to roll over and play dead.

"No, Your Honor," came Young's reply.

I stood. "Judge MacKinnon, maybe I need to clarify. My client, Judge Sheila Harrison Grant, strongly opposes the allegations in the complaint and the disposition of temporary custody. The county will be unable to prove their case, because the allegations have no foundation. The county takes a few random incidents—my client falling asleep and not picking up her daughter, my client disciplining her daughter—a near genius, the tests show, by the way—for underachieving in school, and blows them up into neglect and dependency charges.

"My client, Your Honor, is a good mother, who has unfortunately been swept up in this system because of some newly minted, overzealous school counselor trying to save the world, one child at a time."

The silent courtroom alerted me that I'd probably overstepped my bounds. The judge's tone indicated that also.

"Well, thank you, Ms. Cort. I say, I think we can dispense with your opening statement." The judge paused and sorted through the papers on the bench. "So what we've got here is the agency saying Mom has a drinking problem and parents inappropriately. And on the other hand, Mom is saying that none of this is true?

"You've got my attention, Ms. Grant. Most parents come in here contrite, ready to work on their problems. The agency usually doesn't make mistakes. But there's a first time for everything. Mr. Foster, your witness."

I cringed inwardly. Nothing like the judge admitting her bias up front. I felt like a lone soldier, trying to raise a flag over Iwo Jima. A platoon wouldn't be half bad right about now.

Foster collated his notes, starting again. "Ms. Young, what were the allegations you were to investigate?"

"Objection, Your Honor," I said. "He's trying to elicit hearsay. We are all very aware of the allegations in this case."

"Miss Cort, your objection is overruled. The Juvenile rules permit me to consider hearsay. And since this is a bench trial, I'm sure I can separate truth from fact." To the witness, the judge said, "You may answer, Ms. Young."

"The hotline caller said that Mom was having alcohol issues and was otherwise neglectful toward her daughter."

"Your witness," Foster said to me.

I stood. It was do or die. My approach to this case could go one of two ways. I could keep it short and sweet, putting the burden of proof on the prosecutor. Or, I could do what most lawyers in my position did. Try to obfuscate matters with lengthy cross examinations.

Walking toward the lectern, I made my decision. "Ms. Young, I'll keep my questions brief. Did you personally witness Sheila Grant drinking? Or drunk?"

"No."

"Have you ever seen Ms. Grant act inappropriately toward her daughter?"

"No."

"No further questions." I sat down, hoping the judge would be able to connect the dots when this case was done.

"Mr. Foster, you may call your next witness," Judge MacKinnon said.

"Your Honor, I call Alison Feingold." After Feingold was sworn, she stated her name, educational background and current employment. "How did you come to know Olivia Grant?"

"I met Olivia when she started at Shaker Middle. I was assigned to a group of children. I made a point of meeting them one-on-one."

"How else have you come into contact with Olivia?"

"She was a member of the 'For Girls Only' club."

"What's that?"

"It's a peer counseling group. I wanted to do it to lessen the likelihood of bullying and queen bee behavior at the school."

"What prompted you to call the child abuse hotline?"

"During one of our after-school groups, Olivia asked, 'How do I know if my mom drinks too much?' Then when I talked to Olivia one-on-one, she reported that her mom routinely drank an entire bottle of rum each evening."

Foster paused, allowing the damning evidence to sit with the judge for a moment. I steeled myself to limit my reaction. The visual of a poor child watching her sloppily drunk mama plow through a bottle of eighty proof alcohol wasn't lost on me.

I stole a quick glance at my client. Judge Grant sat as stiffly as the chair holding her. Either she was the consummate actress or there wasn't a lick of truth in what had been said. I suspected it was the former.

Foster continued, "Did Olivia say she feared going home?"

"Yes. She said that not only did her mom drink, but that she was verbally abusive as well."

"What was the verbal abuse?"

"She said her mother was always angry at her for how much she weighed, how she ate, her grades at school. She said her mother had called her 'a sorry excuse for a child' that very morning."

Foster closed his folder with a snap. "Your witness."

"I represent Olivia's mother, Judge Sheila Harrison Grant."

Alison looked at me, then at the judge, her pretty young face full of confusion. "I thought you were the guardian."

I plowed forward in case the judge caught wind of my interrogation sleight of hand. "Have you ever met Sheila Grant?"

"Only when the county workers came to remove Olivia."

"Isn't it true that you've never seen Judge Grant imbibe alcohol?"

"Yes, but…"

"Your Honor, please admonish the witness to answer the questions put before her."

MacKinnon did exactly as I'd asked, keeping Feingold where she wanted her.

"I was asking you whether you'd seen Judge Grant drink."

"No."

"Have you witnessed any interactions between Ms. Grant and Olivia?"

"She, Judge Grant, looked a little cross when she dropped off Olivia one day."

"So your basis for making a complaint to the child abuse hotline was solely the words of a bright twelve-year-old girl who admittedly was underachieving in school?"

"Yes."

"Did you ever suspect Olivia of having attention deficit disorder?"

"No."

"Did you consider it at all possible, with all of your education and training, that Olivia was looking for an excuse not to go home?"

I could see the gears turning in the counselor's head. If only she'd had second thoughts before picking up the phone. "No..." The counselor's voice was markedly less confident than it had been ten minutes earlier.

"Is it possible that Olivia blew a situation out of proportion? Is it possible a bright girl may have manipulated you?"

"I...but..."

"Your Honor," I added a pleading note to my voice, trying to get the judge in my corner.

"Please answer the question with a yes or no," Judge MacKinnon said.

"Yes."

Then I took a gamble. I asked a question where I didn't already know the answer.

"Why did you think Ms. Grant was an alcoholic?"

"From the team meetings I attended, we were worried about Olivia. She was coming to our school from a single-parent home. She was a latch key kid from a poor, predominantly African American neighborhood in Cleveland. It's just statistics that would make her mom, living in a stressful head of household situation, more susceptible to alcoholism."

Now it was time for the show. I walked from the podium back to the counsel table. I ruffled through some papers, pulling out a thick, stapled packet. "Ms. Feingold, here I am holding a copy of the U.S. National Comorbidity Survey. Are you familiar with this study?"

"No."

"Here you go." I handed her copy to Feingold. "Would it surprise you if I told you that the prevalence of alcoholism in African Americans was lower than white Americans?"

"I don't know."

"You don't know. This is a yes or no question. Are you surprised to find out that there are a higher percentage of white alcoholics than black?"

"Yes, no, I mean no..."

"Are you aware that studies done at Howard University show that the perception in the white community is that there is a higher prevalence of alcoholism in the African American community?" I stacked two more stapled packets on the dais in front of Feingold.

"No."

"No further questions, Your Honor," I said as I plunked down next to Judge Grant at the counsel table. I was hardly able to keep the self-satisfied smile off my face. I'd shown Feingold to be exactly as my client had described.

Judge MacKinnon looked at Dick Foster. "Any rebuttal, counselor?"

"Not at this time, Your Honor. But I'd like to reserve the right to call Ms. Feingold later as a rebuttal witness."

"Noted." Judge appeared to be looking at the clock on the far wall behind everyone in the courtroom. "It's twelve-fifteen. Let's break for lunch and reconvene at two o'clock."

At two-fifteen, the clerk pressed the tape recorder buttons with an audible click. "We're back on the record in the adjudicatory phase of the temporary custody hearing in the Olivia Grant matter. Present this afternoon are Mom, Sheila

Grant; her counsel, the prosecutor with a CFS social worker. Also joining us this afternoon is guardian *ad Litem*, Sherry Otis. Ms. Otis, so glad you could join us. I have your written recommendation before me. Has the matter in the other courtroom concluded?"

"Yes, Your Honor. I'd like the opportunity to modify my recommendation based on evidence presented in this hearing."

"So noted, Ms. Otis," Judge MacKinnon said. "Have you given counsel copies of your recommendations?"

Fumbling with the leather portfolio in her lap, Otis extracted two packets. One she handed to Foster, the other to me. While the judge addressed technical matter, I flipped to the end of the report. The conclusion disheartened her. The GAL had gone for temporary custody.

I shoved the open report toward my client and pulled my legal pad closer to beef up my cross examination of the guardian. When I finally looked up, Foster called his next witness.

"Your Honor, I call Jackie Foley to the stand."

Shifting in a suit that looked far from comfortable, Foley rose and took the stand. After stating the preliminaries, she stated that she was Olivia's ongoing worker.

"Can you tell that court what you've done as Olivia's worker?"

"I've placed Olivia in suitable foster homes and when it was appropriate, relative care. I've also been responsible for making referrals to deal with Olivia's special needs."

"Let's talk about her special needs, as you call them. What are they?"

"Olivia came into the county's custody and was diagnosed with ADD by a psychiatrist for the Cleveland school district."

"I know you're not a doctor, but in layman's terms can you describe attention deficit disorder?"

"Olivia's a bright girl but has problems focusing in class. This has shown up in her underachievement."

"What's being done for her ADD?"

"She's getting the medication she needs, Adderall and something to counteract it. Then she and her foster mom were enrolled in classes at Euclid Hospital."

"What's the purpose of those classes?"

"They teach the parent to help the child with organizational skills, focus, time management and prioritizing."

"Have those classes helped Olivia?"

"Yes. She's doing much better in school. Her foster mother said she was able to come home and complete her homework in a timely manner."

Dick Foster closed his folder. "One last question, how was Olivia doing in foster care?"

"She *was* doing great." Foley darted a judgmental look toward my client. That paternity snafu did not get anything off to a good start, I knew. It, along with all the other evidence, branded Judge Grant as cold and callous. "The structure was good for Olivia. They had morning calisthenics, week day chores, homework schedules and everything. Then she was moved to her father—um—Keith Grant's house. I didn't get a chance to visit her there. And, of course, we're going to have to move her again."

"Your witness."

I dispensed with the niceties. This wasn't going to be a cozy discussion about reunification. I needed to discredit this worker's so-called expertise, and I needed to do it now.

"Was Judge Grant invited to participate in the ADD family education sessions at Euclid Hospital?"

"No."

"Despite this, didn't Judge Grant come to the first class? Make an attempt to participate in the class, introduce herself to the teacher, and interact with Olivia?"

"Yes."

"At your request, did the hospital have security escort Judge Grant from the premises, rather than allow her to stay?"

"Yes."

I took my seat at counsel table. "No further questions."

Foster was putting one nail, then the next in Judge Grant's coffin. Each witness was another bang of the hammer. Lyn Byers painted Judge Grant as a mother who didn't do PTA and forgot to pick up her daughter. In haunting terms, she told the story of Olivia breaking into her own house.

My cross examination hammered home the facts, skirting feelings and innuendo.

"So, you've never seen Judge Grant drink, have you?"

"No." Byers' voice was clear.

"You've never seen Judge Grant interact with Olivia?"

"No."

"And if I told you Judge Grant started her morning docket at eight-thirty and sometimes ended well after five, would you think it reasonable that she couldn't attend Mommies and Muffins or PTA meetings?"

"Yes."

"Thank you. No further questions."

"Counselors, how many additional witnesses do we have? Mr. Foster?"

"I have no further witnesses, Your Honor, though I'd like to keep the door open for rebuttal," he said.

"Ms. Cort?"

I stood, smoothing down the wrinkles in my silk suit. "I plan to call three in addition to my examination of the GAL."

"We'll take a fifteen-minute recess. Ms. Cort, be prepared to present your case when we come back."

"Your Honor," I said when we returned from the break. "I call Keith Grant to the stand." I didn't look behind me when someone gasped. No longer accompanied by his girlfriend or lawyer, the walk from the back of the courtroom to the stand looked lonely. He sat wearily and gave his name and address for the record.

"Good afternoon, Mr. Grant. Thank you for testifying today. Did you know that Olivia wasn't your natural daughter?"

"No, not until…no," Keith said, his voice visibly shaking.

"I'm sorry that you had to find out that way. I'm going to ask you some questions about Sheila and Olivia. Are you up to answering?"

Regaining some of his composure, Keith said, "Yes."

"When did you meet Judge Grant?"

"Sheila and I met in high school—Glenville. Her first boyfriend died in Taiwan then we got together. We were married in the summer of nineteen seventy-four, before Sheila started law school."

"When was Olivia born?"

The lines that had etched his face, eased. "She was born on December thirteenth nineteen eighty-eight. We called her our early Christmas gift."

"When did you and Judge Grant divorce?"

"We broke up in early nineteen ninety-one, right before Sheila became partner."

"After your divorce was final in nineteen ninety-two, how often did you visit with Olivia?"

"In the beginning, nearly every other weekend. My mom would pick her up, and I'd stop by. When Mom died, I saw her less." He seemed to shrink back into the chair. "Until this case happened, I hadn't seen her for a few years."

"When you lived with Sheila, did you see her drink?"

Keith nodded. "Not a lot—at least compared to some of the other lawyers she knew. I went to a lot of those events and they served alcohol like it was water. Everyone drank at those events."

"Did you see Judge Grant drunk?"

"No." His head shake was emphatic.

"Did she drink at home?"

"Never."

"Did you ever worry about the safety of your dau—" I caught myself. "of Olivia?"

"No."

"No further questions." I turned to Foster. "Your witness."

Dick Foster rose, no notes in hand. "Mr. Grant, were you surprised to find out Olivia wasn't your daughter?"

"Yes," Keith said, his head sinking in what looked like shame.

"If you didn't know this one important thing about Sheila, how can the court trust your judgment on Mom's behavior? Clearly, you don't know when she's lying or telling the truth. How can we know if you could tell she was drunk or sober?"

I jumped to my feet. "Objection! Not only is the prosecutor asking a compound question, he's practically testifying. The reason Keith Grant is more qualified than any of you to judge my client's behavior is because he's known her most of her life. He didn't waltz in a few months ago and make a snap judgment about this family."

Foster's face turned red. "But what kind of mother doesn't even know her daughter has ADD? This is a special needs—"

Judge MacKinnon banged her gavel on the bench until Foster stopped. "I never use my gavel. Today is not the day I want to start. Counselors, stop this right now. Mr. Grant, you're excused. Mr. Foster, one question at a time. Ms. Cort, no speaking objections. Ms. Cort, call your next witness," Judge MacKinnon

"I call Melanie Whitcomb."

Foster was on his feet before I could get out the last syllable of the witness' name.

"Your Honor, I object to this witness. She's some professor Ms. Cort called in. I don't see how her testimony could be germane to this hearing."

"Maybe you should wait until she testifies before you ask the court to disqualify out of hand," I shot back.

Judge MacKinnon's gavel cracked down several times. "Counselors, no more of this back and forth. You're presenting the case to me, not to each other. Mr. Foster, this is a *bench* trial. *I'll* make the determination of witness credibility, expert status and relevance. Now, let's get on with this. Bring in the witness."

Fresh from New York City, Whitcomb hadn't replaced her all black attire with something more Midwest appropriate. She may have been an attractive woman, but her pale face was mostly hidden by long, dark hair and plastic horn-rimmed glasses. Sworn in, she took the stand.

"What is your educational background and current position?"

"I graduated from Yale and Northwestern Law School. I was appointed to an assistant professorship at New York University Law School two years ago. I research race and the child welfare system."

"Can you tell me about your recent publications?"

"My most recent book is *Black Children and the State*. Previously, I published *Saving our Family Courts*. I've also written about a dozen articles on family law, juvenile law and child custody."

"Objection, Your Honor," Foster said, pulling himself up to his full height. "I still don't see what any of this has to do with Olivia or Sheila Grant."

"Excuse me, I haven't even had the opportunity to get into the substance of this witness's testimony."

Judge MacKinnon banged her gavel again. "Mr. Foster, objection overruled. Ms. Cort, you can continue, but get to the point."

"Professor Whitcomb, in the six years you've been studying foster care, have you found any correlation between race and care?"

"Yes. African American children make up more than fifty percent of the foster care population."

"What percentage of children in the U.S. are black?"

"Less than twenty percent."

"What about time spent in foster care?"

"The average time for African American children is thirty-seven months, while it's only seven months for white children."

"Let's turn to Cleveland. What percentage of Cuyahoga County is black?"

"Twenty-seven percent."

"And what percentage of the children in the county's custody are black?"

"Seventy-six percent. Most children come from the cities of Cleveland or East Cleveland."

"According to your research, why the disparity?"

"It's caused by a combination of factors, most of which center around race and our perceptions of drug and alcohol use. There's a belief, partially spurred on by the crack cocaine epidemic, that blacks use more drugs and alcohol than whites. The truth is that substance abuse is the same across races and socioeconomic class."

"How does this bias play out?"

"In several ways. First, poor women on Medicaid, many of whom are minority, are routinely tested for drugs during health screenings. If they test positive, their children are removed. Second, substance abuse is perceived as more prevalent in the black population, so when indicators of abuse are spotted, it results in confirmation bias and intervention."

"Thank you, Professor Whitcomb. Your witness."

"Professor Whitcomb," Foster's voice held a note of condescension. "You've made some very interesting statements in court today. And I have no doubt there are some biases that should be eradicated from our system. But now I turn your attention to Olivia and Sheila Grant, who are the subjects of our hearing today."

"Your Honor," I was exasperated with Foster's grandstanding.

"I assume there's a question coming, counselor," Judge MacKinnon said.

"Yes, Your Honor. Ms. Whitcomb, have you been paid to testify here today?"

"No. I'm not an expert for hire. I'm a law professor."

"Are you saying you paid your own way here?"

"No, my airfare and hotel are being covered."

"Have you met Olivia Grant?"

"No."

"Have you met Sheila Grant?"

"No."

"No further questions."

I gathered up several sheets of paper and took a deep breath. This was going to be the most difficult witness examination of my short career. "Your Honor, I call Judge Sheila Harrison Grant to the stand."

With what I thought of as extraordinary confidence, Judge Grant strode to the bench.

After Judge Grant was sworn in, I asked my first question. "What's your occupation?" I wasn't above using Judge Grant's position for whatever intimidation it provided.

"I'm a federal district court judge in the Northern District of Ohio."

"Before you were a judge, what did you do?"

"I was a partner at Bennett Friehof and Baker."

"When did you join Bennett?"

"I started as a summer associate in nineteen eighty-one and started full time in the fall of nineteen eighty-two."

"Were there other African American lawyers at the firm when you started?"

Sheila shook her head woefully. "No, I was the first black attorney they hired and one of the first women at the firm."

"How long were you at Bennett before you made partner?"

"I was there thirteen years before I was promoted. Olivia was three at the time."

"How long was it before other people in your class made partner?"

"It was about six years."

"You had to wait more than twice as long before you made partner?"

"Yes."

"During those years you were working for a promotion, what kind of hours did you work?"

"Except right before and after Olivia's birth, I worked more than twelve hours a day, on average."

"Who cared for Olivia?"

"If Keith was out of work, he did the heavy lifting. Otherwise, it was his mom or mine."

"When you were working at Bennett, was there a certain amount of socializing expected?"

"Absolutely. There were summer mixers at partner's houses, Indians games, Browns game, and client dinners."

"Did you drink during these occasions?"

"Of course. I was trying my best to be 'one of the boys.' There was a lot of social pressure to drink. In order to get ahead, I bowed to that pressure."

"Now that you're no longer with Bennett, do you drink?"

"Occasionally," Judge Grant cast a sidelong glance at Judge MacKinnon. "Being a judge is very stressful. Much of the time, you're making life or death decisions by yourself. Sometimes I have a glass of wine to unwind."

"In earlier testimony, Olivia's counselor, Alison Feingold claimed you drank a bottle of rum every night. Is that true?"

"No, I'm not even sure how she came up with that. I do have mixed drinks when my girlfriends come over."

"Would you consider yourself verbally abusive toward your daughter?"

Judge Grant looked properly affronted. "Absolutely not."

"In Feingold's testimony, she said that you'd called Olivia a 'poor excuse for a child.' Is that true?"

"No, it's not. I'll be the first to admit I get angry with Olivia when it comes to achievement. She's a precocious girl, but she doesn't apply herself in school. I'm a firm believer that education can change the path of one's life. I don't want Olivia shirking her responsibility to herself."

"Did you realize that Olivia might be suffering from attention deficit disorder?"

"I don't agree with that diagnosis, first of all. I've read that black children are often over-diagnosed with ADD and ADHD, which goes right along with these kids being overrepresented in remedial classes and otherwise segregated in school. But it's my intention to have Olivia tested again by our doctor. If the diagnosis rings true, I'll do whatever's necessary to help her."

I led Judge Grant through all the steps she'd made to extend visits with her daughter as well as the incident at Euclid Hospital. I hoped the portrait I'd painted was one of a single mother working hard to succeed, thwarted at every turn by others' expectations of what a mother was supposed to be, and 'the system.'

"What happened last October, when Olivia broke the glass to unlock the door?"

"She had asked to go out with some friends to a birthday party. The girl's mom and I agreed that she would get a ride home. Olivia forgot her keys. I'm a working mom, and Olivia's always known the rule: take your keys with you. But she's a kid, she forgets. The party ran late, and I fell asleep while waiting for her.

"You have no idea how sorry I am it happened, especially in light of the implications. But I paid the landlord for the damage, and Olivia learned her lesson. End of story."

"Do you consider yourself a good parent?"

"I do the best I can. I have always provided for Olivia. I love her," Judge Grant made her first show of emotion. She didn't speak for a long moment. "I've always provided food, clothing, shelter, encouragement. I had to be there for her when Keith disappeared. I made sure she went to school every day. Had positive after-school activities."

Judge Grant's voice grew rusty, but she soldiered on. "I love my daughter with all my heart, and I'm the best person in this world to care for her."

There was nothing that could trump a mother's love. "No further questions, Your Honor."

I walked back to my now empty table, and crossed my fingers in my lap. I had no doubt my client would hold up to cross examination, but hoped a little of that motherly love she'd just exhibited shone through her testimony.

Foster rose to the podium. "How long did you know Keith Grant wasn't Olivia's father?" I uncrossed my fingers and gripped my thighs. Somehow the trial had migrated from child neglect to a morality play. I'd never had a lot of sexual partners, myself, but women made missteps. It was no reason to lose a child. If that were the case, many a mother wouldn't have their kids.

"I made a mistake. I wasn't sure if Keith was her father. But for the sake of my daughter and my marriage, I didn't disclose my doubts."

"Who is Olivia's father?" Silence stretched in the courtroom. For long seconds, there wasn't a single sound until Otis entered the courtroom. I looked back as the woman's flaming red hair caught the fading sunlight. "Judge MacKinnon, please instruct the witness—"

"Judge Grant," MacKinnon said. "Answer the question posed."

"I don't know," Judge Grant said, steel back in her voice.

"I find that hard to believe," Foster said sardonically.

I jumped to my feet. "Objection to the prosecutor's characterization of my client's answer. The putative father was served by publication. There is no further issue."

"Sustained," Judge MacKinnon said. The next was directed to Judge Grant. "I'll ask you one last time. Are you going to disclose, in this courtroom today, who Olivia's biological father is?"

"No," Sheila said curtly.

"Well, Mr. Foster, Judge Grant has elected not to give information about the father. She will accept the consequences of that decision. Now, let's move on."

"Okay, *Miz* Grant, isn't it true that you drink to excess every day?"

Judge Grant sat bolt upright. "No, Mr. Foster, that isn't true."

"Isn't it true that you didn't fall asleep on that October night, but that you passed out?"

Judge Grant's head shake was vehement. "No."

"No further questions, Your Honor."

"Anything further, Ms. Cort? Mr. Foster?"

When we answered in the negative, MacKinnon excused Judge Grant.

"I call Sherry Otis as the court's witness," MacKinnon said.

Before Otis made it to the stand, Jackie Foley jumped up and left the courtroom, her phone flipped open and pressed to her ear. Probably another child in crisis, I thought, then turned my attention to the guardian.

Otis defied popular convention, a redhead wearing a mauve suit. The cut of the suit was conservative, but sparkly stockings peeked under the A-line skirt.

Judge MacKinnon spoke to the witness. "Mrs. Otis, in your written report, you recommend I grant the county temporary custody of the child. Having now heard the testimony, would you care to supplement your report?"

Otis made a show of slipping on her reading glasses and scouring her legal pad. "Thank you, Your Honor. After meeting Olivia and Sheila, I have no doubt of their strong bond and love for each other. But love isn't enough.

"Alcoholism is not a problem to be treated lightly. Neither is the participation of a father in a child's life, nor the learning disability diagnosis. I think there's a problem with Sheila and drinking, and I think that her admission would be a huge first step. I'm also concerned that Mom missed the ADD diagnosis. I don't think she's in the best position now to make the necessary accommodation for Olivia.

"Don't get me wrong. I think all of this is fixable. But I think Mom needs some time apart from her daughter to get through rehab and get the training she needs for Olivia's problems.

"Also, Mom should consider getting Olivia's biological father involved in the girl's life. I think individual counseling for the child wouldn't be unwelcome, either."

I stood. "If I may, I have a few questions for Ms. Otis."

Judge MacKinnon nodded. "Go ahead."

"How many times did you meet with Judge Grant?"

"One."

"How many times in the last four months have you met with Olivia?"

"Once."

"You didn't think this case was important enough to meet with the child more than one time, yet you're making a recommendation about her custody?"

"Objection!" Foster shouted.

"I withdraw the question," I said. "Nothing further."

The court treated Otis with kid gloves. "I know you have one of the hardest jobs in juvenile court," MacKinnon said. Guardian was a thankless job, and there was no reason to alienate the few who'd take it on despite the meager pay. "I thank you for taking the time in this case." To everyone, MacKinnon said, "I need to review all of this. I'll be back in a few minutes with my decision."

As MacKinnon made her way to chambers, Jackie Foley burst back into the courtroom, her agitation palpable. I looked from Foley to MacKinnon. But used to comings and goings, the judge sat and began.

"Ms. Grant, I have to make two decisions. First whether, as statutorily defined, Olivia is abused, neglected or dependent. And if so, whether a disposition of temporary custody is appropriate.

"I think it's clear to me, everyone who testified, and to you, that there are certain problems in your home. Olivia's conversations with her school counselor, Alison Feingold, bear that out.

"And Ms. Cort, while I'm sympathetic to the plight of African Americans in foster care, I'm not sure if Ms. Whitcomb's testimony is relevant. If it's true about the percentage of black children in foster care, that's truly sad. However, it has no bearing on this girl, and this mom, and *this* case.

"Anyway, the complaint alleges abuse, neglect, and dependency. When it comes to abuse, I'm not willing to make that leap. I haven't heard enough evidence here today to suggest anything like that is going on in the home. As far as neglect, that's a different matter.

"Part three of the statute says a child is neglected if his or her medical needs are not addressed. It's clear in this case that Olivia's diagnosis of ADD was overlooked. Mom, you missed the boat on that one. Looking at Olivia's IQ, then her school performance, you should have had her tested, diagnosed, and treated.

"Based on the testimony before this court, I'm adjudicating this child neglected. Next, we must deal with disposition.

"Ms. Grant, I have two options. I can place your child in your home under protective supervision or place Olivia in temporary custody, which will mean a foster home.

"I don't know how serious a drinking problem you have, but I can see that you don't have it under control. In this, as in any case, I would consider placement of the child with her father. Either you don't know, or you won't tell us who the father is. For these reasons, I'm placing Olivia in the temporary custody of the Cuyahoga County Department of

Children and Family Services. I've also reviewed the case plan, and I'm making it an order of the court.

"Ms. Grant, I'm aware that you've made no effort to comply with the case plan, as was your right. Now that it's an order of the court, I suggest you get into treatment and get this done. The sooner you complete it, the sooner Olivia can come home. I don't see why Olivia can't be home before summer."

Judge MacKinnon continued, "Let's do the housekeeping. We need to pick a review date. How's June eighth?" No one objected, and the judge's clerk marked the date in the calendar. "June eighth it is. Good luck, Ms. Grant."

45

Disclosure

Casey

January 16, 2002

Not without irony, I thought about drowning myself in alcohol. Good thing no one would take my cat Simba away for imbibing a few too many.

No time to wallow in the biggest loss of my career, that could wait until later. I had to show the client I would press on.

"Judge Grant, I'll file an immediate appeal. There's no way the court could find neglect. There was no clear and convincing evidence."

"Tomorrow," Judge Grant snapped. "I've just lost my daughter. I have to get back to my chambers. I need time to think."

I stuffed papers, folders and everything else in my leather barrister's bag. Pushing the brass clips down into the locks, I gave the approaching Jackie Foley the evil eye.

"Miss Grant? I need to talk to you about Olivia?"

"Can't you give me a break?" Judge Grant made no effort to hide her exasperation. "You won this round. I have your case plan. I'll call you when I'm ready."

I hefted my bag and placed a light hand on Judge Grant's arm. There was no reason for either of us to hang around the courtroom, burning bridges. Judge Grant was right; once the initial anger passed, we'd be better equipped to take the next step.

"Miss Grant, it's not that. Something happened to Olivia," Foley said.

Judge Grant flipped her phone closed, piercing Foley with a stare I hoped was never aimed my way. "What's going on?"

Dick Foster had joined our little circle. Foley looked from Foster to Judge Grant to me, unable to meet anyone's eyes.

"Maybe we could go to the conference room," Foley said tentatively.

"Can you just tell me? There's no reason to beat around the bush, Ms. Foley," Judge Grant said, still poised to leave the courtroom.

Foley wasn't ready to leave, though. She sat heavily at counsel table. I had no choice but to drop my bag and wait. Judge Grant did the same. Foster bounced from the ball of one foot to another.

"I really think," Foley started then stopped. "Okay." A deep but fractured breath made the worker's chest heave. "I just got off the phone with our psychologist.... We think it's possible Olivia was molested in her last foster home."

Judge Grant's phone shattered when it hit the floor. Plastic nicked my ankle, while the other pieces skidded throughout the courtroom. I tried not to cry for this girl I'd never met, or my client when Grant sank to the floor, face in her hands.

Pushing sympathy aside, I went into litigator mode. "What are you talking about?" I rounded on Foley, getting down into the worker's face. "Did the father attack her?" Foley shrank back, but I pressed on. "Is there a history of abuse in this home?"

"At the last home, the other child there, a boy, had an abusive history. We were only keeping him there until we could find a bed at the Bassett therapeutic group home."

A lot of words had left Foley's mouth, but I still wasn't getting it. "What happened exactly?" I asked. I looked down at my client, but Judge Grant had yet to show her face. But the gentle shaking of her wool clad shoulders suggested the mother was crying.

"Valene Winstead called. Olivia disclosed that her foster brother had...seduced...her." I tried not to flinch at the awkward language. But rape was a far less pleasant word. "Dawn Palomo picked her up this morning and took her to see," Foley looked down at the small piece of paper in her hand, "Dr. Konakowitz at Euclid. From what's he's saying, the boy may have had intercourse with her."

At the end of Foley's disclosure, Judge MacKinnon, free of her black robe, came to the bench to collect some papers she'd left. "Court was adjourned."

Before the judge could admonish them for using her courtroom while not in session, Foster made his way to the bench, speaking to the judge in hushed tones. MacKinnon pressed buttons on an intercom, and seconds later, a court clerk and county sheriff escorted them all to the judge's chambers.

Judge Grant sat in one of the two chairs, her face stoic. Foster didn't fight me for the other chair. Instead he and Foley stood, backs to bookcases against the far wall as if waiting for a secret passage to open up and save them from this situation.

"Social worker Foley, am I to understand that Olivia Grant was raped while she was in the Williamses' home?" Judge MacKinnon asked, all pretense and confidentiality gone.

Foley looked pained. "Judge, Your Honor, foster home information isn't supposed—"

"Ms. Foley, do not lecture me in the law. Answer my question."

"Yes. Jermaine, the other child in the home—"

"How did this happen?" Judge MacKinnon barked out the question.

Foley's voice grew quieter. "He...Jermaine came from a traumatic background. His mother was doing drugs and the boyfriend-drug dealer beat him, starved him, and molested him. When the boy's behavior got out of control at the last foster home, we moved him to the Williamses temporarily.

"They're known to be a strict family and Jennifer—that's his worker—thought it wouldn't be a problem to have another child in the home if precautions were taken. Jennifer was just waiting—"

"What's the boy's full name?"

"Jermaine Hickle."

"Where is he now?"

"He's being transported from the Bassett home to the Juvenile Detention Center today."

"Mr. Foster, is your office going to press charges?"

"If the allegations are sustained, of course, we will."

I watched his exchange, speechless. Judge MacKinnon's gaze finally rested on my client.

"Ms. Grant, I can't say how sorry I am about what happened to your daughter. I will do everything in my power to make sure the county does whatever is necessary to ensure that your daughter is safe."

"Like you did for Precious Evans?"

Judge MacKinnon shook her head, perplexed. Who was Precious, I wondered. But before the judge or I could pursue that line of questioning, Judge Grant continued.

"Are you going to send my daughter home?"

"I can't do that. I've already made an order. I'm very upset that Mr. Foster and Ms. Foley didn't see fit to bring this to my attention before we ended this trial—but it may not have changed my opinion."

"How could it not, Your Honor?" Grant asked, her voice laced with scorn. "All the things you've accused me of are not as horrible as what has happened to my daughter in your custody. I mean, everyone's heard all the *terrible* things that can happen in foster homes. Now they've happened to my daughter. Why would any parent want to comply with your crazy demands when you don't have your *own* house in order?" Sheila said.

"Judge Grant, please try to control your temper," Judge MacKinnon said.

"Control my temper? You've damaged my daughter for life. Will she ever get her self-esteem back? Will she ever have normal relationships? Will she ever trust me again?"

"I understand your pain, Judge Grant."

"No, I think you don't."

"You know, you're right. I probably don't. I've been in the juvenile court for a few years now, and I know that it's not a perfect system. Why don't we do this?" Judge MacKinnon paused for a long moment. "Ms. Grant, has your daughter had her first period?"

"Yes," Judge Grant nodded, her face stricken as realization dawned.

"Make sure a pregnancy test was completed with the rape kit. If not, I'm ordering that immediately. The child needs to be able to make an informed choice should it come to that.

"Next, Ms. Foley, I want you to arrange for Ms. Grant to have visitation with Olivia every day for the next week. Olivia's going to need her mother's support."

"Your Honor, you know that at most we have visitation every other week at Metzenbaum."

"Ms. Foley, I'm well aware of the county's practices and procedures. This girl has been injured in your custody. I am ordering you to make the necessary arrangements for this. This is a court order, so you can run it up your chain of command if you must. But you will comply." Judge MacKinnon turned to Dick Foster. "Is this order going to be a problem?"

"No, Your Honor."

"Then we're done here."

46

Appeal

Casey

March 14, 2002

I stood as tall and straight as the columns in the grand courtroom.

"May it please the court," I started, my voice echoing in the rotunda. "My name is Casey Cort, and I represent the appellant, the Honorable Sheila Harrison Grant. Her appeal rests solely on one assignment of error. The juvenile court erred when it found clear and convincing evidence of neglect and awarded temporary custody to the Cuyahoga County Department of Children and Family Services."

As was their right, the three appellate judges hearing my appeal interrupted my carefully crafted speech.

"Ms. Cort, are you saying the testimony of the school counselor was insufficient?" one asked.

"Yes. The single conversation Olivia had with Alison was the only evidence of the mother's alleged drinking problem."

"What about the child's undiagnosed ADD?" another asked.

"The appellant strongly disagrees with that diagnosis."

"Did she get her own diagnosis? Seek a second opinion? We didn't see evidence refuting the county's doctor in the record."

I was silent for long seconds. Had I made a grievous error? Should I have requested a medical exam, hired my own expert? I shook my head imperceptibly. I'd followed my client's defensive versus offensive strategy, and this was the consequence.

Thoughts gathered, I answered, "My client's limited access to her daughter made that difficult. As you can see from the transcript, the county accuses her of neglecting her daughter's special needs, then literally tossed her out of a therapy session that would do just that."

"Thank you, Ms. Cort. We'll hear from the county," a judge said.

Dick Foster rehashed the same arguments about Sheila's drinking problem and Olivia being a special needs child.

"Did you remove the child because of the untreated ADD or because of the drinking problem?" a judge asked.

"The drinking problem is what's in the complaint," Foster answered.

"Did you amend the complaint?"

Foster shuffled through the papers, buying time. "No," he said, his voice hesitant.

"How is it," the judge leaned forward, "that the county's claiming the mother is neglectful for missing the diagnosis?

Isn't that like saying the mother's neglectful because the child was sick? What if she wasn't sick on the mother's watch?"

"It's not only that, Your Honor. The child now has special needs. We're not convinced the mom's equipped to deal with these needs."

"You're going to rest on the idea that a well-educated federal judge with time and resources can't 'get up to speed' on ADD?"

Foster backtracked in a hurry. "No, we're not saying that she can't. Mom hadn't completed anything on the case plan at the time of the trial. The county likes to supervise the parents during this process to assure the child's safety."

"So which is it: alcohol or learning disability?"

Foster ducked the question and argued the same two points again before finally taking his seat. The three judges looked from one to the other and promised to consider the matter. I left the courtroom, energized. I might have a chance to finally get justice for the judge and the girl.

Two weeks later, I was summoned back to the Court of Appeal, an unprecedented move. Quickly, I reassembled my file, the articles from the Plain Dealer and Sun Newspapers concerning Judge Grant and Olivia's coincidental disappearances, and braving the stiff Lake Erie wind, ran to the courtroom. This afternoon, Foster, the judges and I were in a smaller sun-filled room next to the marriage application office. It didn't have the gravitas of the first.

The presiding judge spoke soon after everyone was seated.

"Ms. Cort, we called you and Mr. Foster here, *sua sponte*, because it has come to our attention that the facts have changed. We're taking judicial notice of the news reports and sheriff's report that suggest Judge Grant has illegally removed her daughter from the county's custody.

"It is the decision of this court that in the matter of Olivia Grant, the appeal is hereby dismissed. It will not be said that our court will honor the appeal of a fugitive from justice. Therefore, it is the further order of this court, that the appeal is hereby dismissed with prejudice.

"Ms. Cort, you've done an admirable job here. We were going to reverse the judgment of the trial court. What happened in this case is a tragic perversion of our child protective system. Your client should have trusted the system of which she's a part. But we cannot condone law breakers. If the fugitive returns to this county, she will be taken into custody. The county will be well within its rights to seek permanent custody.

"Court is adjourned."

47

Headlines

March 6, 2002

The Plain-Dealer

JUDGE'S DAUGHTER KIDNAPPED

Cleveland—Recently confirmed federal judge Sheila Harrison Grant has allegedly kidnapped her thirteen-year-old daughter from the custody of the Cuyahoga County Department of Children and Family Services and fled the county on Friday, social workers said.

Grant, whose daughter Olivia was removed from her custody due to her alleged alcohol abuse, was recently confirmed by the United States Senate. She was poised to become the first African American woman district judge to serve in northern Ohio.

After Grant's confirmation, juvenile court Judge Dorthea MacKinnon found Olivia to be neglected and dependent. The juvenile court removed the child from Grant's custody. Olivia's foster parent reported Olivia missing when she didn't come home from school on Friday afternoon.

"I was worried sick," said Marcelle Wormwood who has been fostering children for more than a dozen years. "I don't live in the best neighborhood, but it's usually safe for the children to walk home from school," Wormwood said. "I was just beside myself when I thought some stranger had snatched the girl."

Cleveland attorney Casey Cort represented Grant in her juvenile court matter. "I saw Grant on Thursday afternoon," Cort said. "I have no knowledge of her current whereabouts.

As an officer of the court, I would have been required to report a future crime if I had knowledge of it." Cort would speak no further with reporters. Her statement issued yesterday confirms her lack of knowledge of Grant's whereabouts or any plans of kidnapping.

Neither local, state, nor federal authorities would comment on the pending matter only to say their respective agencies are sharing information and that they hoped to return the child safely to the county's custody.

ABOUT THE AUTHOR

Aime Austin is the author of the Casey Cort Legal Thriller Series. Casey is almost always in trouble. Aime's full time job? Rescuing her. Good thing Aime's got experience. She practiced family and criminal law in Cleveland, Ohio for several years—so she has the skills for the job.

When Aime isn't rescuing Casey from herself, she's raising her son or traveling between Budapest and Los Angeles.

www.ingramcontent.com/pod-product-compliance
Lightning Source LLC
LaVergne TN
LVHW050929080826
845145LV00001B/265

9781644140383